ALSO BY ABIGAIL BARNETTE

THE SOPHIE SCAIFE SERIES

The Boss
The Girlfriend
The Bride
The Ex
The Baby
The Sister
The Boyfriend
Sophie

BY THE NUMBERS

First Time
Second Chance
Baby Makes Three

HARDBALL DUOLOGY

Long Relief
Double Header

CANIS CLAN

Bride Of The Wolf
Wolf's Honor

TAKEN BY THE ALPHA KING SERIES

Taken By The Alpha King

STAND ALONE NOVELS AND NOVELLAS

Bad Boy, Good Man
Surrender
Awakening Delilah
Choosing You
Where We Land

WRITING AS JENNY TROUT

Nightmare Born
Such Sweet Sorrow
Say Goodbye To Hollywood

WRITING AS JENNIFER MORNINGSTAR

All Steamed Up
Bound In Brass
The Pirate, The Bride, and The Jewel of the Skies

THE OGRE'S FAIRYTALE BRIDE

Abigail Barnette

Fablemere

For all my Patreon, Ream, and Kindle Vella readers
who bravely stepped into Fablemere first.

Chapter One

Merlin's Used Books had a hollow, molded plastic sign of a cartoon wizard. Its eyes followed Vanessa Waters as she entered. The storefront in the other half of the building used to be a bodega. Now, the bookshop shared the ground floor of the two-story building with a sensory deprivation flotation tank spa.

Vanessa *hated* the way the neighborhood had changed since she'd moved in twenty years before. She extra hated that out of all of the businesses that had folded to hot yoga studios and artisanal tea shops, Merlin's had inexplicably survived. But it was, unfortunately, where her best friend, Tabitha, worked.

"Hello?" Vanessa's nose wrinkled at the smell of damp paper that she would never get used to. She didn't know how Tabitha could stand it.

"Hullo, Vanessa!"

Trying not to breathe in spores, Vanessa turned. "Hey,

Art. Didn't see you there behind your latest ADA noncompliance."

The gangly Scottish man behind the counter pushed his thick, round glasses up on his hawkish nose and shot her a finger gun gesture that rattled the pendants on his multiple hemp bracelets. "Don't sue."

"That's funny." She did not find it funny. She pursed her lips as she surveyed the piles of library discards and tattered '80s romances. "What's the strategy here? Does the fire marshal accept bribes?"

"You're in a feisty mood." Art walked around the counter, his long, curly white hair bouncing, the lapels of his open Hawaiian shirt fluttering over his white undershirt. "Tabitha's in the back. I'll get her."

"Thanks." Vanessa lifted the cover of a basically prehistoric almanac atop one of the wobbling stacks of poorly arranged books crowding the main aisle of the shop.

Shop, she scoffed to herself. *Hoard, maybe?*

There were shelves, but they seemed to be a loose organizational suggestion, at best. The end of each scarred bookcase wore multiple copy paper signs with curled edges, tape peeling away from the corners. *S-W. Mystery. Magazines. R-U.*

She pitied anyone trying to find something specific.

The floor creaked as she wandered, and she pulled her bag closer to her side to avoid knocking over a thigh-high pile of mix-and-match encyclopedias. Tabitha and Art were talking in the back, their "post-game wrap-up," as Art called the act of tallying up the day's sales and discussing the schedule for the next day.

Though it was difficult to believe that anyone bought anything.

"Hey, we're gonna miss the previews!" Vanessa called. She hated feeling rushed at the beginning of a movie.

How does this place even stay open? she asked herself, as she did every time she came in. *How can he afford an employee?*

Art's loud laugh from the back room, followed by Tabitha's tinkling giggle, indicated that their chit-chat wasn't wrapping up any time soon. Vanessa picked up an atlas and turned a few pages. *Yup. There it is. The DDR.* She slammed the book shut. A cloud of paper dust shot up. Vanessa sneezed, stepped back, and knocked something down.

Since so much stuff was already on the stained, raw wood floor, what was the point of trying to pick it up? But she was raised with manners, so after fishing a tissue from her bag and wiping her nose, she bent and retrieved the book.

It was shockingly heavy, and its brown leather cover was in much better shape than most of the stock. She ran her fingers across the embossed letters on the spine.

"Fablemere," she read aloud. *Maybe it's Latin for something.*

She opened it and found thick parchment pages. It appeared to be handwritten, complete with odd drawings in the margins. It couldn't possibly be a true medieval manuscript. Not in a place that sold bulk back-dated issues of *Popular Mechanics.*

She carefully turned a couple of pages, until she got confirmation. It wasn't a priceless manuscript. There was a full-page photo of…

Grass.

A close-up of grass.

That was odd.

Odder still, the longer she looked at the grass, the more she didn't want to look away or turn the page. Something about it was utterly fascinating.

And as she watched, a small yellow beetle tottered across

the photo.

She flicked it aside.

And *felt* the grass.

"What the—" She moved to slam the book closed. Only… there wasn't a book. Her hands were splayed on the ground. The yellow beetle trundled over her fingers.

She sat up. Took a gasp of clean, fresh air.

No dust. No mildew.

No bookshop.

She blinked up at a gray, cold sky, marked by a rapidly closing scar, through which she could see the flickering fluorescent light above the sales counter.

"No." She stumbled to her feet, waving her arms as the seam crept closed. "No!"

And then it was gone.

No, no, no. This is not happening.

What "it" was, she had no idea. But it *was* happening.

Vanessa felt the side of her head. Then the top. Then the back and the other side. Nothing hurt. No head injury.

Unless I'm in a coma. Yup. That made the most sense. She'd probably been crushed under a bookcase and now she was in the hospital, hallucinating the grassy hillside she kneeled on, and the line of trees at the bottom.

And the looming black mountains far off in the distance.

She sat back on her heels and tried to think of a way to test herself. There had to be a way to tell if this was a hallucination. What was the point of watching all that *Grey's Anatomy* if she hadn't learned something about comas?

"Fuck, how did they wake up Really Old Guy?" She pulled up a tuft of grass. It didn't transform into a handful of butterflies or cotton candy. She counted fourteen pieces, closed her hand, opened it, and counted again. "Fourteen."

Maybe that wasn't a real test. She pulled the strap of her bag over her shoulder.

"Aha!" She jerked the zipper open. "If I were hallucinating," she said aloud to the absolutely no one around her, "I probably wouldn't hallucinate—"

A used tissue.

Her head swam. She dug around frantically in the bag. A tube of lip balm. Her prescription bottle. She held it up, praying the label would be nothing but indecipherable squiggles or big, black text reading YOU'RE IN A COMA.

It said: *TAKE 2 TABLETS BY MOUTH TWO TIMES A DAY lamoTRIgrine 100 MG TAB UNIC*

Only a pharmacist could hallucinate that.

If she wasn't in a coma… where the hell was she?

Something screeched. Like a pterodactyl would screech. She assumed. She'd never met one in person and she sure as *fuck* didn't plan on it now.

Scrambling to her feet, she raced down the hill, her tennis shoes sliding on the damp grass. It had rained recently. That was the smell in the air.

It hadn't rained in days back home.

Nope, not thinking stuff like "back home," she scolded herself. As far as she was concerned, she was in intensive care, having a very dangerous sleep.

Running from the potential pterodactyl was just a precaution.

The shrieking call split the sky again, sending out vibrations that slammed through the air and tossed Vanessa to the ground. She rolled, flipped, rolled again, and came to rest with a dull thud against something solid and furry. And very, very dead.

She scrambled back from the carcass of a huge, ghost-white deer. A foot to the left, and she would have been impaled on its antlers. Its milky blue eyes stared sightless at the sky, and darkened blood stained its snowy coat.

Once, Vanessa had ridden her bike past a puddle with a

dead squirrel floating in it. The deer smelled similar, but so much worse.

The pummeling cry filled the air again, closer now, though Vanessa wasn't sure how she knew that. Some instinct inside her, she guessed, that wanted her to get up and keep running for the trees. She pushed herself to her feet and moved faster than she ever had in her entire life, faster, even than when she'd wanted so badly to beat Mandy Fink at the five hundred meter during sophomore year.

It had been a long time and a hundred or so pounds since high school, though. Her lungs burned, and more lactic acid pumped through her muscles than oxygen. Eventually, she would have to stop and take her chances with the pterodactyl.

Stop saying it's a pterodactyl!

The grass got deeper as she reached the bottom of the hill, and the ground got softer. The grass turned to moss, and the moss slipped away from the dirt beneath it like the skin off a blister. She almost lost her footing when the next ear-shattering screech sounded. The flap of enormous wings stirred wind across her face. Just a few more steps and she'd make it beneath the shelter of the trees, if she could even consider them shelter. The wings made another pass overhead, casting a huge shadow over the ground, and Vanessa made the split-second decision to throw herself bodily into the woods.

And directly into some nasty thorns.

She yelped as the vines scratched her face and arms, and she tried to push and kick her way free, but only succeeded in poking herself more. They tore at her hair, at her arms, and for a moment, she thought she should have chosen death by pterodactyl. But whatever had been screaming and flying was gone now. She took a few deep breaths and worked at extricating herself from the brambles.

Freeing herself ended up drawing more blood, and there were some thorns that had broken off in her skin, but she had her chin hair tweezers in her purse and plenty of hand sanitizer. *I've got this.*

Whatever *this* was.

Climbing to her feet with a groan of pain, she glanced back up the hill. A huge bird hunched over the deer. No, perched on it with giant talons, wings spread over the grisly meal.

And then the bird folded its wings in and revealed dark, matted hair surrounding a woman's face. A woman's bare upper body. No arms, no legs. Feathers and nipples and a blood-smeared, fanged mouth.

Vanessa reeled backward, almost into the brambles again. She found a path through, quickly, hoping the harpy would stay with the easy meal. Branches slapped Vanessa's face as she plunged through the trees, but those were preferable to evisceration by a big-tittied vulture woman.

The trees thinned and Vanessa spilled onto a wide road of hard-packed sand. She was… somewhere, at least. A road would lead somewhere else, hopefully somewhere safe from mythological creatures. If that was indeed what she'd seen. She wasn't quite ready to accept that yet.

Her threshold for acceptance of reality rapidly lowered at the sound of hoofbeats.

Not a truck engine.

Not a dirt bike.

Hoofs, as in horses, and the jangling of stirrups and the creaking of carriage wheels. The first horse came into view, huge and black, topped with a rider in black armor, bearing a black banner. And behind that rider were more riders, and behind *those*, a black carriage, all moving with astonishing speed on the pitted dirt road.

The road Vanessa currently stood smack in the middle of.

Chapter Two

There were two options: get run over or jump aside. One of those options was clearly superior, but Vanessa's brain couldn't grasp which, due to the considerable lag time as it processed everything it had been subjected to, so far.

And that's why Vanessa stood, frozen in terror, in front of a stampede of knights on horseback that showed no signs of slowing for her.

Until a voice called, "Halt!"

The banner-carrier pulled his reins. His horse's hooves carved furrows in the damp sand, skidding to a stop so close to Vanessa that she felt the animal's breaths like a bellows directly in her face.

"Stop in the name of His Grace, Baron Scylas of The Sorrowlands!"

She couldn't tell which of the knights had shouted the command. Their faces were all completely covered by metal grills like the beaks of plague doctor masks. They also all carried long-handled weapons like axes with curved blades and ornate designs punched through the black metal. She put her hands up and took a slow step back to put just a smidge of distance between her and the horse.

There were many things she could have asked. "Where am I?" or "What is this place." But when she opened her mouth, the words that ejected were, "Are you LARPing?"

"Bring her," came a sonorous voice from within the carriage.

Vanessa's hands shot higher. "You don't have to bring me! I'll come peacefully."

The knights weren't swayed. Two of them dismounted fluidly, their blades gleaming like glass, and held their weapons in one hand while gripping Vanessa by the upper arms between them.

"Hey!" she shouted, before she thought that maybe it was a foolish thing to argue with hulking figures carrying anime-worthy poleaxes. "I can walk by myself."

They dragged her toward the carriage, a hulking, black thing almost as wide as the road itself. Eight enormous black horses pulled it, but no one seemed to drive it.

As they passed the team, one of the animals whickered, displaying pointed teeth like a steak knife. The beast regarded her with pupil-less red eyes as she passed.

Up close, the carriage was decorated all over with enameled ornamentation. Carved black bunting draped from the edges of the edges of the roof in scallops topped at each point with a snarling gargoyle's face. It was a colossal goth wedding cake on wheels, and the knights marched her straight to the door.

A slender, pale hand languidly parted the black velvet drapes behind the glassless windows, a ring on each finger. It turned palm up and beckoned, "Closer."

The voice made Vanessa's hearing all fuzzy at the edges, and she found herself stepping forward, easily within that hand's reach. But it retreated, opening the heavy curtains to reveal its owner, equally slender and pale. Only the figure's hands and face were distinguishable in the darkness of the carriage interior, though when they leaned forward, a few long locks of ink-black hair slashed across their face. The person gazed at Vanessa in astonishment.

"A human," they said. "A human, out here in The Mire?"

That wording troubled Vanessa. The way they'd said, "human" as if they'd always heard of humans, but had never actually seen one...

Very troubling.

Whatever was happening to her, she had to at least try to get some footing in the situation. She stuck out her hand to shake the paper-white person's. "Vanessa Waters. Human. And you are?"

They did not offer their hand. Instead, they leaned out of the shadows, a chilling, closed-mouth smile bending their pale lips. "Baron Aerrax Scylas. Ruler of the Sorrowlands. You're a very long way from home, human."

There was that human word again. Vanessa swallowed. "Yeah. I'm starting to suspect that."

"You're filthy." The Baron looked her up and down, the disgusted curl of his lip as he took in her muddied clothing the only "human" expression he'd displayed yet. And then he ruined it with a wide grin of needle-pointed teeth. "And bloody."

Vanessa took a step back, only to feel the prick of what she was certain was one of those huge axes against her head.

"What brings you out here, human?" The Baron folded his hands atop each other on the rim of the window. He moved like a serpent, narrowing his black eyes like a cat.

"A portal?" *Fuck! Fuck, shit, ass, another fuck and goddamn tits!* Why had she said that? This was clearly some kind of medieval land, or really committed roleplay. These freaks would probably burn her at the stake.

On the other hand, the Baron didn't give off the vibe of someone who would be opposed to witches.

"A portal?" he repeated, his voice full of wonder.

Maybe she could walk the answer back. "It could have been like... a window."

He nodded slowly, his unnerving teeth flashing in another wide smile. "You will take me to this portal."

"I can't." Just the thought of going back through the woods, to where that awful bird-woman was feasting, made Vanessa's spine creep. "There's a harpy."

"A harpy!" The joy that lit the Baron's face was in the top ten most terrible things Vanessa had ever seen. He let out a deep, longing sigh. "I haven't had harpy in so long."

Without further command, two of the knights peeled away from the gathering, their metal beaks pointed directly at Vanessa. She raised her arm and indicated the direction she'd come from.

"But the portal isn't there anymore," she said, turning back to the Baron. "The harpy might still be, but if the portal was... I wouldn't still be here."

"How disappointing. But you can still be useful." He flicked two long fingers toward her. "Seize her."

"What? No!"

The knights gripped her upper arms again and dragged her backward.

And then, one of them collapsed to the ground, clattering like someone knocked over a pyramid of canned baked beans.

The Baron vanished behind the drapes just as a shaft of wood as wide as a permanent marker impaled the side of the carriage. The knights reined their mounts into a protective configuration around the vehicle and suddenly, no one cared about Vanessa's presence. One of the knights shouted, "Ambush!" just before everything became a panic of clanging weapons and battle shouts.

Vanessa didn't hesitate. She didn't run in the direction she'd come from; the harpy was there, and two of those knights, if they hadn't already returned. The huge arrows were still striking; a demon horse was caught in the neck and fell, thrashing in the mud in what appeared to be its death throes, only to rise back up. Its rider broke the arrow off and swung fluidly into the saddle once more. Other knights were punctured, huge gouts of black liquid spraying from their wounds, but they recovered in an instant.

Vanessa did not have the luxury of recovery. Her back pressed against the carriage door, trapped between the super creepy Baron guy and a barrage of arrows.

Then, she got a look at the enemy.

They were huge and humanoid, over seven feet tall, at least, and as wide as Volkswagen Beetles at the shoulders. Some of them bore enormous axes, and not fancy ones that looked like they were mostly for show. Huge, double-sided, fuck-off axes they lifted as if the weapons weighed nothing more than a feather.

And the monsters were green. Every single one of them, in shades ranging from green-brown to sickly lime. They were freaking green.

"Gargoyles!" One of the knights called, and the carriage swayed. The hideous faces decorating it were gone, and a shadow passed over Vanessa's head as six burly stone men took to the sky to engage the giant green warriors.

Everybody seemed far too busy to notice Vanessa. And that was when she made the call to bolt. Her only way out appeared to be under. She dove beneath the carriage, praying it wouldn't move.

As she clawed her way across the sand, head down to keep from knocking it against the underside of the vehicle, the wheels rocked. She picked up speed on her hands and knees, clearing the carriage and forcing herself to her feet on the other side.

"The human!" the Baron shouted. "It's getting away!"

Vanessa plunged into the woods.

I was just in the bookstore.

She imagined one of those arrows striking her in the back, right between the shoulder blades.

I was just in the bookstore.

The harpy was in the opposite direction, but there could be more in the forest, right?

I was just in the bookstore.

If there were demon horses and knights and giant green guys, couldn't there be other monsters in the forest?

At the road, someone shouted, "Retreat!" and the

command was so thunderous, Vanessa swore it shook the ground. The shadow of gargoyle wings blotted out the mottled light that reached the forest floor, but she didn't stop running. She kept going, legs pumping, carrying her deeper into the forest. She wouldn't stop. She wouldn't—

She stopped.

More accurately, something stopped her, slamming into her side and carrying her off her feet to collide with the ground on a rib-crushing "Oof!"

A pickle-colored hand the size of her face covered her mouth, and two blunt tusks grazed her forehead as the big body flattened over hers, trapping her in the darkness of some kind of blanket that covered both of them.

"Shh!" the monster ordered, as if she could make a sound with his massive form pressing her into the loamy earth.

Is it still earth, if I'm pretty sure I'm not on Earth?

For some reason, the monster kept shaking her. Then, she realized, glancing up at the creature's wide, yellow, slit-pupil eyes that he wasn't shaking her, he was just *shaking*.

The monster was afraid.

Chapter Three

Pinned between the ground and the immovable boulder of the beast's chest, Vanessa tried to squeak out, "I can't breathe," between the fingers crushing her lips together.

"I said be quiet!" The monster whispered.

They stayed there a long time, until red spots swam in her vision from lack of oxygen, and she couldn't help but wriggle, desperate for air. The battle sounds died down, and someone shouted a command that initiated the jingling and clanking of horses and knights moving down the road, but all of that was barely audible under the monster's heaving breath. Finally, it threw back the covering and looked around, before getting to his feet and quickly brushing himself off in obvious disgust.

"Hey! You're doing an icky dance!" Vanessa pointed an accusing finger at him. "Like I do when an ant crawls on me."

"Will you shut up!" the beast growled. "Do you not understand the concept of hiding?"

"What am I hiding from?" she whispered. Much quieter than the monster did.

A whistle nearby made the creature cock his head and whistle in the opposite direction. There was another whistle, then another, and soon the forest sounded uncannily like a flock of cheerful birds, then faded into silence. More of the monsters appeared through the trees, cloaks of moss and dead leaves on their backs. About twenty of them converged around Vanessa and the monster who'd caught her.

A yellowish-green creature moved into the center of the circle that organically formed. He brushed back his shoulder-length, half-shaved hair and scanned the clearing. "Did we lose anyone?"

"Everyone answered the signal," another asked. This one wore a brown knit cap and had a broken tusk. He lifted one oar-sized hand and pointed to Vanessa. "What the goblin's tits is that thing doing here?"

"It's a human." The monster beside Vanessa gripped her wrist. "I found it running from The Baron."

"Well, it's disgusting," another of the creatures chimed in.

"Get rid of it," another monster called out. "They give me the creeps."

"It's sicking everyone out, Droguk," the first one said with a grimace.

Vanessa looked around the circle. *"Sicking everyone out?"* But if they didn't want her there, that was fine. They were the first monsters she'd encountered that day that would have willingly let her go free.

"I will... get out of your hair, then..." she began cau-

28

tiously, taking a few steps back.

The one who'd caught her, the one they had called Droguk, snagged her arm and pulled her back. "It was with the Baron. When it ran, he ordered his men to go after it."

"Could we use like, she, they, them, her, anything like that to refer to me other than 'it'?" she asked.

And then she laughed. And she couldn't stop laughing. The monsters all looked at her with horror and abject revulsion, and she couldn't stop laughing.

"Ah, fuck," she cursed, doubling over, barely able to breathe. "This is fucking incredible. I'm supposed to be in a bookshop right now."

"Get rid of it, Droguk," the monster who seemed to be in charge ordered. To the others, he said, "Come on. We'll divide up the spoils."

Droguk made a threatening grunt. "You'll divide up the spoils? Without me? I don't think so."

"You want to keep the human," one of the creatures said. "There's your spoils."

Droguk stalked toward that particular monster, dragging Vanessa behind him as an afterthought. When she stumbled, he pulled her up without looking back. "I'll be paid what's mine. If you don't want the human, I'll take it."

"Nobody will be taking it anywhere!" Vanessa dug in her heels. "It needs answers."

A huge green hand struck out and smacked her face. Her head whipped sideways. Her hearing went fuzzy, but she could still plainly hear Droguk snarl at the monster that had struck her. It was knit-cap guy, and the two stood face-to-face, snarling.

Undercut forced his way between them. "We divide up the spoils now and go our separate ways, before this gets nasty."

A few of the creatures lumbered reluctantly into the center of the circle, tossing down bits and pieces of black armor, small pouches, and between two of them, a giant iron chest that landed on the forest floor and semi-buried itself under its own weight.

"No wonder they needed so many horses," Undercut said, nodding toward the chest. "Get it open."

Vanessa tasted blood on her mouth, and gingerly accounted for her teeth with her tongue.

"Are you all right?"

She squinted, trying to get her double-vision to sync up as she stared at Droguk. "Am... no. No, I'm not all right. I've never been less all right."

His prominent brow wrinkled, and he frowned around his tusks.

Vanessa tugged on her ear, which felt as though it had very, very painful water in it. "I think that... guy? Burst my eardrum."

Droguk's expression didn't change.

"What are you all, anyway?" She flicked her gaze to the creature who kneeled in front of the treasure, working at the padlock with a shockingly fiddly little instrument for hands that size.

Slowly, Droguk pointed to his massive torso. "What are we?"

"You're not human, clearly. Otherwise, you wouldn't refer to me as a human." Vanessa added, "Or 'it'."

"We're Ogres," Droguk said slowly, squinting in what seemed like concern. "Gorgrak, how hard did you hit it?"

Fairly hard, Vanessa tried to answer. It came out as, "Frrrrard."

Being struck in the head hard enough to make

30

one's ears ring wasn't a great situation for an epileptic. Especially one already under dire stress. Vanessa recognized the floaty, unmoored feeling of an aura just a second too late to lie down for safety; she hit the ground just before her vision went, but she didn't feel the impact. *Fuck, there goes my license for six months.*

Through the fuzzy, spinning pause in reality, she heard one of the ogres say, "It died of fright."

Another said, "Saves us from scavenging food tonight."

"It isn't dead." Something poked at her side. "It's twitching."

Then her hearing went, and the world went. Only for a moment to Vanessa; one second, she existed, the next, she woke as if from general anesthesia. Her swimming head tried to process her up-close view of the forest litter and some giant, bare, green toes.

Oh, that's right. Remembering where she was always came as a little shock in the post-ictal phase.

This time, it came as a much bigger shock than it ever had before. "Wait..."

"It has the seeing," Knit-Cap growled, jabbing a thick finger at her eyes. As her systems hadn't all come back online yet, she couldn't do anything to protect herself but make a face.

Droguk swatted Knit-Cap's—Gorgrak?—hand away. "You didn't want it. I've claimed it."

"That's why the Baron wanted it," Undercut said, more to himself than to the rest of them. Was he the one in charge?

"Forget what the Baron wants," Droguk argued. "Having a seer will be good for us."

"There is no us," an ogre behind Gorgrak chimed in.

"Unless we've all unionized."

During the ripple of rough chuckles, Vanessa asked groggily, "You have unions?"

They ignored her.

"You can take the human," Undercut snarled. "But you won't have a share in the rest."

"He cannot take the human!" Gorgrak bellowed.

"Shut up!" the Ogre kneeling in front of the chest shouted. "I've almost got it."

There was a click. Then a snap. Then—

"Trap!"

Vanessa flew off her feet and the world went upside down. And bouncing. She shut her eyes, then opened them at the sound of ogres roaring. The area Droguk quickly spirited her away from blackened and screeched, and howls of pain chased them as they moved through the forest at a speed that would have been dizzying even if she hadn't just had a seizure.

My meds! She was upside down, jarring around, and her bag was...

Before she could worry about it further, a dark shape swooped through the trees and got way too close before she figured out it was a bat. She barely managed to fight her arms to her face to fend the thing off. The animal wooshed over her head, and Droguk roared in pain. He stumbled, took a knee, and Vanessa braced to have her neck broken in an inevitable collision with the ground. But with an equally ferocious roar as before, he pushed himself to his feet and ran even faster, crushing thorny brush under his big feet, shoving thick saplings aside like the entire forest was a beaded curtain.

Vanessa sank her fingers into the ogre's cloak and tucked her head between her arms to protect herself from the flap of wings and the slash of fangs.

Droguk ran until the screams faded behind them, until even the bats gave up, then he slid to the ground, spilling Vanessa sideways off his shoulder. There was a loud tear as she rolled up like a crepe in his cloak and bounced across the forest floor.

For a long moment, she didn't move. She didn't try to sit up, or fight her way free, or even open her eyes. The seizure hangover still hadn't worn off and her jostling field of vision wasn't helping her to recover.

"You weigh as much as a sack of stones," Droguk muttered.

The insult was enough to make her fight her way free. She flopped around until she lay on her back, a root wedged painfully in the small of her back. "What the fuck is that supposed to mean?"

It was supposed to mean she was fat. And she was. *That's fair.*

He still didn't need to say it.

Even sitting in a crouch, Droguk towered over her. Of course, she was still on the ground. His brow furrowed. "I could barely tell I was carrying you."

She opened her mouth, then closed it. Not knowing what the hell he was talking about was preferable to trying to figure it out.

Sack of stones. Something about that phrase pricked at her still-muzzy brain. "Sack. Sack! My purse!"

The bag itself was still strapped across her body. The contents...

Sunglasses, chapstick, wadded up receipts dotted the ground directly around her. Her pill bottle was nowhere in sight.

She turned the bag upside down and shook it. "No, no, no..."

33

"What is it?" Droguk asked, shifting to his knees to peer down at her. "Are you hurt? Were you bitten?"

She shook her head. "No, my pills. They fell out somewhere back there. I think. They could have fallen out when I crawled under the carriage or when the harpy—"

"Harpy?" His gaze lifted to the canopy of leaves above them.

"They're my pills," she said. "They're a... a magic bean that—"

The furrow in his brow deepened. "I know what pills are."

"Oh. I didn't know if you had them here." *Here.* "Um, where, exactly is here?"

He tilted his head. "The Mire."

"Right." She nodded slowly. "I know what that is. I didn't fall through a magic book or anything. I'm from The Mire."

"That's very specific. And a lie. Humans don't live in The Mire." He stood and brushed off the knees of his soft leather pants. "What do these pills do?"

"I'm epileptic. The pills keep me from having seizures."

His expression didn't change.

"You know what pills are, but not seizures?" She rolled her eyes. "What happened to me back there? Before the bats?"

"The vision?" Droguk pointed in that direction.

"They're not visions. They're just the product of electric misfires in my brain. And I need the pills to stop them from happening. If I don't take the pills, I could die." Or worse, lose her driver's license permanently.

Droguk looked back the way they'd come. The way

34

the bats were, and the other ogres, who'd seemed just a hair away from violence. He glanced down at Vanessa and, before she could tell him not to, plunged down the path they'd just carved through the forest.

Chapter Four

The sky went from silver to deep gray to blue-tinged charcoal before the ogre returned. He didn't move as fast on this trip, his feet thudding heavy enough to shake the ground.

Vanessa had waited nearly motionless the entire time, wrapped in the ogre's moss camouflage, dreading every crack of every twig she could imagine snapping beneath the claws of the next dire creature that would attack her. She'd thought she would feel safer when Droguk returned, but she wasn't sure what had made her think that, because when he did return, she felt anything but safe. He towered over her and extended his hand the size of a canoe paddle. "Your pills?"

The translucent orange bottle seemed to glow in the twilight. She snatched it up. "Yes. Those are it." she took the top off and shook two tablets into her palm.

No water. She would dry swallow them but that wasn't the real issue. Dehydration was becoming a real threat. She grimaced the pills down and rasped, "do you have any water?"

He fell back heavily on his haunches.

"Hey, are you okay?" She got to her knees. If he didn't have water, she didn't know how to find any. And even if she could pull off *Naked and Afraid: Fairytale Land*, she wasn't sure the water would be safe for her. For all she knew, everything could be poisonous.

Even the air.

She held her breath and gave Droguk a shake.

"I just... need to rest..." His big chest rose and fell rapidly, jerking with every beat of what had to be a truly massive heart.

Don't go into cardiac arrest, she pleaded with him silently. There was no way she'd be able to perform effective CPR on him, at his size. It would be like trying to do chest compressions on a Kodiak bear.

"Is there anything I can do?" she asked.

"No," he replied in a rumbling wheeze. "I just need to rest. Those damn bats—"

"They were still there?" she gasped in horror.

"Keep your voice down," he warned. "Yes, they're still out there. But so are those other guys. Do you want them to find you?"

"Other guys... Oh, the Baron's men?"

"Those aren't men," Droguk growled. "But no, they're long gone."

"Then who are you talking about?" She glanced nervously at the freshly tromped path.

"The raiding party." He huffed and groaned and got to his feet. "We'd better move."

When he stood, a blossom of crimson black shown wetly on his linen tunic.

"You're hurt!" Vanessa reached up as if to touch his wounded side, but he reeled back.

"I know I'm hurt," he said, making a shushing motion at her. "They don't all know that. Imagine if they were nearby and they heard you shouting that I'm weakened."

"I don't understand," she said, but stood up, too. "You were in that raiding party. Why would they attack you?"

"Because aside from the booby-trapped chest full of vampire bats, you were the only thing we seized in the raid. You're the only payoff."

"They'll want to divide me up." Her pills threatened to come up her throat.

"What?" He took a few experimental steps, hissing in pain as he did so.

"For food." They'd already made comments about potentially eating her. If they were hurt and needed sustenance—

But Droguk gave her a look that, even in the fading light, plainly stated that she might as well have accused him of roasting babies like kebabs. "We don't eat humans."

"That guy said—"

"He's a dick." Droguk leaned heavily on an old-growth tree, probably the only thing in the forest that could support him. "We don't eat humans. But they will fight over you. We've spent too much time together, anyway, and the pain from the bat bites won't put them in a better mood. Trust me, you don't want to end up with any of them."

"To be clear, I didn't want to end up with you, either," she pointed out. She'd wanted to end up watching murder shows in bed while simultaneously scrolling TikToks on her phone.

Her phone!

She opened her bag.

"Give me my cloak," he said, ignoring her frantic search.

"Maybe you should leave it with me," she suggested, not looking up from her purse. Maybe she'd put her phone in one of the interior pockets for the very first time? "So I can hide if they come back."

He glowered at her. "You won't need to hide. I'll protect you."

I'll protect you. It was a nice thing to say, but an ominous implication.

"Are you planning to take me with you?" That posed a problem for her. Not that she had anywhere else to go. Other than home, which she couldn't exactly get to from there.

Still, the further away she went from the spot where she'd arrived, the further she was from home. Maybe. She wasn't sure how the rules worked. She didn't come in through a wardrobe or a standing stone. Maybe it didn't matter where she was. Maybe she was screwed everywhere.

"Yes, I'm planning to take you with me," he extended an arm with a grimace. "Come on. You can sit on my shoulder."

She stepped back. "Uh, I don't want to sit on your shoulder. I want to go home."

"Do you know how to get home?" he asked.

"I—"

"You don't even know where you are."

She actually heard a metal-on-metal screech in her

head. "How do you know—I mean, why would you think that?"

"Because no human intentionally comes to The Mire." He waited a moment longer, then withdrew his hand. "Fine. Let's move, then."

Though she didn't plan to stay with this ogre as his long-term possession—they would discuss the "spoils" thing later—she didn't have much of a choice but to follow him.

"You also look terrible," he went on, holding a branch aside for her as if catching the door for her at a convenience store.

Convenience store. She would kill for a Gatorade. The dark blue kind.

"Not just because you're human. Although that is a large part of the problem," he continued. "You're in a terrible condition. Your clothes are ratty and your hair is matted and you have dirt all over—"

"You know—" she barked, then modulated her tone. "You're right. I'm in rough shape. My clothes and my hair got a little messed up when I was running from the harpy. And the whatever the Baron was."

"Vampire," Droguk supplied.

"Vampire. Sure." She nodded, that hysterical laughter from before threatening to make an explosive return.

"You're a human in The Mire. You don't know what vampires are, and you're traveling a road along their border." It wasn't that Droguk was talking to her; he was talking to himself. Until he looked down from the corner of his eye and said, "Why don't you just tell me who you are, why you're here, and how you got here? It's a long walk and I don't care for mysteries."

Visions of burning at the stake danced through

her head. But she hadn't died yet, and there had been plenty of opportunities. "If I tell you something mind-bogglingly absurd, are you going to accuse me of being a witch and torture me to death?"

"Why would I want to kill a witch?" he gasped in horror.

"Where I'm from, they... never mind" She had her answer. "I was waiting for my friend in a bookshop and as far as I can tell, I somehow fell into the book and ended up wherever I am now."

He stopped walking.

And started laughing.

Vanessa raised her voice, hoping he'd hear her over his wheezing roars. "You asked. I don't have enough energy at the moment to try to convince you. But I thought we were being quiet."

That shut him up quickly.

"A magic book?" he said, his voice lower, though he struggled to keep from laughing. "You fell through a magic book."

"It's what happened. I can't make up anything better or more believable. I don't know where I am or how I got here. I don't know what a mire is, and where I'm from doesn't have vampires or ogres—"

Something in the way her voice got higher and thinner as her breathing grew more rapid and shallow must have tipped him off to the extent of her growing hysteria, because all the humor fled his face. "Fine. Fine. I believe you."

It wasn't sincere. She could tell.

But that didn't matter. Humoring her and believing her were functionally the same at that point. His shoulders slumped and he started to walk again. "You're in The Mire. It's a swampy region in the north-west of the Fablemere mainland."

Fablemere! That had been the title! "I'm in a book!"

They'd barely made progress, and he stopped again. "Excuse me?"

"Fablemere! It was the title of the book I fell into. This—" she spread her arms wide and turned in a circle "—is all a book!"

That explained everything! Vanessa laughed in relief and took another little spin. Then she spun right back when Droguk snatched her up by the wrist and snarled, "And the wound in my side? Is that part of a book?"

"I—"

He started walking again and pulled her along behind him. "This isn't fiction, human. This is real blood running down my side. There's real danger out there, and the deeper the night gets, the thicker the danger."

"I'm sorry," she squeaked, and tried to no avail to get her arm into a more comfortable angle. She stumbled and recovered her feet with desperate swiftness; there was no doubt in her mind that if she fell, he would just drag her over the gnarled roots and thorny vines that carpeted the forest. "I didn't mean to offend you. I've just had a really weird day."

"My day was a little out of the ordinary, too," he grumbled. But he did loosen his hold a bit.

"Look, you're bleeding. You're obviously in pain. You should stop and rest," she advised without a shred of wilderness experience.

"I should stop so that the predators can find me more easily?" he countered, never slowing his steps. "You're more likely to die standing still out here than moving. And I don't plan to be out here for much longer. If you won't let me carry you, at least speed up."

To keep up with the pace Droguk set, Vanessa found herself practically jogging, occasionally hopping over obstacles that gave the ogre no trouble. It reassured her that he not only knew where he was going, but he wasn't about to drop dead from whatever gory wound lurked beneath his tunic. The night got deeper, the forest darker, and soon she relied on his hand around hers as a guideline. If he let go, or she did, she was certain she'd be lost.

The ground grew marshy, and her legs were already so tired. Her entire body ached, and she desperately needed to sleep off her earlier seizure. Her shoes stuck in the mud; one popped off.

"Wait, please," she bleated, the weight of the day crashing down on her and pushing her deeper into the—well, into the *mire*—like that damn sad horse in *The Neverending Story.*

And she burst into loud, sobbing, hiccupping tears.

Droguk, who'd said nothing through several long, surly hours of dragging her like a carcass, stopped. "What's wrong?"

"My shoe," she wailed. It wasn't a particularly expensive or fancy or nice shoe. Just a tennis shoe. But it was gone now and there didn't seem to be a lot of shopping options around, and shoes seemed like they were going to be pretty fucking necessary.

The ogre huffed. "We won't find it now. It's too dark."

"I know it's too dark!" Fuck. Not two weeks before, her dentist's receptionist had offered her a little promotional key chain flashlight. She'd thought, *In case I get amnesia and forget who my dentist is?* and she'd *thrown it in the trash when she got home.*

It was all she could think about now.

"I can't keep going without shoes," she sobbed. "I'm sorry, I can't."

"We're not far now." He didn't ask, this time. He wrapped one massive hand around her upper arm and lifted her off her feet. Her stomach plummeted in a weightless moment, then she found herself sitting on one of his broad shoulders. She threw her arms around his head, the nearest thing she could grab at for balance.

"Not far from where?" she asked.

He nudged her forearm up, so that it no longer covered his eyes. "Mudholme."

"Is that a village or—"

He pushed aside a sapling and they stepped onto a wide expanse of flat, steaming swampland. With no canopy of leaves to block it out, the weak half-moon light shone on mirror-like puddles between mounds of tall grass. It would have been beautiful if it hadn't smelled like pickled shit. And in the distance stood the jagged outline of crumbling ruins.

"My castle," Droguk said with pride. "My home."

Chapter Five

Round, flat stones created a path through the swamp. Despite his size and power, the ogre moved swiftly across them, toward the looming ruins.

Vanessa clung to his head and imagined their destination. Slimy walls. Moldy furniture. Spoiled food.

Snails. He probably ate snails.

As they grew closer, though, she spied light flickering in arched doorways, and then, as they approached the gates, actual torches flaming in brackets against the stone.

Two incredibly short figures in pieces of mismatched armor clanked toward them, drawing swords with blades so notched along the edges, they might as well have been keys.

"Halt!" one of them called, brandishing its weapon.

"Igthish, your helmet is on backward," Droguk said wearily.

The creature dropped its sword on the ground and struggled with its helmet, while the other pried a crudely slitted metal pail from its head.

"Master! You've returned!" Pail-head bowed at its waist.

"Open the gate."

The little monsters hurried to a huge wooden wheel attached to the thickest chain Vanessa had ever seen. They heaved and grunted until the wheel budged just a little, then the chain let go entirely. A rung of the wheel caught the one called Igthish by the belt at his waist and tossed him up and over, straight out of his pants. The huge iron portcullis lifted and Droguk strode beneath it.

"Fucking goblins," he muttered, while Vanessa cringed in fear of the spiked gate crushing them into pink jelly.

And green jelly, obviously.

Droguk set her on her feet in a cobble-stone court-yard. The stones under her bare foot were smooth and slick, but everything was surprisingly tidy, if covered with a slimy layer of moisture. No piles of bones, at least.

A door opened across the courtyard, spilling out golden light and two ogre children. They rushed Droguk, and he scooped one up preemptively, before it could collide with his injured side. Vanessa hung back and examined the kids. Both of them wore simple, woven-cloth dresses with aprons. Their hair was braided, one in a single, fat rope that swung down her back, the other in two long vines.

Another ogre emerged, a taller version of the two others. She leaned against the doorway a moment, shaking her head fondly at the sight of what Vanessa assumed were Droguk's daughters attempting to climb all over him. Then, the ogress's eyes landed on Vanessa, and her green face contorted in disgust.

The children chose that exact moment to turn their attention toward the ogress. Following her gaze, they spied Vanessa. And they screamed bloody murder.

"Calm down, calm down," Droguk scolded as the children clung to him and tried to hide themselves behind his legs. "It won't hurt you. It's harmless."

"It's so gross!" the taller of the children wailed.

"I don't want it to touch me!" squealed the other.

"You know, I'm not really in the mood to touch you, either," Vanessa snapped, and silence fell over the courtyard, a silence of mixed shocked and umbrage, if she gauged it right. Not only was the human there, being disgusting, but it had said something that, in hindsight, was even more disgusting.

"I mean," she began, shifting from her bare foot to her shoe and back again. "Not that I would touch you. You're minors and that's..."

Drogruk winced in a species-transcending expression of secondhand embarrassment.

The ogress opened her mouth as if to say something. Then, she looked to Droguk and gasped. "You're hurt!"

"Oh." Droguk lifted his arm and examined his bloody side as if just remembering it. "Yeah. I slashed myself open on a bone-petal thorn. I hope your sewing fingers are feeling nimble tonight."

The ogress gave Drogruk an unimpressed look, then nodded toward me. "Is it sleeping inside?"

"It—" Vanessa took a deep breath and lowered her voice. If they were discussing whether or not she was going to sleep in the cold, wet courtyard or inside near a fire, she didn't want to tilt the scales by being rude. "It would love to sleep inside. In a bed, if possible. And it also would appreciate it if you'd refer to me as 'she' or 'they' instead of 'it.'"

The ogress tilted her head. "And does this human have a name?"

Droguk's brow furrowed.

"Vanessa. We didn't get a chance to introduce ourselves," she answered for him.

The ogress nodded. "Well then, Vanessa. Come along. You can watch me stitch up my foolish brother."

The inside of the castle was as warm and inviting as the light from the doorway had promised. Despite the height and size of the ruins from the outside, there appeared to be only a small portion that was livable. A noticeable chill clung to the perimeter due to the moisture gleaming on the walls, but a round, raised hearth in the center of the room pushed the cold back, and candles on the rough wooden tables arranged around the fire gave the place a cheery light.

It didn't look like a place Vanessa would expect an ogre to live.

"Sit," the Ogress said gruffly, pushing Droguk toward a bench. He sat obediently and shrugged off his cloak and tunic.

And he didn't look the way Vanessa would have expected an ogre to look. Except for the part about being green. The rest of him, though... He was like... like...

Like if Jason Momoa were about a foot broader and dyed for St. Patrick's Day.

"This is my sister," he said gruffly, and Vanessa's face flamed. He had to have noticed her staring. And he stared back, his eyes fully unreadable beneath his furrowed brow. "Drova, widow of Ord. Those are their daughters, Vrada and Od."

Vanessa gave a little wiggle of her fingers in a wave. The kids both cowered behind their mother.

"What brings Vanessa the human to Mudholme?" Drova asked, grimacing at the slash and stain on her brother's shirt.

Vanessa opened her mouth to answer, but Droguk spoke over her. "I found it—found them—during the raid on the Baron. I don't know if they belong to him—"

"I don't belong to anyone," Vanessa spoke up quickly.

Droguk narrowed his eyes. "Beg to differ."

Okay, we will be discussing that *later.*

"What else did you get?" Drova asked, going to a pail beside the fire. She tipped some water into a large wooden mug and pushed it into her brother's hands. "The raiders didn't short you, did they?"

"They didn't short me. She was the only thing of value." He nodded toward Vanessa. "They're a seer."

Drova finally looked at Vanessa, pure astonishment writ across her features. "A seer? Really?"

"No," Vanessa said flatly. "I have a medical condition that everyone has mistaken for a magical power."

"It's a long story," Droguk said.

"It's really not."

"There wasn't any gold?" Drova interrupted. "Goods? Anything we could possibly sell?"

"Nothing. The only trunk we got away with was a trick." Droguk groaned as if the entire night had just caught up to him. His shoulders slumped and he rubbed his eyes with one big hand. "I warned them. I warned them that anything of value the Baron would carry would be inside the carriage. But the gargoyles—"

"Gargoyles!" Drova turned a much paler shade of green.

"Everyone got away," he said, and then, with surprising tenderness, caught her hand and squeezed it. "No one got hurt."

She jerked away from him. "You did, you ass pie." To her taller daughter, she said, "Vrada, bring me my sewing basket."

Vanessa sat silently, watching the family dynamic play out. The younger child stayed close to her mother, darting fearful glances toward Vanessa. The elder kept to her mother's shadow, as well, but showed guarded curiosity where Vanessa was concerned. That curiosity was divided, however, once Drova began to tend to her brother's side.

Vanessa considered them. The adult siblings looked similar. They both wore their gleaming black hair in long braids, and their tusks protruded from the corners of their mouths in a way that was alike, though Vanessa wasn't sure if that was just an effect of seeing someone with tusks for the first time.

Droguk took a sharp inhale when Drova pushed the needle through his flesh. He directed his attention to Vanessa. "You look faint, human."

"So do you, ogre," she responded in kind.

He flinched and made a fist on the tabletop at the next poke. "I didn't introduce myself. I'm Droguk."

"I got that from context. Back in the forest." Vanessa jerked her thumb over her shoulder.

"You were traveling with the Baron?" Drova asked, her concentration briefly flickering over Vanessa.

"Not at all. I just met that dude today and I am not

impressed," Vanessa said, waving her arms in front of her.

"You're only wearing one shoe," Od blurted.

"Helpful question," Vrada deadpanned.

"Girls." The mom tone transcended species; the kids were instantly subdued.

"I'd rather listen to them argue. It's distracting me," Droguk grumbled.

So did Vanessa's stomach. Loudly.

"Did you feed her?" Drova demanded, brandishing the needle again.

Droguk said something that sounded like it was a swear word. "Oh, yes, we had a picnic with the Baron. It was lovely. I'm your brother, by the way, and I'm also hungry."

"Vrada, get the human something to eat," Drova said wearily. "And you, brother, can eat when I'm finished."

"I don't even know what humans eat," the eldest daughter argued.

"The same as we do," Droguk said cheerfully. "Swamp water and snails."

Od laughed.

"I would eat snails right now," Vanessa said, and meant it. She'd been saving room for popcorn at the movie. That was... "What time is it?"

Droguk and Drova exchanged a worried glance.

"It's nighttime," Droguk said cautiously.

"No, but like, do you guys have time here? One o'clock, two o'clock..."

Another look, like Vanessa had asked them if she could borrow the moon.

"There's one night, and one day. We don't have two of anything," Drova said kindly, as if talking to a small child. "Morning, midday, evening, night. Are you all right? Did you hit your head?"

"No. I just—" Vanessa stopped. "You know, I'm just really tired and I'm hungry and I'm not making sense."

"The human Vanessa is going to need a place to sleep," Droguk announced. "We'll put the girls together and she can have Od's alcove for tonight."

Od gasped and hurried toward a curtained-off corner. "Not with my dolls!"

"I won't have it sleeping in my child's bed. If you want to keep it inside, it can stay in the loft with you." Drova grimaced as she looked Vanessa over with open distaste.

The eldest daughter puttered around the hearth, then curtly dropped a pewter plate onto the table beside Vanessa. Whatever was on it smelled delicious, hot, and probably full of swamp water, but that didn't matter. It was some kind of stew, with chunks of vegetables and meat, with side of... purple bread.

Well, lots of things have been different today, she thought, and tore a piece of the chunk of bread to use as a rudimentary scoop, since there weren't any utensils.

"We have spoons," Vrada said witheringly, before setting the implement down beside the plate.

"Are we going to have to housebreak her, too?" Drova muttered.

"Leave her be," Droguk said. "She's tired, she's hungry, and she needs a hot bath."

"And a shoe!" Od called from behind her curtain.

Vrada groaned and dragged her feet as she headed for the door. "I'll get the tub and fetch the water."

"Thank you, Vrada," Droguk called after her in a

beleaguered sing-song. Then his eyes fell on Vanessa. She froze, mouth full of a huge bite of stew, unable to look away. Slight suspicion mingled with amusement in his expression. He studied her for a long moment, while she floundered to simultaneously swallow and figure out what the heck he was looking for. She mouthed, "thank you," to him, and he seemed to nod in acknowledgement, though it was a very subtle one.

Then, his sister picked up a jug from the table and sloshed the contents onto his side without warning. He roared with pain and slammed his fist down on his thigh.

"All done," Drova announced cheerfully, and began to collect up her supplies. "Now, you eat, and I'll see what I can do to make this human less..."

The ogress gave up trying to finish the sentence politely and just walked away instead. Droguk wiped his side with his bloodied shirt and balled it up, as if to toss it into the fire.

"You're going to need that," Drova warned before he could let the fabric fly. "You've only got the one other, and that's what I'm dressing the human in."

"In my good shirt?" he sputtered.

"She's your spoils," Drova said pointedly. "She can wear your shirt."

Chapter Six

"Thank you so much," Vanessa said, squeezing slightly sulfurous water from her hair. "Really, I'm so grateful."

"You were filthy. It was as much for our benefit as for yours," Drova said, shaking out the biggest shirt Vanessa had ever seen. "Here. This will have to do until we can find something better for you."

"I can just wash my clothes," Vanessa suggested, though she had no idea where her jeans, t-shirt, and jacket had gone. The ogress had gathered them all up and hurried them away as soon as Vanessa had gotten undressed.

Drova's expression twisted between disgust and desperation to hide that disgust politely. "We'll just see what we can find."

"Let her keep her clothes."

Vanessa glanced around at the curtains the ogress

had drawn around the tub. It was adequate cover, but walls would have been better.

Droguk sat on the other side of the hearth, his hulking shoulders outlined roughly in silhouette. "She's probably more comfortable in them."

"They're full of holes," Drova pointed out, and she wasn't wrong. The jeans had already been torn at the knee, though. Better to let them assume that had happened in The Mire and not due to a lack of motivation to buy new pants.

Vanessa unwound the linen sheet Drova had given her to cover herself and cast a glance at Droguk. He'd kept his back turned the entire time, despite the curtains between them, and she didn't think he'd suddenly become a peeper. Still, she hurried to pull the shirt over her head while Drova took another long, doubtful look.

"You humans." The ogress shuddered. "Disgusting. Although, not *as* disgusting as some I've seen, with the boney knobs and ridges everywhere."

There had never been a moment in Vanessa's adult life that she'd been called boney. "Thanks?"

Drova made a noise.

Vanessa's teeth started to grind. Not because of her hostess's criticisms. "I don't mean to trouble you, but I need to take my pills."

"I won't stop you," Drova said, frowning as she exited through the curtains.

When Vanessa was sure she was adequately covered—not that it was difficult with the yards and yards of fabric that hung to mid-calf—she exited, too, and stopped short. Droguk had half-turned, a huge wooden tankard in hand. His prominent brow lifted at the sight of her.

"That's more hair than you went in with," was all he said.

Vanessa smoothed a self-conscious hand over the sopping tangle hanging off the back of her head. Usually, she would have washed it with shampoo instead of skin-scorchingly strong soap and followed up with a ton of conditioner and a comb. Now, her cranky corkscrew curls hung in limp snarls. "Yeah, I was wearing a ponytail before. Now it's..."

"Big," Droguk supplied with what seemed like an approving nod.

What she needed his approval for was anyone's guess, but Vanessa returned it.

"Can I brush it?" Od tugged at Vanessa's oversized sleeve.

"You'll get lice," Vrada said boredly, not looking up from the huge book she had open on one of the tables.

"I don't have lice," Vanessa said firmly. Then again, she didn't really want an ogre child to brush her hair. She had no idea how strong they were. One tug could rip her head off. "But I also don't have a brush."

Drova came back from wherever she'd been off to, and she'd brought a comb along, which she planted firmly in Vanessa's hand. "You don't brush hair like that. You'd make a miremouse's nest of it. And Vrada is right, you'll get lice. Let the human do it themself."

"She doesn't have lice," Droguk said, taking a long drink from his mug.

"We'll see," Drova said, and breezed away again. "I'll get some bedding for them, for the floor. I won't have them laying in your bed."

"I didn't want to be in his bed, anyway," Vanessa said under her breath, taking the comb and sitting on one of the benches. Od amused herself with a doll beside the fire, content to brush its woven hair instead. Droguk swirled his mug around and sat in silence, and Vrada was consumed in her book.

It was peaceful and content and horrible because all Vanessa wanted was to be home, in her own bed. Hot tears rose to her eyes as she worked the wooden comb through her tresses, and she tried hard not to sniffle, but finally, a sob squeaked out.

"Did you pull?" Od looked up. "Mummy pulls my hair, sometimes, by accident."

"Yes, that's what happened," Vanessa lied, pasting on a fake smile for the child.

Droguk shifted on his bench, then rose with a stifled groan. "The human Vanessa is exhausted. I'm going to put them in the loft."

"The human Vanessa needs to use the bathroom first." She'd been so detached from her body and deprived of liquids all day that now, in a calm environment that felt bizarrely safe, she finally felt the stabbing pain of her overfull bladder.

Droguk glanced toward the bathtub.

"No, the..." Vanessa searched for an old-timey word that she hoped would translate. "A privy?"

Understanding lit his face. "Right. Well, come with me."

She followed him out of the warmth of the living quarters and into the courtyard, then through a crumbling archway. "Up there," he said, pointing to some steps.

Her eyesight adjusted as she ascended into the near-total darkness. Moonlight illuminated a small room with nothing but a stone ledge with a hole in it.

Great.

Once she finished doing her business directly into

the swamp—far away, she hoped, from where they collected their bathing and drinking water—she made her way back down the uneven stairs.

Droguk leaned against the wall at the bottom, puffing on a pipe that looked suspiciously similar to ones frequently seen in disc golf circles. He saw Vanessa and guiltily tried to hide it.

"Are you..." She covered her laugh with her hand. "Are you getting high?"

"It's been a long day, all right?" he said with a heavy sigh. "Don't tell Drova. She can't do anything to stop me, but she can annoy me about it."

"Your secret is safe with me," Vanessa promised. "What is it?"

"Elf weed." He reached into the pocket of his rustic woven pants and produced a little sachet.

Vanessa took it, opened the top, and sniffed. It was unmistakably cannabis. "We have this in my world."

He grunted in response, and it was her turn to sigh in defeat.

She handed the bag back. "You don't believe that I'm not from here."

"Oh, I believe that you're not from The Mire. I believe that you don't know where you are. And I believe that you need those pills to stop the visions. What I don't believe is the book nonsense." He took another puff from his pipe, then held it toward her.

I'm smoking pot with an ogre. Not how she'd expected to spend her day when she'd woken up, but she accepted a hit gratefully. She needed to take the edge off, too.

"What are you going to do with me?" she asked, coughing on her exhale.

"I don't know. It isn't like I've had a lot of time to

think about it." He took the pipe back.

"You don't eat humans." That was an important point to clarify.

"I would rather eat a bucket full of spiders," he said flatly.

"Oh, great. I fall into a fantasy world where bread is purple and vampires are real but don't worry, out of all the endless, magical possibilities, there are still fucking spiders." She leaned against the wall beside him. "Am I a slave or a servant or a pet or what? What's my role here?"

"For now? You're my captive," Droguk said.

"And that means?"

"That means you stay here, until I decide other-wise." He shrugged. "I've never taken anyone prisoner before, so you're going to have to be patient while I figure it out."

"Right. Can I get another hit of that?" She motioned to the pipe.

He handed it over, warning, "Careful. It's strong."

"Yup." She'd heard that before. Usually from college dudes proud of their ditch weed. "It's not my first rodeo."

"I don't know what that means." He was frustrated. Vanessa could relate.

"Well, my feet are freezing, so I'm going back in-side," she announced after she exhaled. "As long as that's okay? I mean, I'm your captive. I assume I have to run this stuff past you?"

"I don't know. I've never taken someone captive." He took the pipe and nodded toward the door. "Go on. Drova will get you... put away."

Vanessa only made it a few steps before Droguk stopped her. "Wait. Don't tell anyone what you told me. About falling through a book."

"Why? Because you think I'm bonkers?" she demanded, a hand on her hip.

He pushed off from the wall and took two steps toward her. Two steps that filled the gap between them so easily that Vanessa had to tip her head back to look up at his face.

"Because the other guys in the raiding party already know you're here. They already know you're a seer. And the word is going to spread. So, I'd appreciate it if you'd try to not make yourself even more conspicuous by spinning a bunch of strange tales." He stared down at her, unblinking, in what Vanessa interpreted as a silent, *"You got me?"*

"Fine. I won't mention it to anyone." She paused. "But you have to give me your word that if the other ogres try to, I don't know, steal me or something, you won't let them."

To her surprise, he nodded and said, "You have my word."

She didn't know how good an ogre's word was, but it was all she had at the moment.

"Go on. If Drova asks—"

"I'll say you're in the privy," Vanessa promised.

She went inside, where Drova boosted her up a ladder meant for ogre use—the rungs were awkwardly spaced and difficult to hold onto due to their size—and into the loft. There was a bed and a small table beside it with a candle, as well as an open chest with clothing spilling out. The ogress had prepared a pallet from scraps of fur and scratchy fabric, with a thin knit blanket atop it, right at the end of the larger bed.

Like one would for a dog.

At that point, Vanessa was too tired to argue. All she

wanted was to lay down, even on nasty, damp cryptid pelts. She ignored the unpleasant, mildewed smell of her hopefully temporary bed and closed her eyes.

Maybe, she thought, she would fall asleep and hopefully wake up at home.

Chapter Seven

The first day passed in a whimsical blur. Od showed Vanessa around the ruined castle. Drova put her to work with a few chores, but nothing cruel or unusual. Just fetching water, wiping the tables, bringing in firewood, things that Vanessa could manage and actually enjoy if she pretended to be Cinderella, pre-ball. Droguk went away in the morning and took Vrada with him; they returned at midday with some kind of reptilian pig animal that they'd murdered with spears, and everyone seemed quite pleased about the meal it would provide. The sun shone, huge birds made eerie squawks as they wheeled overhead, and the goblins from the gate staggered drunkenly around the courtyard, threatening each other with swords.

It was charming.

Until sundown.

"Something's wrong with the human," Drova said,

nudging Droguk.

Vanessa wanted to say, *No, I'm fine. Don't worry about me.* But she couldn't say anything. She was frozen by a dread so deep, a finality so stark and immediate that she couldn't thaw her neck to even nod.

Reality had paralyzed her. More accurately, the reality that her current situation was reality had paralyzed her. She sat on a stone bench in the courtyard, a bucket of water by her bare feet, and stared straight ahead. Somewhere, outside of the book, life went on. People would be looking for her. She couldn't call into work and explain what had happened. She couldn't check her bank balance to be sure autopay wouldn't run her into an overdraft. She had an appointment with her neurologist on Monday.

And with every passing minute, it seemed like Monday would be spent in The Mire, as a captive of a begrudgingly welcoming ogre family.

"You should poke it with a stick," the goblin Igthish suggested.

The other goblin, which Vanessa now knew as, of all things, "Bob the Goblin," full name, leaned close to her face. His bulging, round, yellow eyes blinked like malfunctioning traffic lights, and his tiny, upturned mouth worked like a little flap ringed with sharp, unevenly spaced teeth as he examined her.

"No," he concluded before Igthis could commence with the poking. "I think he should dunk it in the cistern."

"Don't be disgusting," Drova said, and popped Bob on the head with the side of her fist. "That's our drinking water."

"No one is poking or drowning anything," Droguk called across the courtyard. He was up to his elbows in reptile-pig, Vanessa knew, because the last thing she'd seen before shock had completely overtaken her had been his massive fist pulling handfuls of blackened guts from the animal.

"We don't know what happened to her before she was found on the road," Vrada chimed in. "And she doesn't remember how she got here or where she came from, so obviously it was something bad."

Something? It almost moved Vanessa to speak, and she would have, if she could have. Instead, she recounted all the *somethings* that had happened to her within a half hour of finding herself stranded on a completely different planet. Chased by a harpy. Creeped out by a vampire. Caught in the middle of an armed conflict, then taken prisoner by an ogre. She was so far from where she'd originally arrived, she'd given up all hope of ever getting back there.

And as the sun began to set, her reality got grimmer and darker: she was there, really there, and she had no idea how to get back. She had no idea how to even start.

She was trapped. Probably forever.

She was going to live in a swamp, with goblins and ogres, forever.

"What are we meant to do about it?" Drova demanded.

"Leave them alone," Droguk said simply. "She'll either come around, or they won't."

His casual lack of concern strangely comforted Vanessa. What she needed was to be left alone. To stay frozen in place on the bench, to feel the cold and damp of it seeping into her body. Her thoughts bounced between the physical and psychological discomfort until the very act of remaining motionless, staring into nothing, contemplating her doom became a test of her willpower, long after her initial shock wore off. The sun went down. The beast was butchered. The two goblins feasted on the discarded parts, singing happy little songs about their good fortune and the deliciousness of the creature's organs. Droguk and Drova went inside, and so, eventually, did Vrada, who'd hovered in the courtyard for as long as she was allowed.

Night fell with a cacophony of buzzing, chirping, singing insects; none that Vanessa could identify as crickets or frogs similar to home. Nothing was similar to home.

She wanted to move. She wanted to be comfortable. She wanted to speak, most of all, to explain her pain to someone, but the ogres didn't seem particularly sympathetic. Plus, if she spoke her fears aloud, they were real. If she moved from the bench, they were real. If she warmed herself by the fire and got a good night's rest, she might accept that this could very well be her existence now.

That was the last thing she wanted to do.

It was late when the castle door opened. The goblins snoozed in the rickety stable, snuggled into their moldering straw, and the torches were already extinguished. Vanessa lifted her face to the sky above. In the total darkness, the night showed unfamiliar stars and swirling purple galaxies.

If outer space still exists, maybe I'm still in the same universe as home.

Droguk sat heavily beside her. There wasn't much room, so he bodily nudged her over.

"You're going to freeze to death out here," he said.

"Uh-huh." It was the first she'd spoken in hours, and her throat rasped as if it had forgotten speech entirely.

"What happened to you?" he asked.

Her shoulders slumped, sore from holding herself so tense and still for so long. "I told you what happened to me. You don't believe me."

"I believe that you believe you got here by falling through a book." He made that concession, at least. "But I think that what actually happened was something worse. Something that made you lose your memory."

"Explain my clothes, then?" she snapped. "Explain how I have a plastic pill bottle and rubber soled sneakers in this *Lord of the Rings* ass place." She paused. "Sneaker, I guess. The other one is—"

He followed her gesture toward the castle gate. "Sneaker. Your shoe?"

"Yes, my shoe." She looked down at her filthy bare feet, pale as the moon overhead. "My shoe, my clothes, my purse, the stuff in it. Have you ever seen anyone dressed like me? Who talks like me?"

"I haven't," he admitted. "But I've never been out of The Mire."

"Well, this doesn't exactly look like a haven of synthetics, and I'm guessing there's nowhere else in 'Fablemere' that does." She made finger quotes around the name.

"I couldn't say. Life is simple here. We get up, we do chores, we eat, we exist. We believe in things that we can see." He huffed in frustration. "I can see your strange clothes. I can see the pill bottle. But I can't see this alleged book that you somehow fell through. I didn't see you drop from the sky. All I know is, you were in grave danger with the Baron and now you're here."

"So, what? I should be grateful that you kidnapped

me?"

"You should be grateful that you escaped the Baron," he corrected her. "You didn't meet me until after that happened."

She looked down at her cold, bare toes. "My life is so different from this. When I woke up yesterday, I didn't expect any of this to happen. I'm forty-one, for fuck's sake. I'm forty-one, I have a job, I have a roommate, I have bills to pay. This is the kind of thing that happens to really young people in stories."

"But you're not in a story," he said. "You're here."

"I'm not supposed to be." She thought of her cubicle at work and wondered if anyone would water her fern. Or, where they would put it when it became evident that she wasn't returning. Royal Beverage wasn't likely to keep a distribution associate's desk empty forever. "I need to get back."

"I don't know how to make that happen." Droguk's tone was surprisingly gentle. "If I did, I would have sent you to your home a long time ago. You're creepy and your skin is so pink, you look like you're inside out. Just looking at you makes me shudder with revulsion—"

"Okay!" She pushed herself up from the bench. "I get it. You find me deeply, deeply ugly. So do a lot of humans, you may be surprised to learn."

He shrugged. "Got you off the bench, didn't I?"

"I—" Her mouth hung open.

He stood and motioned to the door. "I saved you some supper. We can't figure out how to return you to your home tonight, and starving yourself won't help. When things have calmed down, I'll take you to the border of the Springlands."

"I'm not from the Springlands," she reminded him.

"I know. But there are humans there. Wouldn't it be better to be around your own kind?" he asked.

Vanessa couldn't argue. She did want to be around her own kind. But she wanted to be around them back on Earth. Back in reality.

That wasn't an option, and her grumbly stomach urged her to go in and eat, despite the fact that she'd gotten a good look at the hybrid pig-beast they'd cooked. Desperate times, measures, etc.

Droguk followed her inside. He poured a mug of something for her that tasted very much like wine, but probably had been made from some kind of weird swamp plant with eyeballs instead of flowers. Vanessa tried not to think about it and gulped it down. She almost asked him if he had more "elf weed," but by the time she'd scarfed down her plate of meat and bread and undefinable but delicious greens, she'd warmed up and didn't want to set foot—especially bare foot—outside. With a normal body temperature and a full belly, all she really wanted was sleep.

Droguk helped her up to the loft, but he didn't go up, himself. She fell asleep to the sound of him puttering around downstairs, pushing in benches and cleaning up dishes.

In the morning, when she opened her eyes, her sneakers sat neatly at the end of her pallet.

Both of them.

Chapter Eight

"So, you don't have a job."

Droguk stopped mid-step and faced Vanessa. He put his arms out and turned in a circle, indicating the fog-thick marshlands. "This is my job. Providing for my family is my job."

They'd spent most of the morning in the swamp, hunting. Usually, Vrada would go out instead, but her mother had needed her help with chores at the castle. At least, that was the excuse Drova had come up with; Vanessa knew the ogress was just creeped out by her.

Droguk used his spear to point to a spot of open water ringed by clumps of dying swamp grass. "This way."

Vanessa followed him, her sneakers squishing and slipping in the muck. She'd never been so happy to get her shoes dirty; Droguk had stopped more than once to pull a huge, fat leech off his bare feet and ankles.

And then, he'd eaten them.

He'd offered her one. Just once. Her involuntary wretch had cleared up that misunderstanding right away.

"But you don't have employment," she went on. "You don't have to get up in the morning and go to an office or something and sit around making money for someone else."

"No," he grunted. "That would be stupid."

"From your lips to his ears," Vanessa muttered.

"Who?" Droguk splashed through a puddle and headed for a huge, hollow log. When Vanessa reached the edge of the puddle, he put his giant hands on her waist and lifted her over it.

"Who who?" She was a little dizzy when he set her down. Due to her current predicament, she'd thought it would be prudent to reduce and ration her daily meds. She wasn't likely to find a pharmacy in The Mire. At some point, the pills would run out, and she'd be in a bad position, so splitting the dose and dealing with the brain zaps had been the best solution she could come up with.

"You said, 'from your lips to his ears,'" Droguk explained, sitting on the log. It sank wetly into the mud under his weight, but it didn't totally submerge.

She climbed onto the log beside him. "It's just a saying, where I'm from. The 'his' is God. You're saying you hope that God hears what the person said, and that he takes it into consideration."

"Do you only have one god?" Droguk seemed taken aback by the idea.

Vanessa shook her head. "No. There are a lot of them. There just happen to be a few different religions that worship roughly the same one. What about ogres? What are your gods like?"

"I'm not religious," he said flatly.

"Oh." She swung her feet, drumming her heels against the log. "I'm not, either."

"I'm not against it," he went on. "I understand that tradition and ritual are important to some. I just don't participate."

She wasn't sure how to respond, so she just nodded. They sat in uncomfortable silence. Vanessa was getting used to that, though she didn't particularly enjoy it. It gave her time to think, and having time to think was what had led to her breakdown the day before.

"Can I ask you a question?"

He made another of his beleaguered grunting noises. Vanessa assumed there was an entire language of them to be learned. He tilted his head to look at her. "What do you want to ask?"

"If ogres don't get along, and if you just want to stay home and survive with your simple little life, why were you in that raiding party?" From what Vanessa could tell, the money didn't seem to be an issue. The family had food, a roof over their heads, and two servants who, while not being very bright at all, seemed to work for scraps.

"Drova's mate owed three raids to Thag. If I hadn't gone in his place, she would have."

Thag must have been the leader, the one with the undercut. "Your brother-in-law was a mercenary or a highway man or something?"

Droguk nodded. "He was from the North. Life is harder there, especially close to the border with the Sorrowland. But travelers are harder to come by there, too. So, a few times a year, raiding parties will organize and strike out on the road. I fulfilled Ord's obligation, so that Drova wouldn't have to."

"You didn't get anything of value." They hadn't even stolen pocket change.

He shifted beside her. "I wouldn't say that. I've got company."

Vanessa snorted. "Yeah. Company that creeps you out."

"Company that doesn't talk incessantly about leaving The Mire for someplace where life will be so much better and more interesting." He inhaled deeply, as if summoning all his patience. "Or trying to tell me how to hunt."

"Teenagers are the same, no matter what their species, huh?" Vanessa mused.

Droguk held up his hand, signaling for quiet. He pointed into the pea soup gloom, to a small green light hovering erratically above the tufts of marsh grass. He looked to Vanessa in warning, then slowly lifted his spear. The light bobbed. He made a cooing noise and the light halted. He repeated it, and the light changed direction, heading straight for them, before disappearing.

Droguk glanced at Vanessa and indicated the small patch of open water in front of them. A bubble rose, then another, and—

The creature burst up through the surface so fast that Vanessa toppled backward off the log. It was another of those reptilian pig monsters, which had turned out to be truly delicious, but was much more ferocious in its live state. It bared long, needle sharp fangs below its snout, and a bioluminescent appendage bobbed on its forehead like a pilot fish's lure. It lashed out with bear-like claws, which Droguk dodged easily. When it reared up in fury, Droguk sank the spear into its throat and thrust straight up; the tip of the spear protruded through the top of the creature's head, and the stocky body went limp.

Vanessa swiped gelatinous muck off her legs and butt. "Holy shit! That was amazing."

Droguk looked over at her, still lofting the enormous animal on the spear. "You ruined my shirt."

She rolled her eyes at him. "I'll wash it. But seriously, you just lured that thing over here and killed it. Like it was nothing!"

"It's not nothing. It's hunting." He gripped the creature's throat and jerked the spear free, releasing a torrent of purple blood. He tossed the spear to Vanessa, and she caught it clumsily, but managed not to slash her face open.

He hefted the beast over his shoulder. "Come on, then. And watch out for those lights. These will grab you and drag you in."

Vanessa jumped and squeaked. "Why are you telling me this *now*?"

"If I told you before, you would have been scared." He adjusted the carcass across his neck like a demented fur stole, holding its front and back feet in his massive hands, and started back the way they'd come.

"I *am* scared!" She hurried after him, hopping onto the mounds of grass as often as possible.

"Well, you shouldn't be," he said cheerfully, never slowing down. "Now, you know that I can protect you from them. There's no reason to be scared."

It was hard to argue with that logic. "And you protected me from the... I can't believe I'm saying this, but from a gargoyle?"

"That's true."

"And you found my other shoe." She looked down at

the already soaked and stained canvas. "Thank you, by the way."

"It was a lot of trouble," he said, though he didn't sound put-out about it, at all. That was something Vanessa had noticed about ogre speech patterns; they weren't mean, just gruff and direct.

It helped her take comments about how disgusting and creepy she was a little less personally.

They walked back through the swamp, pausing occasionally for Droguk to point to a root or leaf with his foot. Vanessa would dig up the plant or snip the stalks and carry them. He educated her briefly on important differences between one type of weed or another, until she stopped him.

"I don't know when I'll use this knowledge. I'm never going to be out here without you," she reminded him as the walls of the ruined castle dimmed the gray-white fog. "I can't kill one of those things."

"Shh," he said, holding up a hand.

Vanessa brandished the spear and whirled, her eyes darting everywhere for a sign of the dread light.

"Someone's here," Droguk said, his low voice eerily soft. "At the gates."

Her stomach plummeted. "Is it the Baron?"

"No. It's not a large enough retinue." Droguk gestured toward the gates. "Whatever happens, you keep your mouth shut and your head down. Don't call attention to yourself. You're an ordinary household servant. You'll go inside and stay put."

She nodded wordlessly.

His brow furrowed, yellow eyes softening with concern. "I'm going to protect you. You just have to trust me."

Vanessa looked at her shoes, then back to him. "I

do."

They walked to the castle at the same pace they'd started out with, as if to say, *"nothing amiss here. We're not concerned."* And when they reached the gate, which was open, and they passed the rickety wagon parked there, Droguk didn't try to hide her.

"Gorgrak," Droguk said in greeting to the ogre standing in the courtyard. To Vanessa, Droguk said, "Take those inside and see what Drova needs. Don't dawdle, or you'll sleep in the swamps tonight."

Vanessa remembered Gorgrak, though not by name and certainly not by his physical appearance, as he hadn't been quite so swollen and bumpy when she'd first met him. He'd clearly had a much worse time with the trunk full of monsters than Vanessa and Droguk. But his knit cap gave him away.

"New serving girl not working out?" Gorgrak sneered, and spit on the ground.

"Don't do that," Droguk said flatly. "What are you doing here?"

"I'm here to take that problem off your hands."

Vanessa somehow managed to not break into a run during the conversation. Droguk had said he would protect her. She had to believe him.

"Looks like you've got problems of your own," Droguk replied.

Inside, Drova was waiting by the door, listening. When Vanessa stepped inside, the ogress motioned to one of the sleeping alcoves. Vanessa moved in that direction, ducking behind the curtain. She sat on the edge of the bed and pulled her feet up, remembering too late Drova's disgust at the very notion of a human touching the places where they slept. This seemed to be a dire circumstance.

"Those fuckin' Sorrowbats, wasn't it?" Gorgrak wheezed as the two ogres entered. "Your sister wasn't very hospitable when I arrived."

"His sister doesn't have time for your nonsense," Drova snapped back.

"I don't know why you came all this way," Droguk said wearily. "The human isn't for sale."

"Everything is for sale."

"But I happen to know that you don't have any money," Droguk countered. "That raid was a failure."

"I may not have it now, but we'll all get plenty, yet. That human you've got there is valuable. And the Baron is willing to pay for it."

Vanessa's blood froze in her veins.

"The Baron?" There was a creak that Vanessa interpreted as Droguk sitting on a bench. "Since when are you on speaking terms with him?"

"Since you ran off with the only valuable thing we stole from him." Gorgrak gave a phlegmy chortle. "First thing we did—when we were healed enough, of course—was send a message to him. If we give him back the seer, he won't retaliate against us for the raid."

"He won't retaliate against me for the raid, anyway," Droguk pointed out. "It was your raid, your band. Your banners they saw."

There was a long, deadly tense silence.

"That band," Gorgrak snarled, "needs the gold that will come from the sale of that seer!"

"If you think that I am so heartless as to hand a human over to a vampire, then you have me confused with a lesser ogre."

"If you turn your back on your kind, you're no ogre." Gorgrak's tone painted a sneer on the picture in Vanessa's mind.

"You're not my kind." There was no animosity in Droguk's voice, which made the remark even more cutting.

Vanessa wished she could see what was happening. The silence stretched on too long. But she couldn't chance a peek; the tension was so thick that a single eyelid twitch would shatter it. Only the embers in the hearth dared to make a sound.

Gorgrak broke first. "Well, it won't be on my conscience then, when I direct the Baron's men your way."

"Will it be on your conscience when you endanger the wife and children of your former friend? The ogre you called your brother?" Drova said icily.

"We have no quarrel with you or with your children. You didn't rob us." Gorgrak paused for effect. "It's this traitor that will be dealt with. And the human."

"Well, you won't deal with me today. So, see yourself out." Droguk said it as though he were ordering away a bothersome child. "Drova, we have a quaglantern to skin."

There was another long pause. Then a shuffling of feet. The door closed. Vanessa still didn't feel safe to move from the alcove.

Droguk was in danger, and it was kind of her fault. She wouldn't accept the entire blame, since nobody forced him to go on the raid or get mixed up with people like Gorgrak, but if she hadn't fallen into the book in the first place, the family wouldn't be in danger from a vampire Baron.

The curtain jerked back, and she let out a startled whoop.

"Pack your things," Droguk ordered. "We're leaving."

Chapter Nine

"You can't leave!"

Vanessa looked past Droguk to Drova. The ogress stood in the doorway, jaw dropped in shock.

"We can't stay," Droguk said, and turned to Vanessa again to repeat, "Pack your things."

"I don't have any things," she whispered. Although that wasn't entirely true; Droguk had gotten her pills and her shoes and—

"Who runs this place if you're gone?" Drova demanded. "The goblins? Are they going to hunt for food and patch the roof?"

"Vrada has hunted with me enough that she practically does it all by herself when we go out," Droguk said. "And the goblins do patch the roof, actually. You just have to tell them to."

"They spend all day falling off," Drova argued.

"Because they love falling off! You just have to keep

them focused on their—" Droguk took a deep inhale and pinched the bridge of his nose. "You heard Gorgrak! If I'm here, if the human is here, you're all in danger."

"No, we're not," Drova insisted. "He said their quarrel wasn't with—"

Droguk marched toward his sister with a snarl so ferocious that Vanessa shrank from it. But Drova did not; Vanessa assumed that the ogress feared her brother about as much as she seemed to fear anything, which was not at all.

"Do you really believe that the Baron will distinguish one ogre from another? That he'll honor the wishes of your dead husband's criminal friends?" he shouted, and Drova's hand flashed out and landed with a smack across his cheek.

"Never." She held up a trembling finger to point it at him. "Never speak of Ord that way. You didn't like him, but he cared for me. He protected me from our parents when you wouldn't. When you ran away!"

Vanessa got the feeling that she was an unwilling witness to a history she had no business learning. She wondered if she could silently inch herself out of the room without being noticed. Somehow, being caught trying to leave in acknowledgement of the awkwardness seemed like it would somehow be more awkward than just sitting there and listening.

Before she could make a decision, Droguk turned back to her. "Get your things."

"Going back to Dun Larvae?" Drova sneered. "Running off to tell on Gorgrak? That worked out brilliantly last time."

"I didn't sell Ord out to Vikthor," Droguk said flatly. "And I know that you don't believe I did."

Drova's shoulders sagged. "You can't leave me behind again."

"I'm not leaving you behind." Droguk uttered that guttural word that sounded like a curse and pulled his sister into a hug. "Yes, I'm going to Dun Larvae to see Vikthor. But I'm coming back. I'll put the human in his care, and the Baron can decide whether or not he wants to pursue the issue."

"He won't be able to get that fancy carriage through The Mire," Drova said with a tearful laugh.

Droguk held his sister out at arm's length. "If we leave now, we'll reach Dun Larvae tomorrow night. I don't believe Ord's friends would allow you to be harmed. You can direct them to pursue me, instead. You might end up with Gorgrak stinking up the courtyard for a while to await my return, but he can protect this place just as well as I can. When things are calmer, I'll return."

Drova nodded, her eyes closed. "I wish you hadn't brought that thing here."

"I'm not psyched to be here, either," Vanessa muttered.

The ogres shot her looks that immediately silenced her.

"Do you have their clothes laundered?" Droguk asked, motioning to Vanessa.

"No. The washers at Dun Larvae will have to take up that task." Drova said this in a tone that implied she didn't think much of whatever this high and mighty "Dun Larvae" was. "At least, stay here for tonight. There's still time to bake bread and smoke some meat for your journey."

"It's two days." But it was clear that Droguk would acquiesce.

"It will give the human Vanessa time to wash her own clothes," Drova added. To Vanessa, she said, "You can't make the trek in just my brother's shirt."

"And I'll need that shirt, myself, at Dun Larvae." Droguk grimaced. "If we can get the Mire muck out of it."

"I'll get Vrada started on the food." Drova snapped her thick fingers. "Human Vanessa, you bring that basket and come with me."

Vanessa slid down from the ogress's bed and went to the ogre-sized basket full of ogre-sized clothes sitting just outside the alcove. Her human-sized muscles burned by the time she wrestled the thing out into the courtyard.

Drova waited beside a huge stone trough, her arms crossed in impatience. "They're not going to find much use for you at Dun Larvae, either. Have you ever washed clothes?"

"Where I'm from, we have machines that do it," Vanessa explained apologetically.

"So do we." Drova pulled a heavy iron thing with a crank and rollers up from behind the trough, which held two basins separated by a wall of thick, scarred stone. The ogress hefted the contraption onto the stone partition and tightened some vise screws. "This side is for soap and scrubbing. Scrub, plunge, feed the garment into the rollers, turn the crank, and it plops out in the rinse. Rinse it, squeeze out the water, hang it on the line over there."

Sounds easy enough. Vanessa began pawing through the basket. She found one leg of her jeans poking out and pulled it with a triumphant, "aha!"

"What are you doing?" Drova blinked at her.

"My laundry."

"You're not doing *your* laundry." Drova placed her hands on her hips. "You're doing *the* laundry. You got us into this mess. Now, you're going to help clean another."

* * * *

Vanessa began the trek to Dun Larvae with two dead arms. Ogre laundry sounded simple, but after all the cranking and wringing and hanging on a line far too tall for comfort, she was certain she had a torn rotator cuff.

Luckily, Droguk didn't expect her to carry anything. But he had expected to carry her.

"You slow me down," he grumbled. "At this rate, it will take us two full days to reach Dun Larvae."

"Well, I don't know what to tell you, but I wouldn't be able to hold onto you all that way, anyway. My arms are useless, thanks to your sister treating me like a god damn front-loader."

"A front what?"

She rolled her eyes. "A washing machine."

"Oh. Well, the laundry *was* piling up."

Was that a joke? Vanessa couldn't tell.

At least, she had her own clothes back. They did a good job protecting her from thorns and scratchy marsh grass, but the walk was boring and wet and uncomfortable, and the sweat and exertion made Vanessa's thighs itch beneath her jeans. She needed something to entertain her. "Who's Vikthor?"

"An ogre who has a soft spot for humans," Droguk said, and his prominent jaw clenched.

He didn't want to talk about it. Vanessa wasn't great with body language, but she could tell. Too bad for him, though, because she wasn't feeling particularly tactful or incurious. "Is that why Drova doesn't like him?"

"No."

"Then why doesn't Drova like him?"

Droguk stopped walking. "You should mind your own business."

"You should keep moving, if you're so worried about getting to our destination." Vanessa put a little skip into her step because she sensed that it would annoy him.

He started walking again, but he didn't stop being grouchy. "Vikthor is an old friend. More of a mentor. He gave me employment and a place to live, years ago."

"So, he helped you? Why would Drova have a problem with that?" It had seemed to Vanessa that the siblings were close and loving. That was a surprise, considering how often fairy tales painted them as bloodthirsty monsters ready to eat up princesses and billy goats.

"Drova is younger than I am. And our home situation wasn't ideal. Our parents... weren't kind. When Vikthor offered me a place in his guard, Drova felt like I abandoned her." His fist clenched and flexed at his side. "She was too young to understand that I was doing it for both of us."

Vanessa regretted asking. "So, is Vikthor like, a king?"

"There is no king in The Mire," Droguk said. "We don't like rulers or being ruled."

"I don't like paying taxes, but I have to. What keeps everyone in line?"

"An unwritten code of honor. Which only works if

an ogre is honorable. That's why we don't particularly like the company of other ogres, unless we trust them," he explained.

"Is that why Vikthor has guards?"

"It's one of the reasons. The other is, Dun Larvae is close to the Strait of Anthor. Lots of trade goes through there, so, lots of piracy." He paused at a thick fallen tree trunk and motioned to Vanessa. She stepped closer, uncertain, and he gripped her waist and lifted her over the obstacle.

"Thanks." She stepped back and noted the way he wiped his palms on his tunic after he quickly released her.

"The Dun Larvae guard protects the coastline, especially at the narrowest point of the Strait. We patrolled the marinas, prevented smuggling, occasionally cleaned up a brawl in one of the taverns." He motioned to a mossy area ahead. "Don't step on that. It's a slor."

"What's a—"

The moss shifted and lifted up, revealing a slug-like head and a lamprey's mouth full of rotating, serrated teeth.

She shrieked and jumped closer to Droguk's side, grabbing his arm like a frightened child.

That made him laugh. It was a weird, rumbling sound like an earthquake. "Don't worry. There isn't enough meat on you to tempt his appetite."

"Because it's all fat, right?" She wanted to storm off, but having seen the slor, she didn't plan to walk anywhere he hadn't stepped first.

"Not all fat," he said mildly. "Your thighs and calves are huge and they're mostly muscle."

"I—" She shook her head. They were two different

species, from two different worlds, with two different cultures. In the short time she'd been around them, Vanessa had learned that ogres were direct and honest. "I know you didn't mean that as an insult, so. Thank you."

In confirmation of her assessment, he looked at her like she'd started speaking in tongues. "Why would that be insulting?"

"Humans are... different." She waved a hand. "It's okay. You didn't mean anything."

He started to walk again, but the slor shifted and she found her feet frozen.

"Are you coming?" he asked.

"Can you just tell me where the other slors are? So I don't step on them?" She took a tentative step forward.

"Come on." He held out his hand.

She eyed him dubiously.

He rolled his eyes. "We'll go much faster if you ride on my shoulder. We might even make dry land to camp for the night. Unless you'd prefer to sleep on the back of a slor."

She let him pull her up, though she felt ridiculous sitting there, holding onto his head for balance while he wrapped his massive arm around her knees.

"What if we get to Dun Larvae—inviting name, by the way—and this Vikthor doesn't want to help me?"

"Vikthor is sympathetic to humans," Droguk said with a shrug that almost dislodged her.

"Not totally disgusted by them in an 'ick, a spider' kind of way?" she half-joked.

"I should hope not," Droguk replied. "He's married to one."

Chapter Ten

As soon as they reached solid ground safe from slors and other marsh horrors, Droguk found them a place to sleep and eat. They couldn't make a fire, because of the swamp gas, but he'd offered to let Vanessa sleep in the crook of his arm. It was awkward, but no more awkward than her extended piggy-back ride, so she accepted.

It was more comfortable than she expected.

The second day was more of the same, but on the other shoulder. They talked about a lot of things, except the one Vanessa had the most burning curiosity about, and that was the very notion of an ogre and a human being married.

It wasn't just about the physical disparity; she had a dirty mind, but for the most part that mind stayed on her own business. But every ogre she'd met so far had reacted to her as though she were repulsive. How did one decide to marry a human? How did they even start dating?

But there didn't seem to be a great way to bring it up.

The sun was setting when the castle of Dun Larvae came into view. It wasn't what Vanessa had expected. She'd assumed they were moving from one heap of moldering ruins to another, but Dun Larvae was a fully intact castle; a stone square with a blunt tower at each corner, sitting atop a hill. Considering there hadn't been anything remotely resembling elevation for the entire trip, Vanessa assumed the hill was man-made. Ogre-made.

A few thatch-roofed cottages lined the road to the castle, and ogres seemed to be closing their houses for the day. Chimneys smoked, cookfires filled the air with savory scents, and mothers called children inside.

"I thought ogres didn't like to be near each other?" Vanessa asked.

"Usually, we don't. Vikthor has made this place different, though." Droguk nodded at an ogre, who gave him a tusk-bent smile. "It helps that he's not a huge dick."

She straightened in surprise. "Oh. You guys say that, too."

Droguk reached up and grabbed her thigh to stabilize her before her sudden movement made her fall. "Of course, we say that. What else would you say if someone was or was not a huge dick?"

"Fair enough." She shifted a little to dislodge his hand. "I can probably walk from here."

He set her down just as another ogre passed. "Droguk. Following Vikthor's example, I see."

"Fuck you, Grathgor," Droguk muttered back. The other ogre laughed, and Vanessa turned, walking backward to watch him go. He nudged an ogress leaning against a doorframe, and she looked at Vanessa beside Droguk and laughed, too.

Facing forward again, Vanessa waited for the inevitable stomach drop that came with such a realization. It wasn't new; she'd seen romantic partners tense up when introducing her to their friends. She'd gone through the humiliation of her mother suggesting she order something different at a restaurant while furtively glancing at an approaching waiter. Vanessa could recognize easily when people were embarrassed of her.

This time, that feeling didn't come. The situation struck her as amusing, in a cheerfully self-deprecating way: an ogre didn't want people to think *he* was with *her*. She covered her giggles with her hand. "Oh my god. You're embarrassed to be seen with me."

"Being seen with a human is embarrassing." Droguk grumbled.

"Especially when you're like, best friends with Vikthor, right?" she teased him.

"I'm not best friends with him. I would be lucky to call him friend," Droguk corrected her. "He's more of a... mentor. An aspirational figure."

Her desire to poke fun at him evaporated. "Oh. I'm sorry, I thought he was like, your buddy or something."

"I don't have buddies." Droguk guided her out of the way of a swift-moving ogre child in a quaglantern-drawn chariot. "Keep walking."

* * * *

Judging by their welcome to the castle, Vikthor didn't know that he wasn't Droguk's buddy. The owner—because they didn't like leaders, Vanessa remembered—of Dun Larvae entered his impressive great hall with his arms open and a slightly dismayed smile on his face.

"I didn't know you were coming!" Vikthor wrapped his arms around Droguk's shoulders with enthusiasm. "I would have had a feast to welcome you!"

"It's better that you didn't," Droguk said. "I think once you hear why I've come, you'd be happier if no one knew I was here. Unfortunately, I was recognized in the village."

Vikthor's thick, black brows furrowed, and his demeanor entirely changed as he stepped back and released Droguk. "Sit. Tell me."

"I went with Ord's raiding party," Droguk began, walking with Vikthor to the huge, crackling hearth. "I came back with that."

Both sets of ogre eyes turned to her. Both tusked mouths turned down at the corners.

"We ambushed the baron's cortege," Droguk went on. "They were with him, albeit unwillingly."

"I wasn't actually with him," Vanessa said, though she had a feeling that perhaps she hadn't been meant to speak in that particular conversation. Fuck it, she was tired being treated like an object or a problem. "I was lost. I fell through a—"

"Thorn bush," Droguk quickly interrupted. "They fell through a thornbush along the roadside as the Baron passed."

"Unlucky timing," Vikthor said with a nod of sympathy toward her.

"The raiding party got away with a booby-trapped decoy trunk and nothing else, while I got away with her. And that's the issue," Droguk said, lifting his massive hands and letting them fall to his knees in finality.

Vikthor followed his thinking. "You can't exactly divide a human up among a raiding party."

Gruesome, Vanessa thought.

"But you can divide up the profit from the sale of a human with talents. And this one is a seer," Droguk told him.

"Ah, and this is where we disagree," Vanessa interrupted again, reaching into her bag for her rapidly emptying pill bottle. "I'm not a seer. I don't have visions. I have seizures. This is the medication I take to control them. And it's going to run out. I need to get back to where I came from—"

"That's not the most immediate issue," Droguk said, recapturing Vikthor's attention. "The raiding party is going to sell her to the Baron."

Vikthor's gaze darted to her again. "Where are you from?"

"They—"

"I asked the human," Vikthor said, his tone sharply reprimanding.

He's married to a human, she thought, taking a deep breath. *He cares about humans on some level, obviously.* It didn't put her at ease, but she still had to answer. "Earth."

They both straightened up, as if in recognition.

"You've...heard of it?" Plot twist. "Wait, Droguk, did I not mention the specific place?"

"No, you didn't. And you sounded delusional." He paused. "Not that you sound any less delusional. You think you came here from Earth?"

"I don't think. I know. I come from Earth. A place where you don't have to walk through monster-infested swamps unless you're doing it for TikTok views, there's a guy on a soap opera with a very similar name to Vikthor's that everybody's grandma was like, in love with, and we stopped believing that epilepsy was a spiritual gift about two hundred years ago." She punctuated it with a laugh that sounded as hysterical as she felt.

"Earth is make believe," Droguk said.

"It's not. I was in the bookshop, then I fell through the book and ta-da, I ended up here." She pressed her fingertips to her temple. "Oof, I'm getting the beginning of what is going to be an incredible headache, so like, can you save me from the Baron or..."

"We can hide you from the Baron," Vikthor said after a moment of deliberation. "But I'm not sure I can help you return to Earth."

"Because you don't believe that I'm from Earth?" she asked.

Vikthor tilted his head. "Does that matter, if I'm sheltering you from the Baron?"

She flinched. "Touche."

"Let's settle this Baron problem first. Then we'll worry about getting you home," Droguk suggested. The way he said it sounded... different. Like he wasn't flat-out denying her story anymore. Or maybe he pitied her because he thought she'd lost touch with reality.

Joke was on him; she'd thought that first.

Vikthor turned in his chair. "Brentan."

The person who entered was tall, over six feet, by Vanessa's estimate, and had the shoulders of a lumberjack. The everything of a lumberjack, if that was the criteria with which she evaluated the human. Everything except the beard. He was even wearing checked cloth, though it was in the form of long robes.

"This is my husband, Brentan," Vikthor said.

Brentan's eyes widened as they darted to Vanessa. "I'd heard that Droguk was here, but no one mentioned a human."

She didn't know why. And she knew she looked like a total weirdo. But Vanessa launched herself toward the first human she'd seen in days.

"I used to say I hated people," she sobbed, snottily, against Brentan's shoulder as she crushed him with desperate arms. "I'll never say that ever again!"

"Oh, for fuck's sake," Droguk muttered.

"Hey, hey." Brentan put his hands gently on her upper arms and pushed her a step back. "We're not friends like that."

"You're right." She nodded and sniffled and reached into her bag for her dwindling supply of tissues.

"She hasn't seen another of her own kind in a while," Droguk said tightly.

Embarrassing herself was bad. Causing someone else's second-hand embarrassment was excruciating.

"What brings you?" Brentan asked Droguk, giving Vanessa a sidelong glance as he moved to his husband.

Droguk lifted his hand toward Vanessa, then let it fall in defeat.

Brentan nodded sympathetically. "It always is."

"I can explain it all later. At the moment, we need to hide these two. And expect a less pleasant visit." Vikthor stood and motioned to Droguk. "We'll put you in the dungeon."

Vanessa panicked. "In the—"

"It's not that kind of dungeon," Brentan said, and Vikthor cleared his throat loudly.

Droguk muttered something under his breath.

"An ogre sex dungeon." She nodded, making eye contact with no one. "Sure. Lead the way."

Chapter Eleven

As far as dungeons went, the one at Dun Larvae wasn't that bad. It was like something out of a movie set in the middle ages, but not one of the realistic ones. The slate floor was mopped and tidy, the stone walls dry, and there was no odor of prisoner excrement or tortured screams.

If it were a themed AirBnB, Vanessa would probably have rented it.

"The dungeon hasn't been an actual dungeon for a century at least," Brentan told her as they walked. "We repurposed it. I promise, it's comfortable, even if it is a little small."

Behind them, Vikthor told Droguk, "It's secure, that's the important part."

"Do we really think this Baron guy is going to storm the castle and knock down doors?" Vanessa asked.

"No," Vikthor said, and Vanessa's trepidation lessened. Then he increased it by saying, "He would send gargoyles."

"I know Vikthor loves you like a son," Brentan said to Droguk as he pushed open a thick, iron-banded door. "But this can't be a permanent solution."

"Brentan—" Vikthor began tersely.

The human put his hand up. "No. If the Baron is after them, their presence puts my home and the ogre I love in danger. I'm going to speak my mind."

"It was never my intention to endanger you, in any way," Droguk said. "We'll leave as soon as I know she's safe. And if there's any threat, we'll take our chances out there."

Vanessa nodded fervently. They might end up out in the swamplands again, at the mercy of the Baron's men, but she wanted to delay it as long as possible.

Droguk ducked to fit through the doorway and Vanessa followed him into what was, as promised, a comfortable, small room.

With just one bed.

Vanessa's eyes went painfully wide. "Uh-oh."

"What?" Droguk asked.

She shook her head and looked away. "It's a trope. From stories. 'And there was only one bed?'"

The two ogres and one human stared at her in silence.

"Well," Vikthor said finally, clapping his hands together. "You've traveled far. We'll bring you something to eat. Stay here; you'll be well-hidden from the Baron's monsters, should they come. If you hear anything suspicious, you douse the lights."

"Of course," Droguk said with a nod. "And thank you, again. Both of you."

Vikthor nodded, and Brentan turned away, closing

the door behind him.

"Well, this is..." Vanessa turned in a circle. Her gaze fell on the manacles hanging on the wall. Manacles that were far too big for a human. "Huh. So Vikthor is the—"

"What?"

She whirled to face Droguk. "Sorry, I didn't realize I said that out loud." To avoid looking him in the eye, she glanced past him, at a bowl piled high with bright and appetizing items. "Is that fruit?"

He turned. "Of course it is. Apples, oranges, bananas..."

"No. No, those aren't apples and oranges and bananas." She moved past him. For one thing, none of the fruits were the color orange. Magenta, pear-shaped things with fluorescent-yellow spikes, a round object that could have been an orange if it wasn't purple, and tiny, radium-green melons nestled like accents in the stunning array.

That was just sitting around in a dungeon.

"Did you ever notice..." she began, drifting to the table and picking up one of the magenta fruits. "Of course, you couldn't have noticed. Where I'm from, there are always random bowls of fruit hanging around in fantasy movies and shows. This whole world feels like a story."

"Well, I hope you're entertained," Droguk scoffed. He sat on the bed, and it creaked under his weight. Vanessa had noticed that Droguk was tall and big, even compared to other ogres.

"What I don't understand is... why do you have a fruit called an orange, and it isn't orange?" She tossed the magenta object back and forth between her hands. "But you have the color orange, right?"

"Obviously." He pointed to the hearth. "What color would we call embers? Speaking of, one of us needs to start a fire. I'm guessing that would be me?"

She waved a hand, lost in thought. "Whatever. Hey, when I say 'orange' like the fruit and 'orange' like the color, are you hearing two different words? Or is it the same word for both?"

"What kind of a question is that?" He picked up some logs and tossed them into the fireplace. "Orange is the color, and orange is the fruit."

"Just answer, is it one word or two different ones?"

"Two different ones!" He snatched up fistfuls of twigs and bark from the tinder box. "What does it matter?"

"It matters because it means something is translating for me." She sniffed the fruit, then took a tentative bite. The yellow spikes popped like pomegranate seeds, and the juicy magenta flesh tasted like rose petals. "But it's not translating everything. It doesn't change this fruit into something more familiar, and sometimes I don't understand the words you're saying. I'm pretty sure they're swears that don't have a direct translation?"

"I have no idea what you're talking about." He arranged the tinder and logs and picked up a flint lighter not unlike the ones she'd used to light Bunsen burners in high school. It sparked a few times under his hand, and the dry twigs caught, crackling.

"You knew about Earth." And he'd known the name for it, though if everything was being translated for her, who the hell knew what they called it.

"From bedtime stories. Human tales. Things we tell our children to warn them or teach them morals." He waited until the first flames licked at the firewood before he stood up. "It's nothing to concern yourself with."

"I'm very concerned with it," she corrected him. "We're talking about the place I came from—"

"We're talking about the place you *think* you came from." He ran a hand over his hair and made one of the frustrated curses. "I don't know what happened to you out there. Maybe it was one of your visions—"

"I don't have visions!" she snapped at him. "I have seizures. I have a medical condition—"

"Fine! Then maybe your medical condition caused you to, I don't know. Hit your head on something and dream you're from Earth. I've seen you have one of these seizures. You fall down." He shook his head and turned away.

"You think I'm crazy," she said quietly.

"No." He sat in the lone wooden chair beside the hearth. It was more human-sized than ogre, and he looked ridiculous, like and adult sitting in a seat meant for a kindergartener. "I'm afraid I am."

Before she could ask him what he meant, the door opened again. No knock, though why anyone would think they needed to, she had no clue. It wasn't like anyone would expect them to be indecent.

To her shock, it was Vikthor who entered with a large platter of roast meat, with vegetables and bread and cheese—thank god, they still had cheese!—arranged around the perimeter. In his other hand, he carried a huge pitcher. He took note of her expression and explained, "I've sent the servants away. There's no reason to have them here, poking into our business and spreading rumors."

"I'm so sorry for this inconvenience," Droguk apologized again.

"You're never an inconvenience," Vikthor said firmly. "You need help, as I once needed help. Ignore Brentan. He isn't angry; he's frightened. He just can't admit that to himself, yet. He's not the master of Dun Larvae."

The shackles on the wall seemed to indicate otherwise.

"And I say that you can stay, and that we will do whatever is needed to stop the Baron from taking this human," Vikthor continued. He looked her up and down. "I know what it means to feel tenderness toward these creatures."

She wanted to say, "none taken," but she couldn't find it in herself to be snarky to her host. Not when he was vowing to keep her out of the Baron's hands.

"We can't stay down here forever," Droguk said. "We'll be on our way soon."

"You may reconsider how long 'soon' is." Vikthor paused. "Should I send a guard out to Mudholme?"

"No. Gorgrak said that my sister and nieces were safe. He was Ord's friend, and an ogre of his word, even if he's a piece of bogland trash. I believed him when he made that oath." But Droguk sounded awfully unsure for someone who believed. "Besides, if you send your guard, that will only lead them here."

"True." Vikthor looked around the room and set the pitcher on the small table beside the door. "You should have everything you need until morning."

"Except a bathroom," Vanessa spoke up. When Droguk shot her a sharp glance, she shrugged. "What? I have to go."

"I'll bring you a chamber pot," Vikthor said. "I hope you don't have the customary human shyness."

She did. But desperate times.

Vikthor left them. She didn't want to be the first to touch the food; it seemed too greedy, and deepened her fear of seeming ungracious.

"I do appreciate all of this," she said, her voice almost a whisper.

"I know you do." Droguk picked up the entire table, platter and all, and moved it near the bed. He scooted the chair over, as well, and indicated that she should sit. Together, they started picking over the dinner, Droguk pulling large strips of meat off the stringy roast with his fingers. Vanessa followed his lead, and nearly moaned in pleasure at the taste of the greasy, tender roast.

"This is amazing. You guys must have crockpots here," she quipped.

"Of course we have pots. And crocks. How else would we cook or store our food?" he asked.

"It's not a—" She stopped herself. "Never mind. Why don't you tell me one of your stories about Earth. Something you told your nieces, maybe? A favorite of theirs?"

He grumbled a little. "I don't know any stories."

"You must," she insisted. "You basically positioned yourself as an expert."

"Well, I'm not an expert, and I don't tell stories." He nudged some kind of stuffed pepper-looking thing at her. "Eat this. You need vegetables, too."

She watched him as he ate, never looking up at her again. He seemed to loathe her company, but he'd brought her all this way, just to protect her. Now, he was worried about her diet.

"I can't figure you out," she murmured, more to herself than to him.

"Then don't." He glanced up, then back down at the

piece of bread he pushed through the juices from the meat. "If it makes you feel any better, I can't figure you out, either."

It didn't make her feel better, but at least she knew they were in the same boat.

Chapter Twelve

"Vanessa!"

She closed her eyes tighter.

"Vanessa! Human!"

Something rocked her back and forth, and she swam up from her sleep.

No, not sleep.

Her head was all muzzy, disconnected from her body in a way that was all too familiar. She opened her eyes and the shapes around her were all sized incorrectly. The bed was too long, the body beside her too large. Alice in Wonderland Syndrome, her neurologist called it.

"Eat me," she mumbled, thinking of the cake. Specifically, the one from the 1986 television movie that had traumatized her so badly, she'd hid under the kitchen table until grandma had coaxed her out.

She didn't feel good. "I want grandma."

"She's not here. And I'm not going to eat you," a deep, rumbling voice said. "You're having one of your vis—seizures."

It came back in pieces. The harpy. The gargoyles. The ogres.

The furniture wasn't too big because of a neurological problem. She was just trapped in a fantasy world where her condition was getting worse.

She groaned and tried to sit up, but a big hand in the center of her chest pressed her back down.

"Easy. Easy," Droguk soothed her. "You're just coming out of it."

"Left side." She tried to roll, tried again, and he finally released her. "I have to be on my left side."

Positioned this way, she was face-to-face with him. And his face was terrified.

"You weren't breathing," he said. "That's what woke me up."

"You heard me stop breathing when you were asleep?" His reflexes and awareness impressed her.

"I heard a long pause between deafening snores. And then you were violently trembling." With surprising gentleness, he smoothed her hair back from her forehead. "Are you all right? That was worse than what I saw in the woods."

"Sometimes, I stop breathing. If it's a bad one." And she could expect more bad ones, and worse to come. Eventually, her medicine would run out. Between the stress and the lowered dose, it barely helped her, now. "I can usually feel them coming on, but if I'm asleep, obviously I don't. And even if I do feel one coming on, I can't always ask for help."

"I wouldn't know how to help you if I tried. All I could do was...wait." His sigh made the ropes beneath the straw mattress move.

He didn't like feeling helpless. Vanessa knew that the moment his brow creased, as he tried to decide his final word, to know when to stop voicing his fears. It was a reaction that Vanessa was so familiar with, she felt like she could read minds, at least where her epilepsy was concerned.

"That's really all you can do. I mean, you can time the seizure, if you had a watch. But what would be the point? If it lasts longer than two minutes, do you call an ambulance?" she asked with a shrug. Her back teeth ground; she had no control over that motion. Her jaw always gnashed and her legs crawled with ants after a particularly bad seizure. This one sounded like a grand mal, from his description, and it wouldn't have been his shaking her that brought her back to life. It was pure luck that she survived, every single time.

"What's an ambulance?" He pronounced the word carefully, but incorrectly.

"A doctor," she simplified. "You have doctors, right?"

"Of course, we do. There's one in the village. Should I get her?" he asked, already moving to get out of the bed.

She caught him by the arm. "No. No, there's no reason. She probably couldn't treat me, anyway."

After a long pause, he said, "I didn't know what to do."

"People often don't." She was the one who'd almost died, but she was comforting a bystander. Every damn time, that's what happened. He had an excuse, though, unlike people in the real world, who didn't bother to learn things and were more likely to jam a wallet in her mouth than actually save her life. "It's not your fault."

"Your pills are supposed to stop those from happening," he pointed out.

Pushing herself up to sit, she let out a long sigh. "Yeah. Well, I'm not taking them as regularly as I should. And I'm not taking the appropriate amount. They're going to run out soon, and I was hoping I could just get by on what was left, for a while. That's why it's so important that I get back to Earth—"

"We have to find a way to get more," he said, cutting her off the moment she mentioned her home. "There has to be someone in Fablemere, somewhere, who can cure this."

"Maybe a magic potion?" What she wouldn't give for something like that, something that could cure her instantly, and she would never have to worry about it again. Never go to sleep wondering if she'd wake up in the morning. Never be prevented from driving for six months because of a break-through seizure, or embarrass herself in a high stress situation because her brain just went overactive and zapped her into oblivion for thirty seconds of shaking and pissing herself.

Droguk didn't dismiss the magic potion suggestion outright. "There is a university where all the physicians of Fablemere train. If the doctors there are qualified to teach other doctors, surely they know everything about medicine."

"Yeah, you'd think that," she said with a snort.

"We could go there," he suggested, in such a way that Vanessa was pretty sure he'd already made up his mind. "It could solve two problems. We'd have to travel across the Divide, which will get us further from the Baron's men. And the university is neutral ground.

We'd just have to get there—"

"How much travel would this take?" she interrupted him. "Because I don't know how much more I can do. Anything stressful just makes my condition worse."

"It's far," is all he said.

She swung her feet down onto the cold stone floor. "I just want to get home. I just need to get back to Earth. Even if you don't believe me, it's where I'm from. It's why I'm so different."

Droguk mimicked her position, sitting beside her and holding the edge of the mattress, just as she did. He radiated warmth in the chill of the room.

"I don't know many humans. Just Brentan," Droguk said with a shrug of his massive shoulders. "But I believe that you're different. I don't think there could possibly be anyone as strange as you, anywhere."

It sounded like a compliment. She didn't know why. But she'd take it, especially since it seemed like he was softening toward the concept of an Earth dweller in his reality.

She was about to make a retort when a stabbing pain ripped through her head, just behind her eyes. Pressing a hand to her temple, she sucked in a whining breath and held it until the pulsing sharpness passed.

Droguk's hand shot to her back to steady her. "Are you—"

"Fine," she gasped. "I'm fine. Just a weird pain I get sometimes, afterward."

Her heart raced in blinding white behind her lids, beating in time to the throb of the ice pick through her brain. It disappeared as quickly as it had come on, and she straightened, blinking at the moonlight streaming through the tiny, barred window near the ceiling. "It's still night."

"You should sleep," he said, laying back. He patted the mattress beside him. "I'll keep watch."

"You don't have to." After all, he'd known she was in trouble even in his sleep. She snuggled down into the still-warm spot she'd vacated and let him pull the thick fur blanket over them both. Since she'd slept atop his arm and chest like he was a giant bean bag out in the swamp, it was far less strange to simply sleep beside him. He'd offered to stay on the floor, on the blanket, but that would have meant a freezing night for them both.

"Thanks for letting me sleep by you, even though I'm so gross to you," she said, flipping her pillow to the cool side.

He made a grumbly noise. "You're not gross. You're just... different. Pink. And weird looking. That doesn't mean I want you to freeze."

She closed her eyes, but that nagging feeling that she might not wake up intruded on her momentary peace.

"Are you all right?" Droguk asked.

Her body was stiff with anxiety. She took a breath and tried to unclench her muscles. "Yeah. A little shaken up, is all."

"Do you still want to hear a story?"

She blinked. "An Earth story?"

"A human tale, yes."

She twisted to lay on her back. A shaft of moonlight illuminated his tusked face, his rough features that had been so grotesque to her when she'd first laid eyes on him. He didn't look so horrible to her, now. "Sure. Since you're offering."

He laid on his back, too, and they stared up at the

ceiling and the darkness together. "In days long past, there was a prince. A proud, spoiled prince, who, once he became king, learned quickly that he wasn't suited to rule. He surrounded himself with those who wished for his power, who used him like a puppet to their dire ends."

"This could be literally any dude on Earth," Vanessa interjected.

"Do you want to hear this, or not?" Droguk asked.

"Sorry."

He took a breath and continued. "One of these evil men was a karl-rove, a terrible wizard with the power to—"

"Did you just say Carl Rove?" Vanessa gasped.

"Again, I'm telling you the story you requested—"

"No, it's just that…" she sighed. "No, please, go on. I'm sorry, I promise I won't interrupt you again."

He hesitated in clear distrust before going on. "Together, the king's viceroy and the karl-rove hatched a plan. They would plant the seed of war in the mind of the king. They told him that an enemy kingdom planned to wreak mass destruction on the land. It took little convincing to make the king believe their lies, and less convincing still to make his subjects believe it, as well. They clamored for war and fed their young men and women to it for a century."

A little less than a century, Vanessa corrected him silently.

"But soon after the war began, the king learned that he had been tricked. Too proud to quit his endeavors, he declared his campaign a success. The people were unhappy, and a curse of shame was placed upon him. He locked himself away, creating portrait after portrait of each of the subjects lost to his ambition, but the curse was never lifted, and his legacy of death and failure plagued him until the end of his days."

She waited until she was sure the story was finished to tell him, "His days haven't ended, where I'm from. He's still alive. And he's still painting. That part is right. But how did you learn this story?"

"It's been told since before my mother was born. Before my grandmother, even," he said.

"And you tell this story to children to what? Teach them not to believe everything they hear?"

"I suppose that's one moral they can take away from it," he said, rolling onto his side to face her. "It's a parable against war more than lies. One never knows when they might get chosen from a lottery to marry an elderly king. Or maybe they might happen upon a stone in the woods and pull an ancient sword from it. So, it's necessary to be prepared."

"For a time when you might accidentally become a king," she clarified.

"Exactly. You never really know when it's going to happen."

"Sometimes, it seems like it's never going to happen," Vanessa said. When she was met with silence, she added, "It's a joke. There was this queen on Earth who was around for like, ever."

"Kings and queens don't last quite as long here," Droguk said. "You're better off never having power. It comes with consequences."

"Another huge difference between your world and mine." She took physical inventory of herself. Her jaw had stopped gnashing. Her legs still felt like she needed to get up and run for miles to stop the electricity running through them, but it was lessening. And her sleepiness was starting to outweigh her fear of not waking. "Thank you for the story. It really helped."

"Well, don't expect it every night," he said gruffly, turning onto his other side to face away from her.

She got comfortable and closed her eyes, willing to try sleep again. But before she drifted off, she asked, "Remember how you said before that you don't have any buddies?"

"No, I don't remember saying that," he said, his voice thick with impending sleep.

"Well, I remember it," she said. "And you're wrong. I'm your buddy."

He didn't answer her. He didn't have to.

He didn't really get a say in the fact that she'd decided they were friends.

Chapter Thirteen

The next morning, Vikthor and Brentan invited Droguk and Vanessa to breakfast. They took secret passageways to get to the sitting room in the private apartment, which was thrilling for someone who rarely got to experience secret passages, and the parlor was a welcome change of scenery, anyway.

They ate fruit and bread and porridge, and the morning sunlight streamed cheerfully through diamond-paned windows. Maybe it was unfair of Vanessa, but she attributed the beauty in the dark wood furnishings and elaborate velvet drapes to Brentan. Having seen one ogre house, they didn't seem that picky about aesthetic.

Smearing berry-colored butter on her bright orange bread, she looked across the table. "This is delicious, thank you."

"We'll have to pack some for you to take with you,"

Brentan said pointedly. "When you leave."

Vanessa looked down and swallowed the bite that had turned into razorblades in her mouth. She wanted to remind him that she wasn't there just to impose on him, and that it would have been nice to have some human solidarity and companionship. But whether she intended to or not, she was imposing on him, and he'd clearly chosen to live away from other humans, so maybe he didn't give a damn about solidarity. He just wanted to live his life in comfort, without worrying about other people's troubles. She couldn't blame him for that.

"That will be soon," Droguk promised. "We have to leave. By tonight, if possible."

Vanessa didn't look forward to more travel, but it was better than rotting in a dungeon. Even a nice one.

Vikthor shook his head and poured himself juice from a carafe on the table. "Don't be foolish. You'll meet the Baron's men on their way here if you leave now."

"We're not going back to Mudholme," Droguk clarified. "We're going to Lua. To the university."

Vikthor fumbled his glass. Brentan snatched it quickly, so it didn't spill.

"Why would you need to go to Lua? What's there for you?" Vikthor demanded.

Droguk was calm in the face of his mentor's sudden, forbidding concern. "The human Vanessa needs pills to stop her seizures. They're getting worse. She had one last night and I thought..."

The choked sound that cut off his words surprised Vanessa.

He passed it off as something caught in his throat, holding up one finger as he sipped from what she knew was an empty glass. When he put it down again, he continued. "I thought she had died. And without the medicine, she will. I think the doctors at the university can help her."

"Doctors," Vikthor harumphed. "I've never understood the obsession with them."

"They keep you alive," Brentan said into his cup.

"Not only will a journey to Lua take her out of the Baron's reach, they could save her life there," Droguk said.

Vikthor shook his head. "There is no place out of the Baron's reach. Not even Lua. And at least here, I can defend your claim of ownership of your prize. West of here, there'll be no such protection. She'll be snagged and sold off as soon as you arrive in Murkwater."

"We'll forge a bill of ownership," Droguk suggested.

"Um, how about we don't present me as if I'm your property," Vanessa objected.

Brentan shook his head. "You don't want to be a human on your own in Murkwater. Trust me."

"Even a bill of ownership is tricky. There's no respect for law or property in the Mire. You know that," Vikthor said to Droguk.

"You own enough land that your signature will hold weight," Droguk said.

"Wow, so some things are exactly the same here," Vanessa muttered, and took a sullen bite of her bread. She'd gone a whole seventy-two hours without being referred to as someone's property. It had been a nice break.

"There *is* one law that's respected in the Mire," Brentan said, his gaze flicking between Droguk and Vikthor. "An oath to the gods?"

The words sucked the atmosphere out of the room

in an instant. The ogres and human gave each other charged looks that Vanessa didn't understand and very much did not wish to. They were in a silent communication of grave importance, and the less she was involved, the better.

It seemed like a long time before Droguk spoke. "No. That's not an option."

"Suit yourself." Vikthor sat back in his chair, hands out in a gesture of helplessness. "If you insist on going to Lua to save this human's life, what good would come of it if they were kidnapped on the journey?"

"It's not the worst idea," Brentan said.

Three gazes fell on Vanessa in wordless debate.

She shrank down in her chair. "What's not the worst idea?"

Droguk let out a heavy sigh. He couldn't even look at her. He actually put his elbow on the table and shielded his face with his hand like a blinder. "They're suggesting that we take a binding oath."

"Is this a...marriage thing?" She'd read too much fanfic to not grasp the implication of the words.

"Exactly," Brentan said. "If you two took a binding oath, you'd be safer out there."

"Oh, because I'd be some man's property?" She sat straight up in her chair.

"Ogre's property," Vikthor corrected her. "And no. Gender doesn't matter—"

"That's good, because I don't have one of those," she interrupted.

"What he's saying," Droguk said, still hiding behind his hand, "is that on your own, you're unprotected in the lawlessness of the Mire. If the Baron's men decided to take you, they could. I wouldn't have recourse or the resources to rescue you."

"Possession is nine-tenths of the law," Vanessa said uncomfortably.

"I don't know what that means." Vikthor pushed his chair back and stood. "You're both more than welcome to leave this place without the protection of a binding oath if you want to lose this human to the Baron. But I say again, if the point is to save her life, why not take a basic precaution?"

"It's not just a precaution." Droguk dropped his hand. "It's a serious commitment. If I swear an oath to the gods, I have to keep it. There aren't any loopholes—"

Brentan scoffed. "There are always loopholes."

"Not for me!" Droguk protested. "I never wanted to be bound to anyone. I just want to live my life in peace and quiet. Instead, I'm going on raids and running from the Baron, all to save some human?"

Heat burned in Vanessa's face. While she could tell herself that she'd never asked for his help, and that he'd pretty much forced that help upon her, shame consumed her. She was an imposition. Her very presence was a danger. And the person who'd put her into this embarrassing predicament was pissed off at her?

She jumped to her feet, her heavy chair making the most awful, scraping noise. "I never asked you to rescue me!" she snapped at him and stalked to the door of the secret passage.

"Vanessa, wait," Droguk called after her. And beyond him, Vanessa heard Vikthor say, "I'll get the mystic. Just in case."

The light blocked out suddenly, and she turned in the narrow passage to see it filled with Droguk.

"That sounded bad," he began.

She cut him off. "It didn't sound bad. It sounded

honest. I just wish you would have honestly told me exactly how you feel about helping me. Help which, if you will recall, I did not ask you for!"

"I know you didn't. I know. And I'm sorry. Not for helping you, but... my honesty hurt you. And wounded your pride."

"My pride?" She turned away, feeling along the wall for the staircase opening. She found it, but tumbled forward, he caught her with one hand splayed on her stomach and pulled her back. She brushed him away. "Why would my pride be wounded?"

"Well, I...rejected you," he said.

"You didn't reject me!" The unbelievable gall of him. She grabbed the chain that served as a railing and carefully found the edge of each step with her toes. Going up had been so much easier. "You can only reject me if I want to do the oath thing with you, and I don't."

At the bottom of the stairs, he reached over her to push the door open, and they stepped into a dungeon hallway. It took a moment for her eyes to adjust, but when they did, she turned and glared up into his ugly, green face. "And I have a lot less to lose. Your binding oath? It doesn't exist in the real world. So, I don't have to follow your rules. The oath is totally insignificant to me, and I still don't want to do it with you!"

He didn't reply, but he didn't look away from her, either, and his lack of response grew heavier between them by the second. But she wouldn't be the first to break.

"Brentan is right," he said, his shoulders slumping. His voice was hoarse and sad, and it pierced Vanessa's heart. "We have to get you to Lua. It's the only chance you have. I got you into this the moment I grabbed you in the forest. If I had let you run—"

"A gargoyle would have eaten me," she said quietly.

"What?" His face screwed up in disgust. "Why do you think everyone wants to eat you?"

"I don't know. The harpy would have eaten me. I'm pretty sure the Baron's horses would have eaten me."

"The Baron would have eaten you," Droguk grumbled. "What I'm saying is, you're my responsibility. If that means swearing a binding oath... I'll do it."

"Did you not listen to me about two minutes ago? When I was hurting your feelings?" she asked.

"I heard you. And you said that the oath doesn't mean anything to you. That makes it easier, I think. It's a binding of convenience."

"Fuck." She closed her eyes. "It's Marriage Of Convenience. I thought it was Only One Bed."

Only One Bed had been a simple fix. They'd just slept beside each other, with no sexually charged banter or sudden admission of long-denied feelings. Marriage Of Convenience wasn't as easy to solve, especially when it sounded like the only practical solution.

"Okay." She let out a long breath. "Binding oath it is."

Chapter Fourteen

"If someone asked me what I thought I would be wearing at my storybook castle wedding, I would have said a suit of armor, if I had rescued the princess." Vanessa plucked at the sleeve of her mud-streaked t-shirt. "Or a beautiful gown, if I *was* the princess."

"Well, you're not a princess. And you're not marrying one," Brentan said, frowning over her shoulder in the mirror. "And I don't have any gowns or suits of armor."

They stood in the parlor where they'd had breakfast, but the table had been cleared entirely away and the rest of the furnishings pushed to the perimeter of the room, to accommodate the fact that three ogres and two humans would be crowding in at any moment.

"I guess wearing half the swamp is appropriate when you're marrying an ogre," she said, facing her fellow human. He immediately pressed a cup into her hands. She sniffed it. "What's this for?"

"Fortitude." He poured his own cup, drank it down with several huge swallows, and filled it again. "We have to have a delicate conversation."

Vanessa narrowed her eyes. "About what? Is this going to be a weird ritual? Am I going to have to bathe in animal blood or something?"

"No, nothing like that. I was just wondering if you had given thought to..." Brentan's voice trailed off, then he sighed. "You've thought about it, right?"

"About..." Vanessa circled her hands. Then, she stopped.

Had she thought about...

No. He couldn't be serious.

But he was serious, so they couldn't be talking about...

"Are you trying to give me a birds and the bees here?" she asked.

Brentan frowned. "Why would I give you bees? Where would I get them from?"

"That's not—"

"I'm talking about fucking," he said.

She choked on the sip of wine she'd taken, then wished she'd done a spit-take instead. She coughed and laughed, waving her hand. "There isn't going to be any of that. This is a Binding Oath Of Convenience."

"That's not how it works," Brentan said. "You have to complete the oath joined as one."

"Figuratively," she said.

"No. You're binding yourselves together as one. So, you need to be as one to truly bind yourselves." Brentan swore under his breath. "This is uncomfortable."

"It's uncomfortable for *you*?" She wobble-legged her way to a chair and sat down cautiously. She thought of the sheer size of Droguk, the width of his big hands, and she gulped down the rest of her wine.

Brentan hurried to pour more. "There are some things you're going to want to know."

"Oh, there are many things I want to know," she said with a panicked laugh, though she didn't actually want to know any of those things.

Brentan grabbed a chair and pulled it up beside hers. "You need to be prepared for differences in ogre anatomy."

Oh god. She felt the blood draining out of her face and directly into the very back of her brain. *Seizures never happen when you need an out.*

"First of all, it's big. You know...it?"

"I know what you're talking about!" she snapped. "How big?"

He looked around the room for a size comparison then gave up, and instead brought his hands up, thumbs and fingers in a c-shape. He touched his fingertips and thumbs together and gave her an apologetic grimace.

She shot to her feet. "Are you fucking kidding me?"

"Don't worry, don't worry," he quickly reassured her. "You only have to do it once."

"Sure, just the once, and then I never walk again due to my crushed pelvis!" This was how they were going to keep her alive and unharmed? Maiming by ogre cock?

"It's not like you have to take the whole thing. You don't have to take the—" He cut himself off.

Vanessa blinked at him with furious expectation. "The what?"

"There's a... a bulb," he said uncomfortably. "It's just a part of an ogre's dick. It's this egg-shaped bulge, wider at the bottom, and it's meant to—"

"I read fanfic, I know what it's meant to do!" She slumped back into the chair and covered her face. "This is a fucking nightmare."

"Droguk is not expecting a night of wild passion, I'm sure. You just need to be technically joined for that final bit of the oath, and then you can stop." If Brentan thought that was a bright side, his internal dimmer switch had been turned all the way down.

Sex with an ogre. Unavoidable sex with an ogre. Ritualistic, unavoidable sex with an ogre. Her stomach turned. "And you all watch?"

Brentan recoiled. "No. Oh, old gods, no. Why would we want to?"

"It's part of the oath thing!" She gestured to the floor in front of them. "I thought that meant we did it in here, during the ceremony or whatever."

"No." Brentan's face betrayed every ounce of distaste he had for that notion. And for Vanessa, for making him imagine it. "Why would anyone watch to watch that?"

"I don't know! I wouldn't!" she borderline-shrieked. "I thought maybe to prove that it happened? Otherwise, how are they going to know?"

"The oath mark?" Brentan squinted and slid his head forward.

"Again, I'm not from here. I don't know what that is."

He pushed back the sleeve of his tunic. A sigil of a twisting line twining between two straight ones marked his skin in ink-black. "Everyone's looks different. See the curvy part here? If you draw my mark side-by-side with Vikthor's, they fit together."

"Oh." She rubbed her arm. "And that's not something you can fake? We couldn't just draw it on?"

"No. It's not like a tattoo. It gives off energy, and it can be tested. Watch." He rubbed his thumb, banded by a simple gold ring, across the mark. It sparkled and fizzed and sent up a halo of illumination like the Northern Lights, only shorter. Then it faded back to black. "Any metal will work. Except pewter. I don't know why."

That part didn't concern Vanessa. It didn't matter if metal would make the oath mark jump up and sing a little tune. She still couldn't get out of this. If she wanted to survive, she was going to get hitched to an ogre.

Only until I get back to the real world, she told herself.

"There's just one more ogre-dick related thing you should—"

There was a knock at the door, and Vikthor opened it. "Everything all right in here?"

"What was the other thing?" Vanessa whispered, but Brentan ignored her.

"Yes," Brentan answered for both of them. "How'd it go?"

Vikthor's eyes darted to Vanessa, then back to Brentan. The ogre cleared his throat. "As well as could be expected. He was shocked, to say the least."

"And you told him the part about the—" Brentan drew a rounded diamond shape in the air.

Vikthor nodded emphatically. "I described it exactly as you told me."

Vanessa hid her face behind her hands. "I am...mortified."

"It's nothing to be embarrassed about," Vikthor assured her, stepping fully into the room. "Personally, I would have liked to have known about the differences before Brentan and I—"

"Different differences, though," Vanessa muttered. She couldn't bear to put her hands down. At least her clammy palms were cool against her flushed cheeks.

"I don't understand how you're so embarrassed when just seconds ago, you were willing to do it in front of us," Brentan said.

That got her to face them. "I was *not* willing to—"

Droguk entered the room behind Vikthor. Vanessa assumed her spouse-to-be was just as shaken and horrified as she was because he wouldn't even look at her.

He was followed by the ogre Vanessa assumed to be the mystic. His skin was a sickly pale gray-green, like a houseplant that didn't get enough sun. His back was hunched, his face lined with deep crags, and bushy white brows shaded his nearly invisible eyes.

"This is our couple?" The mystic looked to Vikthor for confirmation.

"That one," he responded, pointing to Vanessa, then to Droguk. "And that one."

From a satchel tied around his waist, the mystic produced a handful of sand. He drew an impressively perfect circle with it on the ground. "Come along, then."

Droguk moved to Vanessa's side and took her hand. He still wouldn't look at her.

He was her only ally, and she felt suddenly very alone. Tears stung her eyes and a lump formed in the back of her throat. She whispered, "I don't know what I'm doing."

And the big, green hand around hers gave a squeeze.

That was enough to ease some of her apprehension. She took a deep breath and stepped into the circle with him.

"Now, let me see," the mystic muttered to himself, and drew a length of golden cord from the satchel. He shook sand from it, then shuffled forward and wrapped it around their joined hands. "Now, say the words."

Vanessa stared at the two beady little holes barely visible beneath the old ogre's brow and realized he'd been prompting her.

"I'll go first," Droguk said. He turned to Vanessa and looked somewhere near her eyes. Mostly at the top of her head. "I am yours, wholly. I will protect and nourish you, body and spirit. I will help and encourage you to be the best version of yourself that you can be. I will sacrifice my life before I let harm befall you."

Okay. These are actually really nice—

"And we will be one until decay and rot robs my flesh of the oath mark I will bear for you."

There it is.

Haltingly, she began, "I am yours, entirely—"

"Wholly!" The mystic barked.

She leaned slightly forward and hissed, "They mean the same things!"

Droguk gave her hand a tug.

"Wholly," she corrected herself, and pushed down the sick feeling in her gut. She didn't want to be there, but disrespecting the ceremony was churlish and immature. "Sorry. Can someone guide me through it?"

Droguk lifted his free hand and, to Vanessa's shock, tilted her face up with a crooked finger under her chin. Her eyes met his kind ones, surrounded by a face that had stopped looking fierce to her, but she didn't know quite when that had happened.

"I am yours, wholly," he said again.

Her mouth went oddly dry, but she squeaked out, "I

am yours, wholly."

"I will protect you and nourish you, body and spirit."

"I will protect you and nourish you, body and spirit," she repeated. Was his hand trembling in hers, or was she imagining it?

"I will help and encourage you to be the best version of yourself that you can be."

No, it was her hand that trembled. She loathed public speaking, and even just three witnesses to this awkward recitation of intimate words were too many. But she made it through, even the rot part, though she'd mentally added, *until I go back to the real world.* That was the only moment she couldn't maintain eye contact with Droguk.

"Very good," the mystic mumbled, and Droguk looked sharply at him, as though just remembering that the old man was there. "The oath has begun. Go from here and seal your vows to each other before the next sunrise."

The mystic moved around them in a counterclockwise circle. The sand disappeared beneath his feet. He unwrapped the chain, but Droguk didn't release her hand.

Brentan opened the door to the secret passageway. As they passed him, he put his hand on Droguk's shoulder. "I took a lot of wine down there. And a little something extra."

Droguk nodded and said nothing, which made Vanessa wonder if they weren't supposed to speak. Maybe that was part of the ritual. She kept her mouth shut and let Droguk lead her through the passageway.

Once they were in their dungeon room, Droguk went straight to the table where several pitchers waited.

He picked one up and drank directly from it. His

tusks somewhat obstructed the action, and a slender rivulet of wine ran down from the corner of his mouth. He put the pitcher down, wiped his mouth on the back of his hand, and announced, out of breath, "We need to get severely wasted."

Chapter Fifteen

It wasn't a smart idea to get chemically altered when she'd been cutting back on her medicine and having recent seizures.

However, ogre dick.

Vanessa claimed her own jug of wine. She used a cup, though. By the time Droguk packed a pipe with elf weed, she was on her second pour.

"Here." He handed the pipe to her and lit a taper in the hearth. "We need to take the edge off."

"Agreed." She didn't know where to look or go, so she stood beside the table. He went to the bed and sat cross-legged at the end, clutching his wine. The silence was relentlessly terrible, so she took a deep inhale from the pipe and shook out the taper to douse it. Without exhaling, she said, "We don't know each other."

"No, we do not," Droguk agreed, taking a deep hit

from the pipe. He coughed a little as he passed it back. "Don't let that go out."

"Maybe if we did some get-to-know-you conversation, we'd feel better about..." She gestured helplessly to the bed.

His eyebrows raised, and he pointed to the shackles on the wall. "You mean, you don't want to be chained up for this?"

She almost choked on her inhale then realized he was kidding. She blew out a cloud of purple smoke. "You might want to wait for a different partner. I'm not well-versed in all that."

"Neither am I. I'm actually... I'm not versed in any of this. At all." He cleared his throat and looked away.

"Oh, you mean you're..." That was interesting information. Then again, there hadn't been a wealth of non-related ogres back at Mudholme. "I'm sure it's all going to be fine."

"Maybe. But—" He cut himself off to take another huge gulp of wine. "I need to know something."

Vanessa hadn't expected to become a sex ed teacher, but since she was the only one in the room who'd ever *had* sex, she didn't see much of a choice. She nodded solemnly. "Anything you want."

He looked her up and down. "We—that is, Vikthor, I mean, he—I can't—"

"I know you're nervous, but you being this nervous is making me more nervous," she interrupted him.

He sighed. His shoulders slumped. "Please, don't be offended. But I don't know any human well, besides what I know about Brentan, and Vikthor couldn't tell. I was wondering what you had under there."

She followed the direction of the finger he pointed at her midsection. "Oh, you mean..."

"Yes." Droguk cleared his throat again. "Vikthor told me about both. I'm just wondering what you've got."

"Vagina. The innie kind," she said, and turned away to fill another glass.

"Oh. That's a relief." Droguk said with a deep sigh.

"Glad to be of help?" Her hand trembled as she took a drink.

"I hope I didn't hurt your feelings. I just didn't know. You said I could call you 'she' or 'they,' but you thought things weren't being reliably translated."

"Yeah, I go by both." She sat beside him, on the corner of the bed, because that's all that remained after he'd taken up the whole end with his body. "There are basically two sets of physical workings for humans, but a whole bunch of different genders. I'm the kind that...well, I don't really feel like I have one. So, what other people call me doesn't matter as much. I look like what people where I'm from would call 'she,' so I roll with it."

"Your world sounds complicated," Droguk said.

"It can be." It didn't have to be, but that was a discussion for another time. And then, it struck her: "You believe I'm from a different world, now?"

He puffed on the pipe, coaxing the dying ember in the bowl back to life, then handed it off to her. "I don't know what I believe. I know that you're not from the Mire. I know that you're strange. But for all I know, humans are strange by default."

"They are," she agreed. "What about ogres. Are you like other ogres, or are you a big grumpy weirdo?"

"I'm not usually grumpy. Just when my life gets turned upside down," he said, and gave her a sidelong glance. "But no, I'm not like other ogres."

"Yeah? How?"

He thought for a long moment, staring down into his pitcher as if the answers would be written on the surface of the dwindling wine. "I'm ugly."

"I couldn't tell," Vanessa admitted, though it pained her to say so. There was something so sad about the way he'd said it, as if it truly bothered him. She wished she could object and tell him he was stupid for thinking that. "If that helps at all."

"What about you?" He looked over at her, all nearly three-hundred pounds of her, with her double chin, her frizzy curly hair in desperate need of shampoo, her perimenopausal acne. "Are you ugly for a human?"

"No," she said firmly, without hesitation. "I'm actually the standard of human beauty. You're very lucky."

He smiled, clearly not believing her. "We'll talk about lucky when I'm not about to consummate an arranged binding with an odd-looking creature."

She giggled and lifted her cup. "Same."

They sat silently for a long time, drinking and passing the elf weed between them.

Finally, Droguk said, "Are you feeling it yet?"

"I am..." She took a big breath and held it to fortify herself. "I'm gonna say something very hurtful. So, prepare yourself."

His empty pitcher clattered to the floor, and he braced his hands on his knees. "Is it, 'no amount of intoxication could make me want to do this?'"

Their eyes locked. Vanessa wasn't sure what she was supposed to feel. She didn't hate him. He'd done nothing but protect her since the moment they'd met. But she didn't have to hate him to be apprehensive. Or to think he looked pretty gross.

And judging from the determined grimace on his tusked mouth and the helplessness in his eyes, he was going through exactly the same thought process.

She opened her mouth to say something. A laugh rolled out.

Droguk's eyes widened, then he laughed, too, seemingly caught by surprise. And then they were both laughing and falling back onto the bed. The wine and the elf weed were doing their work.

"This is ridiculous," Droguk said, wiping tears of mirth from his yellow eyes. "It would be one thing if we were like Brentan and Vikthor. They're in love. We're just—"

"Buddies," Vanessa reiterated from the night before. She sat up. "Oh my god. Guess what?"

He looked at her expectantly but didn't sit up.

"There's this thing where I'm from. Fuck buddies. It's when you—"

"I can figure it out from context," he said, holding up a hand. "I'm not even used to you being my friend yet. Let alone the other part."

"Well, we're gonna get there fast." Despite the strangeness of their situation, it pleased her to know that he thought of her as his friend. That was probably drunk talk. Or she'd misinterpreted the remark via drunk thought. She flopped back and studied his face. "I haven't seen many ogres, but I don't think you're ugly. That Grothgrunk dude was ugly. You don't look anywhere near as bad as him."

"That's...not his name. But I don't want to talk about him." Droguk reached out with one thick finger and touched Vanessa's bottom lip. She moved back just a little, and his gaze met hers again. "Vikthor told me some of the customs that humans have, that he learned from Brentan. Is it true that humans... put their mouths on each other's mouths during sex?"

"It doesn't have to be during sex," she clarified. "It's a kiss. It's to show affection. And it doesn't have to be on the mouth. Friends kiss each other on the cheek, people kiss babies' heads all the time."

Common sense scrambled above the rising tidewaters of her intoxication. "Wait! Wait, we can't do this. I don't take birth control and I assume you don't have condoms here in storybook land—"

"Of course, we have condoms," he scoffed. "They're made from the filmy layer of the muckthorn tree's bark. The sap—"

"Do you have one here, Mr. Muckthorn?" she cut him off.

"No, but it doesn't matter. Humans and ogres can't conceive together, any sooner than a human and fairy could. Or a pixie and a troll." He gave her a doubtful look. "Why would you think that would work? We're all totally different species."

"Literally decades of urban fantasy novels." Her stomach sank in dismay. That would have been a great lifeline out of this.

This thing you're trying to get out of is *your lifeline*, she reminded herself. No, not the lifeline. The anchor. And Droguk was willing to be that anchor for her, without her ever asking. He'd seen that she was in need of help, and he'd given it to her freely.

And he was willing to go through with this absurd mating ceremony.

He reached out, put his hand on her upper arm. "I think it's time we got this over with. Before we pass out unconscious and have to try again tomorrow."

"Right."

"I'm going to kiss you," he said with a deep, fortifying breath that Vanessa could only interpret as him working up his courage. He held up his fingers. "On the count of thr—"

"You only have three fingers," she said with a little "Ha!"

Grimacing, he dropped his hand. "You have too many fingers, by the way. I was meaning to tell you."

"Sorry." She winced. "Sorry, I won't observe anything else."

"On the count of three," he began again. "One, two—"

She focused on his tusks. "Wait!"

When she sat up, he followed, making a noise of exasperation. But he did wait for her to explain.

"I'm the one with kissing experience, right?" she pointed out. "So, I need to be the one leading this. Let me just..."

She looked him up and down. Even when she climbed onto her knees, she was still too short to reach him comfortably.

One strong hand swept her onto his lap, to kneel on his thighs. "There. Does that work?"

Dizzy and breathless from the sudden movement, she braced herself with a hand on each of his shoulders. "That's not hurting you?"

"No," he scoffed. "I told you, you only weigh as much as a bag of stones."

It wasn't an insult, she realized. Or, it was, but he hadn't been calling her fat to insult her. Some of the dread squeezing her ribs loosened; she hadn't even realized she'd been worried about that.

His big hand supported her back. "I don't want to hurt you."

"I don't want you to hurt me, either. So...let me take the lead." She cupped his face with her hands and tilted her head. It seemed almost impossible with the tusks, but eventually, she had to give in and be okay with touching them. They pressed flat against her cheeks as she brought their lips together.

Maybe it was the wine. Maybe it was the elf weed. But whatever it was...

Kissing Droguk wasn't so bad.

Chapter Sixteen

For it being his first ever kiss, Droguk was really great at it. His mouth was as warm and soft as a human's, and after loosening up from the initial shock of contact, he got...

Into it.

Vanessa wasn't complaining; it was a scorchingly good kiss. Or maybe, it had just been such a long time since she'd gotten laid, she could settle for an ogre.

He moved gently back, gazing up at her with wonder. "That wasn't bad."

"It's only strange if you think about it," she said, breathing a little hard. "So don't think."

She kissed him again, this time running her tongue over his bottom lip. A shiver went through him, and he pulled her tighter to his chest. His tongue brushed hers in timid exploration.

It was...

"Oh my god." Vanessa twisted her face away. "Is your tongue forked?"

"Is that bad?" he asked, reaching up to cover his mouth.

"No. That is not bad at all." Not that it would be to her benefit; it wasn't like they'd have to do anything like *that* to fulfill the ritual.

"Then let's keep going," he grumbled. "We were starting to get somewhere."

She doubted he'd get *anywhere* with the amount of wine he'd chugged down, but maybe whisky dick wasn't a thing in fairytale land. She leaned in for another kiss, and this time, he wasn't shy about using tongue. Or the forkedness of it. Any semblance of letting her take control was out of the window once he understood the mechanics. He kissed her breathless, dizzy, fully unaware of her surroundings. He shook the very foundations of what Vanessa expected from a kiss.

And then he calmly leaned back and said, "That feels really good."

"Then why don't you guys do it?" she panted.

"The tusks, I assume."

That was her assumption, as well.

"You don't have tusks, though, so..." And he dove back in.

He kissed her like...he liked it.

After a while, she didn't even mind the tusks. Her hands roved over his back, as much of it as she could reach, then up into his hair, which fell through her fingers like strands of pure silk. With her eyes closed, he could be anybody. An extremely well-built anybody. With a slight dental anomaly.

He bunched her shirt in his hand at her back, and

something tore.

"Oh," he breathed against her lips. "Sorry. I think I ruined your shirt."

She looked down. Not totally ruined, but the neckline was definitely wider than it had been before.

"I'll get you a new one," he promised.

"Just don't be so strong." That was the only word for it.

"I'll try, but you're like parchment and glass." He made a hopeless rumble deep in his chest. "I'm afraid I'm going to hurt you."

"I'll just slap you if you get too rough." It seemed like a sensible solution.

"I mean it. I'm really concerned. Vikthor says humans aren't as fragile as they look, but you're so soft." Droguk ran his hands up and down her sides, his fingers sinking into her hips. "And small."

"But I have a very freaky history when it comes to sex toys." Didn't seem like something that should have come in handy, but life was full of surprises lately. She grasped the back of her collar and pulled the shirt over her head, tossing it aside.

Droguk's eyes widened.

"We were going to have to get naked, eventually." She still had to fight the urge to cover herself, though.

"You're confrontingly pink." He held his hands away from her.

"Well, you're—" she swallowed down a wine burp. "You're green."

"I am," he agreed, and nearly toppled her from his lap trying to pull his own shirt off.

"Whoa!" she scrambled to hold onto him. And to not accidentally end up wearing his shirt. The alcohol and smoke had made their movements dicey and unpredictable.

Laughing, he caught her in the same arm he'd used to throw his shirt aside. She lost balance on her knees and crashed into him, skin-to-skin, and the sensation hit her like a shockwave.

Droguk made that noise that sounded like a swear word. He pushed her gently back to take in more of her, to trace a stretch mark on her breast, then one on her side. "You're striped."

"It's because—"

"It's beautiful," he breathed, with another reverent touch.

Vanessa braced herself against his shoulders again, then let her hands drift down to the warm firmness of his chest. She followed her fingers with her eyes, then lifted her gaze to his.

"You're not ugly," she said.

He covered her hand and held it flat to his chest, as if he didn't want to lose her touch. "And you're not an odd-looking creature. I shouldn't have said that."

"Probably shouldn't have brought it up again, now," she said, pulling a face that would have been expressed verbally as, *"Yeesh."*

"Sorry." He palmed the back of her head and brought her down to meet his mouth again.

And she was lost. Completely lost in the heat of him, the urgency with which he devoured her, the way he'd grown bolder but still held her carefully, like she was a soap bubble he couldn't bear to break. She'd thought of his strength as being brutish and clumsy, but she couldn't have been more wrong. Droguk wasn't some mindless beast who would squash her without a care. He knew exactly who and what he was, who and what she was. And the differences didn't seem to bother him, now.

Turning her head from him, she rasped, "If ogres don't kiss...what do they do?"

He lowered his head to her shoulder, grazed his tusks over the curve. "We bite."

"Better not do that then." She held her breath as the tips of his tusks scratched her, his tongue tasted her.

"But you're good enough to eat," he growled playfully into the hollow of her neck. "Isn't that what you thought ogres did?"

"I thought ogres had Scottish accents and talking donkey friends," she giggled. Then, realizing he wouldn't get the reference, she redirected, lowering her mouth to his jaw and giving him an experimental bite there.

Judging from the low, appreciative sound he made, he liked that quite a bit. So, she gave him another gentle bite, lower, on the thick column of his neck. His grip on her tightened. She kept going, sliding her mouth along his skin, teasing with her teeth and sinking into spots that got a reaction.

"Fuck," he mumbled against her throat.

"That's the idea," she whispered back.

He gripped her hair and pulled her head up. The intensity of his gaze must have punctured her lungs, because she suddenly couldn't breathe.

"This is probably the only time we're ever going to do this." He wet his lips. "Can we..."

"Make it good?" she suggested.

He nodded, almost ashamed. "I'm embarrassed to even ask. If it's an imposition—"

"I would rather enjoy this than endure it," she decided.

"Then can I see you?" It was a plea made like he

couldn't dare hope. "All of you?"

She slid from his lap wordlessly and unbuttoned her jeans. She pushed them down; her underwear was still drying from laundering them after her bath. They weren't exactly sexy, but she was beginning to understand that what human men found attractive wasn't the same for ogres. She kicked off her sneakers, stepped out of her pants, and stood in front of him.

The awkwardness of how they'd begun this came crashing back, and her face and neck flushed. *Oh yeah, have a hot flash right now. That won't ruin the mood.* But it was just the effect of his stare, roving over her body as if he were taking in some majestic wonder. Her hairy legs, her hanging tummy, the fat rolls at her sides, all of it seemed to entrance him more.

"Stripes," he said again, and she heard appreciative lust in his laugh. "I had no idea humans hid such beauty beneath their clothes. Why?"

"Modesty?" She thought quickly. "You know, you don't want to share your greatest attributes with just any old person. It has to be something intimate." *Like a gym changing room or a doctor's office.* She could have snorted at the self-deprecating thought, but she didn't.

Droguk didn't know that back home, she was hardly a ten. Maybe a five, on a good day, with a lot of make-up. But to eyes untrained by a lifetime of being told that a human with a body like hers was undesirable, she was apparently—

"Perfect." He shook his head, mouth agape in disbelief.

It was too much. She'd long since given up on wishing for the "perfect body," ever since she realized that there was no "perfect body" for someone with no definable gender in a world where gender was irredeemably entwined with biology. But that acceptance had made it difficult to imagine herself as desirable. Dating apps had not helped.

"I said the wrong thing." His face fell, and she realized that a tear had escaped down her cheek.

"No, you said the right thing. It was..." She hiccupped a laugh. "Perfect. To steal your word."

He got to his feet. The low ceiling of the room made him that much larger. She took a step back.

"I'm just taking my pants off," he reassured her, as if that could be reassuring. "It seemed fair."

"Sure." Her eyes went to the ceiling.

With absolutely no ceremony, he said, "There."

She looked down and...there it was. An ogre dick, standing as tall and thick as her forearm. The green of his skin darkened as it rose up his shaft and blended into a deep plum color near the head. He shimmered with iridescent wetness, and her first thought was, *I know he's a virgin but that's a lot of precum for just a little making out.* And then, she felt like kind of a stud.

"And you're like, fully erect right now." Vanessa clarified.

"Well, no. There's the bulb—"

"Right, right." She held her hands up, feeling a little hysterical. She took a step closer and reached out to lay her palm against his chest. His indrawn breath lifted her hand, and she pulled back.

But he covered her hand with his own and pressed it back where it had been. "It's okay. I want you to touch me. And I want to touch you."

"Well, good news," she said, her skin throbbing where it laid against his. "Because I want that, too."

Chapter Seventeen

"Where?"

The word didn't make sense for a second. Nothing made sense to Vanessa in that moment. Her brows scrunched together and she stared up helplessly into his yellow eyes, trying to understand.

"Where can I touch you?" Even whispering, his voice was a deep rumble.

"Wherever you want." But she guided his hands to her hips.

He took a ragged breath as his thumbs touched the stretch marks on her sides. "You're so soft."

She ran her hands over his forearms. "And you're very... firm. Wow. You're like, pure muscle."

"Is that something humans like?" And though he asked it in general, Vanessa knew what he was actually asking. Did she like *his* body, or was she disgusted by him?

She tipped her head back to look him in the eye. "I don't know what other humans like. But I like it."

His green face darkened with a purple flush.

"Here." She guided his hand between her legs, parting herself around his thick finger. His eyes went wide. She rubbed the length of it up and down her clit, then helped him crook his knuckle to find her opening. "Go ahead."

His finger was ridiculously thick, and she moaned with relief as it penetrated her. He hesitated at the sound, but she grabbed his wrist to urge him deeper.

"That's good," she promised.

"It's so... small." He tentatively withdrew his finger and pushed it back in. "There's no way I'm going to fit."

She held onto his arm for support as his rough fingertip moved over her g-spot. "Without getting too graphic, I know it will."

He never had to know about her modest collection of fantasy-creature sex toys. Or their circumferences.

Oh no. They're going to find that stuff in my apartment when they declare me dead.

There was no guarantee she'd ever go back to the real world, so she refused to be distracted from what might be the last sex she ever had.

She took his cock in her hand. It was slick with his copious precum, and her palm tingled as she tried to wrap her hand around him. She kept her eyes on his, concentrated on his finger stroking in and out, the raging pulse that reverberated up her arm, faster with each glide of her fist.

"You can add another," she whispered.

His eyes widened, but he did as she asked, pushing another thick finger into her. The intrusion stung a little, but it was totally necessary; she hadn't had sex in a while, and it was good to stretch before strenuous activity.

"It's so wet." He withdrew and pushed them into her again.

"Yeah. Just imagine what that's going to feel like on your—"

"I'd rather not imagine that. Right now." He took a deep breath. "I'm just trying not to spend in your hand."

"Spend?" That was an interesting word. "What an elegant way of putting it."

He huffed a laugh. "I feel like you're making fun of me, but as long as you keep doing what you're doing, I don't mind."

"I'm not making fun of you," she promised, and tightened her grip a bit. "But I'm *having* fun."

"The fun might be short-lived." He grimaced. "I don't want to rush you, and I don't know how this works in humans, but I'm sure that if you keep that up, we're going to be significantly delayed."

She let go of him and he carefully slipped his fingers from her. She squeezed her thighs together against the emptiness.

Have I totally lost my mind? she wondered. Because she was no longer thinking of how strange it was to fuck an ogre. She was focused on the fact that she very much wanted to fuck this ogre. It was her stupid vagina. It had no idea that it was just getting petted and primed by a fairytale monster. It just wanted more and it couldn't be reasoned with.

"You know, since you're inexperienced, maybe I should be on top. Just in case you get carried away and like…" *Rip through my guts like tissue paper in one thrust*, she did not say aloud. "Well, I just know how to do it."

"I know how to do it," he muttered defensively, but conceded, "You're right, though. Maybe you could be on top?"

"Good idea." She gave him a little push backward and he fell heavily onto the bed. She climbed up between his legs and tried to throw one of hers over him, but it left her in an awkward position.

Not that the entire enterprise wasn't an awkward position, but her libido was more than willing to problem solve.

She crawled onto him, perching on his thighs the way she'd done when she'd kissed him, and inched forward. "I can't quite..." She brushed her bottom against him accidentally, and he groaned. It was impossible to spread her bent knees wide enough to straddle his waist. "This way won't work. What if you..."

She eyed his erection again, the ferocious length of it and the tapered bulb midway down the shaft. "What if you laid on your side, and I..."

He rolled up, and she scooted closer. "Hold my legs."

"Like this?" he asked, securing her ankles in one hand.

She propped both her thighs against his hip, careful to avoid the healing slash in his side, and wriggled until her aching core was flush against him. Her hands trembled as she took hold of his cock to position him. "Just like that. But no sudden movements. You have to let me lead."

His entire body shivered. "Understood. Please, just—"

The dripping tip of him touched her.

She'd been struck by lightning. No. She'd fallen off a cliff. No, she was...*having an orgasm?* From just that one little touch? She clutched the sheets in her fist and cried out, her back bowing so hard, her spine cracked. Sounds tore from her mouth that she'd never heard herself make before.

He wasn't even inside her.

"What the fuck was that?" she panted, her thighs trembling.

"What do you mean?" His eyes were squeezed shut tight, his neck corded with effort. Something warm gushed over the hand still grasping his cock.

"Did you just—" Fuck, another one was about to happen. She rocked her hips and the tapered head pushed in, widening her faster than she expected, but she didn't have control over the driving need to get him inside of her. The pleasure rippled over her like rings on the disturbed surface of a pond, and she gave herself up to it.

He rested his forehead against the top of her head, gasping. "I thought Brentan told you—"

"He told me about your weird-shaped dick! He didn't say anything about—" She was going to pass out. Her limbs jerked and her cunt clutched down; Droguk pushed further inside, a movement so small it could have been accidental. He groaned, and another hot burst flooded her. Impossibly, it made her even more sensitive than before, and she ground her opening on the bulge in his shaft. It wasn't too big, she decided. The problem was that she was too empty, and he was too big and hot and hard to resist.

"More," she moaned, and he obliged, panting, sinking deeper, and the whole thick, round bulb popped inside. He hissed and bucked, and she grasped onto his arm, biting her nails in as the relentless pleasure took her under again.

"Oh, fuck me, you're tight." His massive fingers dug into her thigh. There would be bruises there tomorrow.

Let him break me, she thought, her mind drifting in an ecstasy-drunk haze. *Let him fuck me to pieces. As long as he doesn't stop fucking me.*

"The words," he rasped, shuddering with another climax. "We have to say the words to complete the binding oath."

She tried, really tried, to process what he was saying, but it was difficult to focus while trapped in a torturous cycle of endless orgasm. "I—"

"Just repeat after me." His voice went tight, and he squinted his eyes shut. "I am yours, wholly."

"I am yours," she moaned, and in that moment, it was utterly true. "Wholly!"

"I will pleasure you and satisfy you—" He groaned, grinding deeper into her. His cock jerked and he whined, "—body and soul."

Fuck, just this alone is going to satisfy me for life. If it didn't kill her. "I will pleasure you and...satisfy you...body and soul."

"Our bonds are forged. Our oath is sacred. Our joining is...eternal." The last word came out like he was being strangled.

Eternal? That cut through the fog. But she had to say it. They'd come this far. Everyone claims their marriage vows are forever, she reminded herself. She waited for the next peak to fade into the electric, over-sensitive valley before she attempted to speed through the words. "Our bonds are forged, our oath is sacred, our joining is eternal. And I'm seriously about to die from too many orgasms, so you can take it out now!"

"I can't," he roared in frustration. When he tried to withdraw in demonstration, the problem became entirely clear; she yelped in pain as the wide base of his bulb tugged at her opening. "Now we can't... be separated..." He flexed inside her and fuck, it felt so good.

Her mouth was thick and her voice hoarse. "What do you mean, we can't be separated?"

"We're joined until... it's over." He let out a ragged cry, thrusting deeper.

"How long does it last?" She arched her hips and saw white hot stars as the bulb pressed harder against her g-spot. "Oh fuck, I can't stop coming!"

"Neither can I!" he growled, clearly irritated with her. "Why did we do that?"

"We were horny! We mad bad choices!" The last word ascended on a scream that nearly tore her vocal cords from her throat.

Droguk gripped the thick wooden beam that served as a headboard. It cracked under his fingers as he held on.

Reaching between them, she found the astonishing length of him that hadn't entered her. He rocked his hips in short, jerky motions; it must have been taking every ounce of his self-control not to thrust too deep and impale her.

"I can't," she sobbed finally. "It's too much. It's too much."

He buried his face against the top of her head. "Just hold on. It only lasts—" he hissed and stiffened. "It'll probably only last until nightfall."

Nightfall! That was hours away. Wasn't it? Vanessa couldn't tell the time and, when the next wave of release hit her, she didn't care, anyway.

There was no use fighting it. Crushed in Droguk's massive arms, Vanessa let herself tumble into an ecstatic abyss.

Chapter Eighteen

The best sex she'd had in her life. And it had been with an ogre.

She glanced across the table at Droguk, then quickly averted her gaze. They hadn't made eye contact since the night before, even when they'd woken up in each other's arms, still loosely joined. Even when they'd examined their oath marks.

Vanessa's was a sort of t-shaped line that reminded her uncomfortably of an IUD diagram, and Droguk's a pinched rectangle with a missing side. They weren't beautiful, like Brentan and Vikthor's, but she figured they couldn't reasonably expect beauty out of what was a transaction. The marks didn't look like they would fit together, though, and neither of them suggested trying.

They only spoke when totally necessary. For example, when Droguk asked her what she wanted for breakfast, and when he offered to fetch and heat water so they could wash, a definite necessity after all the... fluid.

And that's what finally broke the ice. She looked up, studying him as she chewed a bite of some kind of mystery sausage. "Magic cum?"

Droguk snorted in shock, clapping a hand over his nose and his mouth as he coughed and choked.

"I didn't mean to make you snarf." But it was pretty funny.

"Brentan was supposed to tell you about that," Droguk wheezed.

"We got interrupted. He also didn't get a chance to tell me about the being-locked-together part." She hoped he didn't see her shiver at the thought of it. In fact, her t-shirt was a little thin. She crossed her arms over her chest, just in case.

"Well, we only had to do it that one time," he said, his gaze dropping to his bowl of porridge. "So, we don't have to talk about it."

"Fair."

They sat in silence. It wasn't until both of them had finished their breakfasts that Droguk announced, "We're leaving today."

"Already?" She knew they would leave, eventually, but she'd hoped to get a little time to recover.

"We can get to Murkwater by nightfall. We might even get there early enough to book our ferry tonight." He paused. "You don't know where any of this is."

"I don't. And I probably should, right?"

He pushed his bowl aside and looked around their room. "It will be easier if I draw it."

She wasn't sure what he thought he would find; it was a sex dungeon, not an Office Depot. "What about in the ashes?"

He glanced to the fireplace. "All right. Come here."

She kneeled beside him at the edge of the hearth, uttering a, "sorry," when her arm brushed his.

"It's fine." He cleared his throat. Picking up a piece of tinder, he raked some ash toward them and began to sketch the stick through them. "Fablemere is made up of two continents, split by The Divide. We're in The Mire, which is here—"

She watched as he drew a lumpy sort of circle-ish shape, and a jagged kidney bean beside it.

"—and we need to get to Lua, which is here." He pointed to the southern end of the kidney bean.

"What's this part? Just water or something?" She pointed to the space between the bean and the kinda-circle. "Do we sail?"

"That's The Divide. And this part that you want to sail down? That's the Smuggler's Sea. Does it sound like somewhere you'd like to sail?" He turned to her with a little smirk that loosened the awkwardness between them. "We'll take the ferry from Murkwater across the straits here, then travel by road. It will be a long trip, but safer than what we've done so far. At least, as long as we stay ahead of the Baron."

"So far, so good, right?" Vanessa eyed the distance warily. "How long will this take?"

"If we have good weather for a crossing tomorrow, that puts us at two days, including today, to cross the Divide. From there, maybe a week?"

Her knees were screaming. She got to her feet. "All right. A week of walking. That is not going to kill me at all."

"I can carry you, some of the time," he offered.

"I don't suppose they make horses big enough for

you to ride on, huh?" she asked with a nervous laugh.

"None that I've ever met." He got up, too. "Murk-water is dangerous. No matter what happens, or who says what, you can't do any of that, 'I'm not owned by anyone' nonsense—"

"Nonsense?"

"—because you won't survive five seconds if some-one thinks you're up for grabs and on your own," he growled, which surprised her. "Could you just let me protect you? Without arguing?"

"I haven't—" she stopped herself. Maybe she had argued with him. A few times. She could concede that much. "You're right. You're right."

"You say you're from a different world," he went on, more to himself than to her. "If I found myself in a dif-ferent world, I would listen to the people in that world and I would assume that they knew best."

"Great. I'm glad you have that all planned out. I, however, was not afforded the opportunity for fore-sight!" She rubbed her temples. "I can't believe we're having an argument the day after our wedding. The honeymoon is over before it even happened."

"Honeymoon?" He tilted his head, and his un-bound hair fell forward, brushing the ash. She lunged forward without thinking to prevent it from getting dusty. He sat back quickly at her sudden movement but caught her before she could topple into the fire.

"Sorry. Your hair." She steadied herself on her knees and shuffled back, wincing. Stone and straw were not great to kneel on. Getting stiffly to her feet, she an-swered his question. "A honeymoon is a trip people take after they get married in my world. Not usually a trip to flee a vampire."

"What a boring world you come from." The corner of

his mouth twitched. "Come on. Vikthor's putting some packs together for us."

* * * *

Now that the oath bound them and they were leaving, Vanessa and Droguk didn't need to hide anymore. A mix of ogres and goblins went about their daily castle duties, not bothering to disguise their curiosity as they passed the odd couple waiting in the yard.

Vikthor and Brentan exited through the huge, iron-banded doors, accompanied by a knee-high goblin visible only from the waist down as it carried a pile of provisions.

"Hey, we have things like this in my wor— village." She cleared her throat and hoped nobody focused on her slip-up as she took one of the bags the goblin carried. It really was just like a hiking backpack you'd see on people at home who were goofy enough to go hiking. *I guess that goofy person is now me,* she thought with dismay, though in her defense, she was hiking for a reason, not just to wander around in the woods and gaze at distant rocks.

"There's enough water for the hike, and a little food, but you'll need to stock up in Murkwater. Or the other side of the strait," Vikthor said, reaching for a pouch on his belt.

Droguk preemptively shook his head. "I can't—"

"Don't argue." Vikthor pressed the pouch into Droguk's hand. Coins jingled.

Needing money on the trip had never occurred to Vanessa. She didn't want to argue against accepting it, if they needed it; she certainly didn't have any money, and she had no idea if Droguk carried any. But it felt wrong to her Midwestern soul to just let someone finance her flight to safety.

"Hey, we're oath bound, now," she began. "If the Baron shows up, he can't take me, right? What if we stayed for a couple more days and did some work for you? Some housekeeping or..."

She looked around the bustling courtyard. There were plenty of servants.

"Your mate will take the money and he'll stop being obstinate about it," Vikthor stated firmly.

Droguk grumbled and shouldered his pack, but he stopped rejecting the cash.

Vanessa examined her own backpack. There was a bedroll attached to the top, and straps to slip over her shoulders, though when she did, the whole thing fell straight to the ground.

"Ah. Ogre-sized," she said, looking sheepishly for a way to adjust the straps.

Droguk picked up the pack and jerked it about, but Vanessa couldn't see exactly what he was doing. Whatever he did, it fit her when he was finished. She would have to get used to the weight, though; it wasn't as though she'd carried a backpack since college.

"Be careful out there," Vikthor warned. "Not just in The Mire. I don't know what will await you on the road to Lua."

"Or if there is a road to Lua," Brentan added grimly.

"No road?" It seemed impossible that a medical facility with the capability to cure her would be located in a place that wasn't developed enough for roads. Maybe that was xenophobic of her.

"Most reach Lua by dragon," Brentan said.

Dragon? A dorky little thill gripped her heart. "There are dragons?"

"You seemed surprised that there are ogres and goblins and vampires," Droguk said dryly. "Why rule out dragons?"

"I'm not ruling anything out," she said, but her brain still throbbed with excitement. Dragons. There were dragons. She might see a real, actual dragon.

On the other hand... "So, why aren't we taking a dragon?"

"Because I don't have that kind of money," Droguk said.

"Dragons are notoriously gold hungry," Brentan added. "They charge high prices for their services. Very few peasants find themselves flying to Lua."

Peasant? She almost vocally objected to the label. Then she remembered that she worked for a company with a literal crown on its logo. And she paid rent to a guy called a land*lord*.

Her rent. Fuck, she wasn't going to make her rent.

Did that even matter?

"Thank you for everything," Droguk said, offering his hand to Vikthor, who pulled him in for a hug instead.

"It was very nice meeting you, Vanessa," Brentan said.

"I won't hug you," she promised.

He smiled. "I'll consider that a thank you gift."

"Vanessa." Droguk motioned to the castle gate. She gave their hosts a small wave, hindered by her thumbs tucked beneath her backpack straps, and followed Droguk out of the castle yard.

"All right," he said, his eyes fixed on the road ahead of them. "Let's go to Lua and save your life."

Chapter Nineteen

Murkwater smelled like its name. The refreshing sea breezes got lost somewhere around the muddy banks of a low tide, mingling with dead fish and human body odor and so, so many sea gull droppings.

Vanessa still had her hand sanitizer, but it was running low, and she didn't even know if the bacteria in Fablemere were the same as back home. She couldn't reach it from her perch on Droguk's shoulder, anyway.

Droguk took a big, savoring inhale. "Smell that."

"I can't help but smell it." She pulled the collar of her t-shirt over her nose. "I tried to breathe through my mouth, but then I could taste it."

He laughed. "Not a fan of seafood?"

"Not if it smells like that." She patted the top of his head. "Let me down."

"I'm not a cragowl," he grumbled, stooping to swing her down from his shoulder.

"I don't know what that is."

"It's a bird? That you saddle and ride?" His brow furrowed. "You don't have those in—"

"No, we don't. You could have just said 'horse.'" She staggered, her legs numb from sitting all day. "By the way, your stamina is impressive."

He looked sharply down at her.

"Carrying me! Your carrying me stamina!" It seemed that every time they tried to speak to each other, they said something that could be construed as a remark on the night before.

The day before.

The night and day before.

He actually did have impressive stamina in that regard.

And Vanessa was not thinking about that. Neither of them were going to think about it. Except for every single time their stilted conversations forced them to think about it. When that happened, Vanessa tried very, very hard not to think about the fact that he was thinking about it.

It was impossible not to think about it.

"Let's see the ferryman," Droguk said, and kept his eyes firmly on the small bridge ahead of them.

Murkwater was a town paved predominately in boardwalks. The massive wooden pylons holding up the wattle-and-daub buildings were stained to varying degrees by marks of the tide, and barnacles clung to the darkest parts of the exposed surfaces. Gulls screamed overhead.

"Oh wow. Where I'm from, you usually see those in Burger King parking lots," Vanessa mused. Maybe that was a sign that she needed a vacation when she got back home. If she got back home. "Hey, do you guys have any tropical places in Fablemere?"

He grunted a questioning sound.

"You know. Palm trees. White sand beaches. Crystal blue water that's perfect for snorkeling?" Of course, judging by what she'd seen of the land so far, snorkeling would probably result in being eaten by some type of creature.

"The southern part of the Smuggler's Sea, maybe. But you'd be robbed blind before you got there. Or pressed into service on a ship." He motioned to a street sign Vanessa had no hope of reading. "This way."

It was difficult to tell where the docks of Murkwater began, due to the entire place being a giant dock. There was something of a marina positioned far, far down a long boardwalk, over the shore and out into the windswept waters. The occasional gust blew Vanessa sideways, and her pack kept her off balance. The wood underfoot was slick; her shoes slid and she almost went down.

Droguk caught her by the arm and righted her. "Be careful. I didn't bring you all this way to drown you."

It was considerably colder over the water. Vanessa's teeth chattered and she kept her arms crossed, hunching over them in a desperate attempt to conserve body heat. Her jacket wasn't any help; the wool held onto the spray from the crashing waves. By the time they reached their destination, her curls hung limply in her face and she couldn't stop her teeth from chattering.

"Hello?" Droguk called, approaching a dubious-looking watercraft. "Anyone aboard?"

"This is the ferry?" Vanessa whispered, eyeing what appeared to be fresh tar patching the rotting hull.

"It's one of the few that will allow ogres aboard," he

explained, gesturing to a sign tacked to the post at the end of the vessel's gangplank.

Righteous anger rose in Vanessa's chest. "But that's discrimination!"

"It's a weight concern," Droguk said. "And a size concern."

His face instantly flushed, and Vanessa turned away.

Luckily, a man came down the gangplank and saved them. At least, he appeared to be a man, before his gills inflated behind the gray stubble on his parchment cheeks. "Can I help you?"

"How much for passage across the straits?" Droguk asked.

The ferryman took a deep breath through his gills and blinked his eyes. Vertically. "You missed the last crossing. But I can take you in the morning for seven gold."

"Is that a lot?" Vanessa whispered.

Droguk ignored her. "We'll be here before midday. I'll pay you then. Where can I find an inn that will accommodate us both?"

"I don't have use for inns," the fish-man said, scratching one bushy sideburn. "Live under my ship. But I've heard The Pink Pixie ain't too choosey about clientele."

"Thanks." Droguk nudged Vanessa and they retreated down the pier.

"We're not actually getting on that thing tomorrow, right?" she whispered to him.

"Did you look at the ferryman?" he asked. "Did he seem like someone who doesn't understand water?"

"He might understand water, but that doesn't make me a better swimmer." Especially not in storm-ravaged waters like the ones churning around them. Her toe caught a warped board, spilling her forward.

This time, Droguk didn't have time to catch her. She slammed face-first into the ground.

"Fuck!" She sat up on her knees, but Droguk had already scooped her up under her arms to pull her to her feet. She blinked away involuntary tears and clamped both hands over her stinging nose.

Droguk slid the pack from her shoulders and looped it over his forearm, frowning down at her. "Let me see."

Reluctantly, she lowered her hands. Somehow, it hurt less when it was covered up. "Is it bad?"

Judging from Droguk's expression, it was. "It's not good. But it's not life threatening. Here."

"Ack, no!" She flinched from the blunt green finger approaching her face. "What are you doing?"

"I was going to wipe all that blood—"

"Not with your bare hand! Jesus." She lifted the collar of her t-shirt, which had already seen better days, so it didn't matter that she wiped blood across it. She winced. "What's one more bruise?"

He looked away uncomfortably, and she remembered the dark marks from his fingers digging into her thighs.

"I wasn't referring to—"

"Let's just get out of the spray, before you really do end up in the sea." He held onto her the rest of the way down the dock. Not holding hands, really, more like gripping her forearm, but it helped her stay up.

The Pink Pixie wasn't that difficult to find; they advertised on nearly every corner with cheerful, brightly painted signs bearing an illustration of a very busty, very bewinged woman with bright pink hair, smiling and raising a foaming mug of ale.

"Wow. So, is she going to be there or..." Vanessa remarked, wide-eyed.

"Keep walking," Droguk said gruffly.

There wasn't much of a choice; the boardwalk was packed to creaking and swaying with a teeming mass of all sorts of creatures Vanessa only recognized from fairytales and Jim Henson projects. She could tell a goblin from a fairy, and she was pretty sure they walked past a vampire lingering on a corner, but as far as she could see, Droguk was the only ogre. He attracted a few stares, but for the most part, everyone seemed to be minding their business.

"There!" Vanessa pointed ahead of them at the busty pixie sign dangling above a doorway.

"I see it," Droguk called over the heads of some people she assumed were elves, due to their pointed ears. Somehow, the two of them had gotten separated in the crowd. "Don't go so far ahead."

It wasn't as if she could stop and stand still in the flow of traffic; she ducked under the awning and slipped through the door. No one even spared her a glance. Then, Droguk bent down to enter, and the place went utterly silent.

"I thought this place was supposed to be ogre-friendly," Vanessa whispered over her shoulder.

"You have crusty blood all over your face, and you just came in here with an ogre."

"Oh..." she said slowly. "So, they think..."

"That I attacked you." He nudged her forward.

The inn was exactly like any tavern Vanessa would have imagined in a D&D game. A hearth with a big, bubbling pot of what was probably perpetual stew, golden light bathing the pipe-smoke-stained walls, the thick, gnarled beams that support a second story;

it could have been a theme restaurant and Vanessa wouldn't have known any better.

A small, human-shaped thing with dazzling wings flitted toward them. Standing on the ground, she might have come up to Vanessa's hip. She was not, however, the pixie from the sign. She lacked the huge boobs and pink hair.

Hers was blue.

The pixie frowned at Vanessa's blood-smeared face. "You look worse for the wear."

"I slipped on the ferry dock. Almost went over, but he caught me," Vanessa said, hoping to dispel the hostility she felt steadily creeping through the tavern. She sheepishly swiped her sleeve across her face then instantly regretted it. "Ow."

"My uncle went that way." The voice that spoke up belonged to a grizzled-looking human with a beard and dirt-blackened nails on his fingers. "Slipped and went straight in. Waves took him down. You're lucky you had your friend there."

A murmur of commiseration went around the tavern, and the tension in the air loosened its grip. It seemed everyone in the inn had lost someone to the treacherous marina or knew someone who had. The tide had turned to sympathy, and Vanessa took advantage of it.

"We're oath bound to each other. Just got hitched yesterday," she said, grabbing Droguk's heavy wrist and hauling it up to show their marks.

The innkeeper's pointed ears twitched, and she clapped her hands in delight. "Congratulations!"

"We're on our honeymoon," Vanessa went on, batting her eyes up at Droguk. "Isn't that right, darling?"

He grumbled a cautious, "Yes."

"An ogre and a human. Oh, it must be such a romantic tale. How you met, I mean." The innkeeper's round face flushed with joy and expectation.

"It was." Vanessa realized that the fairy wanted to hear that romantic tale. She supposed saving her from the Baron, then from a group of angry ogres, then the whole desperate-trek-to-save-her-life thing could reasonably be interpreted as romantic but spilling a lot of detail about where they planned to go and what they planned to do seemed like a bad idea.

And the pixie was still looking at her.

"Her carriage lost a wheel in the muck," Droguk said, startling Vanessa. "It was sinking fast. I couldn't save the carriage, but I did save her."

"Although, some days, I think he regrets not saving the carriage, instead." Vanessa pushed playfully at his side. She couldn't say that he was better at improvising than she'd expected, because she hadn't expected him to play along, at all. "Now, he's saddled with an accident-prone spouse for eternity."

"Well, that does explain the state of you," the pixie said. "All right. Well, don't knock my ceiling down with what you get up to, and you've got a night here on the house."

"What?" Droguk looked between Vanessa and the pixie with wide eyes. "For free?"

"You can use what you would have spent on some better clothes for your partner. They can't walk around looking like that." There was a hint of recrimination in the pixie's voice.

"Gosh, thanks!" Vanessa beamed at the pixie. Then, she turned to Droguk and gave him a bright smile, too, playing into the love-struck newlyweds act. "See, honey bear! I told you this place looked like the best one."

She could clearly hear him express his revulsion with a questioning, *"Honey bear?"* even though he didn't say it.

He did arch a brow at her that indicated they would probably talk about it, later.

Chapter Twenty

Vanessa woke alone in an ogre-sized bed. She sat up, blinking in confusion and scratching her frizzed-out hair.

Beach-y waves might be a summer trend, but the damp salt air was hell on her curls.

"Droguk?" She slid to the floor, wincing at the stiffness in her joints. Marathon ogre sex followed by a day-long hike was a younger man's game.

A quick glance around revealed his pack exactly where he'd left it, so she didn't immediately panic. But it was morning, and people were shouting in the streets.

Well, not *people.*

She used the chamber pot, happy to have some privacy, for once. Then she washed up with the freezing water in the jug beside the basin and tried to comb her fingers through her hair.

What she wouldn't give for some shampoo.

The door slammed open, and she jumped. Droguk stooped over to enter and tossed a wad of fabric onto the bed. "Cloak."

"Yes. Cloak," she said with a grave nod. "Cloak. Bed. Fireplace. Droguk make good words."

"It's early, and I have a headache," he grumbled. "But you're going to need that, so you don't freeze on the boat."

"What about you?" She picked up the cloak. He definitely hadn't spent all their gold on it, she could tell from the numerous patches. Still, it was heavy and probably much warmer than her still-damp jacket. "Aren't you going to get cold?"

He shook his head. "Ogres run hot. You know that by now."

Of course, she knew that. She knew it from the night they slept in the swamp, when he kept her warm by nestling her in the crook of his arm. She knew it from the night before, too, when she'd woken sopping with sweat and kicked the blankets off frantically, although that could have just been a hot flash.

But her mind didn't go to any of those instances first. She had to forcefully pull her memories away from how hot and hard his cock had been, the heat of his release bursting inside her over and over—

"Vanessa?" There was a note of alarm in his voice.

She shook herself back to the present, her face flushing. "Yeah. Sorry. I checked out for a second."

"Are you going to have another 'seizure'?" He made air quotes around the word.

Ogres make air quotes?

"Fingers not needed," she said, narrowing her eyes. "And no. I mean, yes, sometimes they start with staring, but that wasn't what was happening. I was just…"

She would die before she told him what she'd been thinking of.

"Let's go. Get an early start." She tried to throw the cloak over her shoulders, but the wet air made her ache more than usual. The bed hadn't helped.

"Here." Droguk moved toward her, ducking to avoid the beams in the slanted thatched roof. He wrapped the cloak around her and fastened it with a toggle at her neck. Then, he drew the hood up and patted her head. "Now, you look like a scoundrel."

"I look like a wandering hermit," she said, frowning down at her clothes in dismay. The holes in her shirt certainly weren't getting any smaller.

"Well… we are wandering," he said with a grim set to his mouth. He gestured to the door. "Let's go. We'll get something to eat on the way."

They left the inn—Vanessa thanked the pixie profoundly for the free room—and wandered into the grimy sea of monsters and creatures outside. Her stomach roared loud enough for Droguk to hear it over the street sounds, and he gave her a raised eyebrow before stopping at a stall and purchasing two huge, round, spongy white buns. He handed one to her, warning, "Careful. The filling's hot."

"Is this…" she sniffed. Whatever the filling was, there was fish in it; the scent escaped the breading. She pinched a piece off and tasted it. "Oh my god! We have this! We have this back in my—"

"Hometown," Droguk snapped.

"Oh, right," she said, sheepishly glancing around to see if anyone had been listening. "Well, we do have this. We call it bao. Bao!" She whooped with joy and tore a big bite off.

"You'll choke yourself," he warned. "And don't eat too much."

"Why, you don't want a fat spouse?" She gestured to her body. "Too late."

"You could stand to gain some weight," he grunted, but he didn't disguise his slight, lop-sided smile.

Fondness and heat mingled in his expression, and Vanessa felt weirdly light beneath her ribs, like a balloon lifting her up. Was he flirting? Should she flirt back? What would the point be? But also, what would the harm be?

"That's how I get those stripes, you know." She meant it to be coy; sassy, even. She hadn't flirted with anyone in a long time. Maybe that's why he looked away, that little smile gone so fast she wondered if she'd imagined it.

"Don't eat too much," he said again, scratching his neck. "Don't want you puking all over the deck."

* * * *

It wasn't her, Vanessa wanted to point out testily, that had been in danger of puking all over the deck.

They'd paid the funny little Ferryman and climbed aboard his dubious, barnacle-crusted vessel, and taken up a spot on the slick, open deck. A few other passengers had gotten on, eyed the human and ogre sitting on the floor, and chose to loiter elsewhere. Droguk had picked a place near a railing, and that turned out to have been a wise decision because after only ten minutes into their voyage, Droguk was feeding the fishes.

"Hey, buddy," she said, standing at arm's length from his heaving back. "You get all of that out of your system?"

He lurched forward. Usually, the sound of someone throwing up would also make Vanessa throw up, but the gurgling roar Droguk made was so fully inhuman that it didn't affect her. That left her with the job of comforting him, a thing she'd never had to do for anyone before, due to her strong aversion.

"Is there something I can do?" She patted his back half-heartedly.

He shook his head, mouth clamped shut tight.

Vanessa looked around. There was an open barrel with a dipper beside it. She approached, hoping it was water, and when it was, she hoped it was *fresh* water. Unless ogres could drink salt water; it had never come up.

She glanced around, trying to catch the eye of another passenger. They all looked away. Raising her voice, she called out, "Is this for everybody?"

"Human," Droguk growled. "Just bring me the water."

She scooped up some water and refrained from complaining about being called "human." The rule was, she just went along with whatever he said or did, and he wouldn't let her get killed. It was a fair trade.

"Here." She passed him the dipper and tried not to think about the number of pukey mouths that had touched it before. Droguk rinsed and spit, and Vanessa gladly turned away to give him privacy.

"Thank you." He handed her the ladle and shuffled across the deck to sit down heavily. Vanessa returned the implement to its place and went back to his side.

"If you get this seasick, why did you suggest a ferry?" Vanessa asked.

"The alternative was a dragon that we can't afford,"

he reminded her. "Unless you planned to get a job wiping down tables in a Murkwater tavern for a few decades to save up?"

"The alternative was sending me alone," she pointed out. "You don't have to torture yourself—"

His hand shot out too fast for her to move. He gripped her arm and turned it palm-up, knocking her cloak aside to reveal her new, mystical tattoo. "You think it's torture to protect my mate? We're bound. Did you listen to a word of the oath we took?"

"Yeah, but that's like, symbolic, and it was to get me out of the Mire safely." It was a weird sensation, having to argue with someone about protecting her, but he was in misery.

"Look, we're already on the fucking boat!" he snapped. "I'll have to take another to return, anyway, and I could use the break. So drop it."

Drop it, like he dropped her arm when he turned away in disgust.

A phlegmy snicker drew Vanessa's attention. She noted the way Droguk's eyes cut toward its source, a short creature with shiny white skin like a boiled chicken bone and huge eyes on the sides of its round head. It covered its mouth, a gash of sickly black-red across its bulging face, and giggled into its hands.

"Do you have a problem?" Droguk asked, pushing himself up on one knee.

The creature's mirthful, malicious gaze flitted to Vanessa and back, and its giggling intensified. Bristly spines rose up in a strip down its back and trembled with its laughter.

"Is something funny?" Droguk demanded.

"Nothing. Nothing, nothing," the creature said, and scrabbled off across the deck.

Droguk's eyes narrowed as he watched it. "Fucking ghouls."

"Ghouls? Is that what he is?" Vanessa whispered.

"What?" Droguk shook his head. "No. That was a puckwudgie. He's a ghoul because he's creeping around, leering at us."

She glanced over at the puckwudgie, who flopped down next to a goblin and pointed toward them, snickering, before they both dissolved into laugher. Then, she understood: they were making fun of her and Droguk. Because they were together.

The realization came to her at the same moment Droguk lurched to his feet.

"Wait!" The last thing they needed was for Droguk to throw a passenger overboard or get *them* thrown overboard; Vanessa would *not* be walking a plank, and she could only imagine what the sharks were like here. She lunged for Droguk... and he lunged for the railing.

"I thought you were defending my honor," she said with a relieved laugh as he projectile vomited overboard.

His back sagged between his shoulder blades as if they were too weak to hold it up. "They should be praying to whatever sea god is keeping me incapacitated and giving thanks that I can't pummel them into jelly. I would, if I weren't feeding the fishes."

He retched, and she rubbed his back in small circles. "I know you would, buddy. I know you would."

Chapter Twenty-One

The Ferry docked at a marina in Shinewater, a town whose name was spelled out in a huge mosaic of rocks and shells above the tidemark on a sloping beach. Even from the deck of the dilapidated ferry, Vanessa could tell that the place they'd arrived was much nicer than the place they'd departed.

The sun blazed cheerfully overhead, so big and round that Vanessa expected it to turn and reveal a friendly cartoon face beaming down at them. The temperature was perfect, with gentle breezes wafting the scent of sugary baked goods out to sea.

"I thought I was sick before," Droguk muttered as they reached the end of the dock. Vanessa ignored him. She'd spent the past few days in conditions either dank, grimy, waterlogged, or underground. Shinewater looked like a damn theme park in comparison. The thatched-roof buildings were painted pastels, and each window held a window box overflowing with vibrant flowers. Vines twined up chimneys, and plump, happy-looking, mostly human creatures strolled the clean cobblestone streets.

"It's like a cookie village," Vanessa breathed, half-certain that if she took a bite out of the corner of a house, it would be gingerbread.

"Don't get attached to it. We're not staying long," Droguk reminded her. "We're getting provisions and moving on."

"We can't stay for one night?" she asked as they joined the flow of foot traffic out of the marina. "These people look like they might break out in song or something."

Droguk's lip curled in disgust. "Exactly. Don't wander too far from me. The less time we spend here, the better."

Vanessa let Droguk lead the way, though soon it became apparent that he was just guessing which direction they needed to take. As they walked, she noticed heads turn to look at them, smiles freezing as they passed.

If the citizens of Shinewater were going to sing and dance, it became increasingly clear that the song would be about the spooky strangers who'd just arrived in town.

She tugged Droguk's sleeve. "Hey, do you notice how... conspicuous we are?"

"There are plenty of humans here. And ogres. Nobody's looking at you." He paused in front of a greengrocer's stall.

The greengrocer was green.

"See?" he said, gesturing to the ogress behind the bushels of produce.

"Can I help you?" she asked, eyeing them both dubiously.

"He was just trying to reassure me that people weren't staring because he's an ogre and I'm a human," Vanessa said.

"They're staring because you both look like you've just rolled out of a dung heap." The ogress jerked her chin at Droguk. "I see a mark on you. Are the two of you—"

"Bound, yes," he said gruffly.

"Hmm." The ogress nodded, grimly surveying Vanessa's appearance. "You should be better to your human mate, ogre. Letting them walk around in rags, filthy like that. It's shameful."

"Thank you for the advice," Droguk said, and steered Vanessa away from the stall.

"Buy it a comb, too!" the ogress called after them.

Droguk held Vanessa at arm's length ahead of him and walked them both across the street. At the corner, he stooped down to Vanessa's eye level. "We'll be able to work faster if we split up. I need to buy a map and a guidestone. Can I trust you to handle the food and water?"

"Yeah, give me your canteen," she said gesturing to his pack. "And don't worry about the food. I'm excellent at picking snacks for a road trip."

He said nothing, but his expression said enough.

"What, are you going to give the job to the other guy you're married to?" she asked, and put her hand out palm up. "Coins."

He fished out some gold for her. "Please be realistic about the amount of food we can carry. And... don't do or say anything weird. Don't tell people where we're going or who you are or where you think you came from—"

"Droguk, I don't think I'm going to have time to have deep, life-changing conversations with people while I'm trying to buy chips, okay? And give me some credit here. I'm not helpless. Back in my world, I tied my own shoes and everything." She watched his gaze flick to her feet, where her laces were fully untied. With a scowl, she bent to correct them. "They came undone while we were walking."

"Just make safe choices, please?" His words walked a line between pleading and commanding.

"Yes, mom." She brushed off her creaking knees as she stood. "Where do we meet up when we're done?"

"Take the main road south. I'll meet you at the city gate." He hesitated, as if reconsidering the whole arrangement, then sighed. "Just don't make me worry about you, all right?"

Worry about me? She considered teasing him, but he seemed too sincere for that. He took the binding oath seriously. She wouldn't mock him for it. Reaching up to squeeze his shoulder, she said, "Sure thing, buddy."

He nodded and stepped back, then turned away and moved swiftly down the street.

Vanessa didn't know what he thought he had to worry about. She'd survived an encounter with a harpy and with the Baron. Buying some bread and cheese wasn't exactly running with scissors. She tilted her head up and followed her nose, literally. There was a bakery nearby, judging from the scent. She wondered what cookies were like in Fablemere, or if they'd somehow improved on cupcakes.

It was nice to explore her new surroundings outside of the framework of "fleeing" or "trying not to die." At the bakery, she explained to an elf that she was off on a journey—she didn't say to where, per Droguk's instructions—and that she needed something portable.

Well, she said she needed lembas, but despite being an elf, the guy had never read *The Lord of the Rings*.

She took the same tactic—minus the pop culture references—at every stall and amassed a collection of savory and sweet. With two loaves of bread for each pack, a considerable amount of cheese, a small crock of jam, some dried meat, and nuts that looked like almonds but tasted like marshmallows, her pack was stuffed full as she headed toward the city gate.

Vanessa wasn't sure why it caught her eye, but she found herself standing at the mouth of an alley that vibrated with an incongruous atmosphere. First, it was the only dark place she'd seen so far in Shinewater. It was the only alley, really. Second, it was damp-looking and smelled like wet garbage, another feature that really stuck out in the storybook-perfect town. Most intriguing, though, was the shadow-cloaked sign hanging between the buildings, swaying gently on creaking chains.

She moved toward it as if in a dream. Because she recognized the sign. It wasn't plastic and hollow and lit from within by one sickly yellow bulb that was not up to the task of advertising. But it was the same illustration, the same wizard that she hated, with the creepy eyes that always followed her into Merlin's Used Books.

It couldn't be a coincidence. The dingy stone walls of the alley didn't match the facades of the buildings on either side, as if it had been copy-pasted into the wrong part of an image. Vanessa entered the mouth of the passage carefully, noting that the door beneath the sign should, if it followed the rules of physical space, lead into the flower shop operating out of the storefront.

Unless it was a portal, like from the old *Dungeons & Dragons* cartoon she'd watched on Saturday mornings as a kid.

Vanessa grabbed the door handle. And froze.

Droguk. She imagined him waiting at the city gate for her. Watching the road nervously as the sun got lower in the sky. Sitting in the dark, thinking of all the terrible things that might have befallen her. *"Just don't make me worry about you, all right?"*

Wasn't this whole journey about saving her life, though? Returning to her world would do that far more effectively than a road trip to a place where they might not even be able to help her. Wouldn't Droguk want that for her?

In the cartoon, the portals disappeared before the adventurers could reach them. This was probably her only chance to get home.

But Droguk would never know that she'd left. Maybe he would go to the authorities, whatever kind of authority they had in Shinetown. Would they organize a search party? How long would he wait for her before he gave up and went home?

She looked up at the wizard. Even the stars and moons on his robe were the same color and pattern as the sign at Merlin's. It couldn't be a coincidence.

Droguk would think that the Baron had gotten her.

Would that stubborn ogre do something foolish like try to rescue her? He'd already taken a significant risk trying to help her. What if he got himself killed? She couldn't just leave without telling him.

But her life was on the line. If ever there was a time

to be selfish, surely it was when one's life was on the line.

She took a deep breath. Pressed her thumb down on the latch. *I don't have to go through the portal. I just have to confirm that it's there.*

But she didn't know what she would do when confronted with the chance to escape Fablemere.

"Fuck it," she whispered, and jerked the door open.

Chapter Twenty-Two

It wasn't a portal.

Vanessa's shoulders and spirits sagged. Maybe it was disappointment. Maybe it was relief. She had no desire to interrogate the emotion she felt at finding herself on the threshold of what appeared to be a new age store.

Someone, a very short someone, emerged from the back of the shop through a tinkling curtain of bells. Vanessa's first impression was that she'd just run into E.T. during the part of the movie where he'd dressed up in the blonde wig. The figure shuffling toward her was short, brown, and topped with a long mop of frizzy graying-blonde hair.

"Welcome, welcome," it said in a voice that could only be described as "smoker's cough, but make it a language." And it was wearing the wizard's robe from the sign.

"Hi, I'm sorry. I thought this was... someplace else." She blinked back tears from her eyes. "Nice robe, though."

"You're here now," the creature said. "Let Mommy Udacha tell you your future."

"Uh..." Vanessa looked back over her shoulder. "You know, today has been a little weird for me. Most of the days lately have been weird for me. Every day, I would say. And this situation doesn't seem likely to mitigate any of that weirdness. I think it's safe to say that it will add to it. So, thank you, but I should be going."

"It will take but a moment!" The little fortune teller whipped a scarf from a crystal ball on a small, round table. There was a chair on either side. She patted one seat and a poof of dust rose visibly into the air. "Come on, now. Sit."

Nothing was stopping Vanessa from leaving except the authoritative voice and the awkwardness of the interaction. Those things won, as they often did when Vanessa was faced with them. She went to the chair and sat obediently.

The creature extended one spindly hand and cleared its throat. Unsuccessfully, by the sound of it.

"Right." Vanessa dug into her bag and dropped a gold piece into the shopkeeper's outstretched palm. "Is that enough?"

"It'll do." The creature leaned over the crystal ball, wrinkly face crumpling in concentration. "I sense you have been on a journey."

What gave it away? Vanessa thought, tugging at the straps of her pack.

"And a long journey ahead," the fortune teller went on.

Shinewater was a port. Travelers must have passed

202

through it all the time in the middle of their trips. It wasn't even a lucky guess. It was just a guess. Vanessa was a bit disappointed; it seemed like in a place like Fablemere, a place that had real magic, there wouldn't be scam psychics.

The ball began to fill with mist. That was a nice touch.

"You're going to Lua," the psychic said. Probably another guess unless there were many cities on that side of the divide. "And when you arrive... They won't be able to help you."

"Oh?" But there were doctors in Lua, and Vanessa knew she couldn't be the only person who traveled there looking for a cure. She wondered how many desperate, sick people had been dissuaded from seeking help just to line this little gremlin's pockets.

"There is someone who can help you. But you're moving in the opposite direction." Gnarled hands waved over the crystal, and the mist evaporated. "I can't read you."

"How convenient." She couldn't help it if she wasn't impressed, but she knew a cold reading when she experienced one.

The creature narrowed its eyes. "It's not me that's the problem. It's you. You don't belong to this world."

"How could you tell?" Vanessa quipped, gesturing to her ragged clothes and muddied sneakers.

"You don't believe that I can tell your future?" The creature shook its head. "I can tell your past, then. You came from a world beyond our own. And now, you're trapped here. You've acquired strange allies to survive, but you have one that you've overlooked. You'll meet again, soon enough."

"Still pretty vague," she said, digging into her purse

for some of the silver and copper she'd received as change for her earlier purchases. "What do you want? Because I'm not paying you... more than this."

The fortune teller balked at the coins in Vanessa's palm. "Keep it. You need it more than I do."

"Well, thanks. For whatever this was." Vanessa turned and headed for the door but paused on the threshold. "Hey. Just out of curiosity, where did you get your sign?"

"The sign was here when I bought the place. Can't reach it to take it down," the creature sniffed.

You could get a ladder. But that wasn't the point. It was so similar to the sign outside of Merlin's Used Books. It had to be a sign.

A metaphorical one. Vanessa already knew that it was a *sign*.

"Who did you buy the place from?" she asked.

The little psychic shrugged. "Some wizard."

"Was his name Merlin, by any chance?"

The creature blinked. "No. Merlin's been dead for centuries. This one was named Arthur."

* * * *

It's not the same Arthur. She shook her head to herself as she walked, eyes firmly on her feet as she plodded along the cobblestones. They'd become more annoying than enchanting, just like everything had since her run-in with the Sylvia Brown of storybook land.

It's not the same Arthur, she reasoned, because that would be ridiculous. I would be a ridiculous person if I believed that Arthur the bookstore guy was a wiz-ard.

Arthur the bookstore guy who owned a magic book.

A magic book which, frankly, he should not have left just laying around, especially if he was a wizard and knew what the book was.

No, the Arthur she knew was an obnoxious, middle-aged Scottish guy who thought he was a surfer and dressed like Michigan was Hawaii. He was *not* a wizard. Unless Scotland existed in Fablemere.

She stopped in her tracks. Most of the people—creatures—she'd met so far had sounded like they had accents. Except for the ogres. They'd sounded as American as apple pie and unsecured firearms. But everyone else sounded like they could have been from England or Ireland or...

She refused to think about it.

In other news, Merlin apparently existed, or had existed, in Fablemere. That was pretty cool, and much more fun to focus on. She'd ask Droguk about that on their trek.

Vanessa had brooded so hard and for so long that she hadn't realized she'd reached her destination until something in the stretched ripped collar of her shirt snagged her and pulled her back.

"You won't get far without this." A green hand waved a map under her face, and she looked up to find Droguk smirking at her in amusement. "Is your pack breaking your spine? Is that why you can't lift your head?"

She let out a breath of sheer relief at the sight of him. When tossed into a sea of uncertainty, a familiar face could be a lifeboat.

They needed to get somewhere with less water, so she could avoid maritime metaphors.

"I was thinking," she said. Someone jostled her as

they passed, and Droguk growled at them, putting one huge hand around her back to shield her.

"Let's move out of here. Get down the road and let the crowd thin." He gestured to her pack. "Give me that. You need a break."

Her shoulders and spine were crying out, and she knew Droguk was capable of lifting about three hundred pounds with one arm, so she let him take it. He carried it like a purse over his shoulder and guided her through Shinewater's towering, sand-colored stone gate.

A thick forest met the city wall on the opposite side, but the road cutting through it was still paved. Plinths stood at intervals with the sooty remains of fires atop them, and Vanessa assumed that was to light the way for travelers in the night. It was all very Roman Empire.

When the traffic on the road was less congested, Droguk pulled her aside to stand beside one of the plinths. He opened the map and pointed to Shinewater. "This is where we are—"

"Obviously."

He arched an irritated brow before continuing. "Lua is down here, and the road..."

She watched his thick fingertip trace the path through the forest, a straight, bold line that faded into squiggles before an abrupt end.

"Um..."

"That's as far as the road goes," he said with a heaving exhale. "After that, it's beanstalk forests and rocky outcrops all the way to Lua. The mapmaker couldn't include any of the roads in the city, though. His surveyor hasn't returned from his most recent expedition."

"I don't know if I like the sound of that." Vanessa's voice was thin and high.

"The lack of roads?"

"The people not returning," she said with a roll of her eyes. "That should be a bigger concern for you than the lack of roads."

"It's not." He said it so easily. As if there weren't a bit of fear in him at all. "People do come back from Lua. Not as many as you might expect. It's a difficult journey. I assume weaker creatures, like people, don't want to make the trek back. I'm an ogre. I can make it back."

"What's it like to be so confidently right all the time?" Vanessa asked.

"Satisfying." Droguk folded the map and tucked it into his pack. He jerked his chin in the direction they'd set off in. "We've got a day of this, maybe, before it gets rougher. Then, the worst part will be the forest."

"Yeah, fill me in on that," she said as they began walking again. "Beanstalks, did you say?"

"They lead to the realm of the giants," he replied with a dismissive wave of his hand.

"Giants are real." Why wouldn't they be? It was nice that these new discoveries no longer made her choke on her heart.

"They're not as big as people say, by the way." Droguk sounded personally affronted by the idea. "They're only slightly bigger than ogres."

"I believe you, buddy." She gave him a friendly smack on the arm. "You're impressively big."

Fuck. That was the worst possible phrasing.

Worse, he cleared his throat, a universal sign of changing the subject with purpose. "There's a village

207

down the road. I'd like to reach it before nightfall. Get a room at the inn."

"Sounds good. Do you think there'll be any chance of a bath? Because I'm quickly becoming...not great smelling."

"I hadn't noticed," He grunted in response. "But pick up the pace. Nobody's going to draw you a bath in the middle of the night."

The mere thought of cleanliness would keep her legs going long after her feet were worn down to stumps.

Chapter Twenty-Three

As it so happened, the inn did have a bath.

For a fee.

And they didn't have any rooms available, anyway, and certainly none that would accommodate an ogre. So, Droguk found them a spot to camp for the night, near a steam he pronounced, "Just as good as a bathtub."

Vanessa took serious issue with that proclamation, but desperate times called for desperate measures. In the fading light, she began to strip off her shirt, then hesitated. "Maybe I should wear these in. They could use a wash. Do you think they'll dry by morning?"

Droguk was very preoccupied in laying his enormous bedroll out just right. He barely looked up. "I don't know, but it doesn't matter. Check my pack."

She moved suspiciously toward the two backpacks leaning against a nearby tree. Inside the larger of the two, she found...clothing?

"What's this?" She shook out a white linen shirt, not nearly big enough for an ogre. Then, a jacket much nicer than the cloak she already had. It was silvery-blue leather, with big cuffs at the ends of the sleeves like a pirate would have, and long tails that were more like a skirt than a coat. And there was a matching pair of trousers and boots.

"You needed clothes," he said, stopping to tend the fire. "I wasn't fulfilling my obligation to you as your mate."

"Oh." The clothes were well-made, way fancier than anything she'd seen at Mudholme. "This might be... too much. I mean. It's beautiful. I love it. But wasn't it expensive?"

"We have enough," he assured her. "And the lack of facilities for ogres on this route seems like it will save us a lot of money."

"That's not ideal but thank you for the clothes. They're really nice." Nice in a way that made her chest ache.

"You deserve something nice," he said, his voice barely more than a rumbled whisper.

She didn't know what to say. She placed the clothes carefully atop the pack and went back to the edge of the water, kicking off her shoes and tossing her shirt aside along the way. "If I get eaten by an alligator, avenge me."

"I don't know what an alligator is, so it's probably nothing you need to worry about," Droguk said, point-edly turning his back.

"Fuck!" She leaped back from the water's edge, teeth already chattering.

"It's the temperature," Droguk finished with a little

chuckle.

She winced and slid a foot back in. "I don't care. I've been sweating my balls off all day and I have no idea when I'm going to get a chance to bathe again."

"You don't have balls."

"Figure of speech." She whooped as a sudden drop plunged her in up to her waist. Droguk instantly spun, had already reached the edge of the water before she turned and saw him charging to her rescue.

"I'm fine! It's cold," she assured him.

His gaze flicked nervously up and down the banks. "Just don't stay in there too long. I don't know what's in this area."

Now, she glanced nervously around the banks, too. "Are there quaglantern out here? Slor?"

"Not muddy enough for slor, and quaglanterns can't abide moving water," he said, his eyes on her again. As they lingered, she remembered she was standing there topless. She crossed her arms over her chest and he averted his gaze to the sky, continuing. "There could be vodnik, nixie, nursery bogge, gwragedd annwn, leeches, snapping turtles—"

"That's plenty. Thanks. I got it." She took a deep breath. "I'm going under. If I don't come back up—"

"Avenge you," he finished for her, and turned back to the fire.

It wasn't that she was an exhibitionist, but Vanessa would have felt much better if he would watch her. But his reaction time was pretty excellent, so maybe having his back turned wouldn't matter. Either way, she wouldn't linger. Dunking under was like plunging into a bucket of needles, and she surfaced too shocked to make a sound. Without soap, there wasn't much to do but rinse off and scrub at herself with her hands, so she finished up quickly and raced back to the shore and her bedroll.

"Wait, you'll get it all wet!" Droguk warned, but Vanessa didn't care. She hopped in and wriggled closer to the fire, like a worm.

"Go check out the food I brought," she urged him. "And praise me for the good job I did."

While he did that, she burrowed down tighter in her sleeping bag. Maybe dunking her head had been a mistake. Her hair would be more tangled and it would take a long time to dry, even beside the fire. She sat up, tucking the bedroll around her chest, and finger-combed through her curls.

"Yes!" Droguk exclaimed, rustling through the pack. "This is my favorite cheese!"

She wasn't sure why that pleased her so much. *Road trip snack champion, undefeated.*

He brought the food over, humming happily. At least, the ogre equivalent of humming, which was more of a low, menacing grumble. But he was happy, and Vanessa was relieved that she could make him so. "It's the least I can do. I accidentally put you in a sucky position. I know cheese can't possibly make up for it, but I hope it helps a little?"

"I don't know, it might make up for it. It's very good cheese." He settled on the ground beside her and tore a loaf of bread in half. "Here."

"Thanks." She tucked her knees up and gathered the bedroll tighter around her bare shoulders. "Should we sleep in shifts? So we don't get eaten by anything?"

"What could possibly eat me?" He gestured to himself.

"I don't know. Like, a swarm of something? Or a dinosaur?" She took a bite of her bread and reached for the cheese.

He passed it to her reluctantly. An ogre-sized bite had severely diminished the size of the wedge, and she suddenly doubted that she'd bought enough for the trip.

"Dinosaurs," Droguk said, shaking his head with a chuckle. "That's nonsense."

"Oh good. I go to a fairytale world and end up with like, the one creationist in the whole place." At his lifted brow, she sighed. "It's not worth explaining. But dinosaurs are real."

His eyes widened. "You're joking."

"You have dragons, and you can't believe in dinosaurs?" What were dragons if not, well...dinosaurs?

"Fair," he conceded. "How do you fight them?"

Oh. He thought she meant... "We don't have to. They died out centuries ago. Well, some of them. Others evolved into birds and lizards. Alligators are dinosaurs, I think. And crocodiles."

He nodded thoughtfully. "How did they become birds? Did a wizard do it?"

"Time did it." She was about to tell him that wizards didn't exist in her world, but after the weird Arthur coincidence, she couldn't be certain. And she didn't want to mention any of that to Droguk. She'd brought enough weirdness into his life, already.

The night seemed to grow colder, even by the fire. By the time they were finished eating, her teeth chattered so much that she just gave up trying to chew without biting her cheeks.

"Are you all right?" Droguk asked, appearing perfectly comfortable.

"Just chilled." To her aching bones. And the wet bedroll wasn't helpful, anymore.

Droguk nodded decisively. "Get out of that. Spread it out so it can dry and get in mine."

When she hesitated, he rolled his eyes and grumbled, "We're mates. We've done more than sleep next to each other."

That made her feel a little warmer.

He looked away while she disentangled herself, spread out her sleeping bag like he instructed, and got into his. Then he climbed in beside her and curled around her like a giant electric weighted blanket.

Fuck, I hope I remembered to unplug mine, she thought, images of her apartment going up like a tinderbox haunting her. She bounced her foot nervously.

"Stop wiggling," Droguk all but growled.

"Sorry."

He shifted his arm under her head, cradling her against him like he'd done in the swamp to keep her warm and off the ground. The familiarity put her at ease, and the feeling of his bare skin against hers was surprisingly comforting. Within minutes, she was warm and sleepy and, hopefully, not as wiggly.

* * * *

Vanessa woke to the chirping of songbirds and a cheerful, clear dawn.

And an empty sleeping bag. Droguk must have gone off somewhere to relieve himself. She got up and tromped in what she hoped was the opposite direction and did the same. There was something freeing and primal about venturing into the woods naked and marking her territory.

When she returned to the campsite, Droguk still hadn't returned. Odd, but not anything she was going to worry about. She went to his pack and shook out her new clothes, hoping they would all fit.

Like magic—probably, it was magic—the breeches, shirt, and exquisite coat fit perfectly. Even flattering-ly, from what she could tell. But she could really use some kind of reflective surface to judge.

Not that looking nice was important to her. Who was she trying to impress?

Still, she ventured down to the stream in the hopes of getting a least a hint about what she looked like.

She reached the edge of the water and gave a quick scan up and down the banks for slors or—

Masturbating ogres.

There was no mistaking what he was doing. Droguk stood in the reeds about ten feet down from their campsite, massive dick in massive fist, eyes closed, pumping fast.

Vanessa made a startled noise without meaning to. That's how she got caught. His eyes flew open, and his hand went from stroking to covering himself in a nanosecond.

"Sorry!" she yelped over his shout of surprise and indignation. She scrambled up the bank and back to the campsite. There were so many constructive things to do, like put out the fire and roll up her sleeping bag and die of utter mortification.

Droguk stomped back into camp, not making eye contact with her.

"Sorry," she said again.

"It's nothing. Let's get moving," he snarled.

Judging by his temperament, he hadn't...

"You could go back and finish," she suggested, not adding, *if it would put you in a better mood.* "I didn't mean to interrupt—"

"I said, let's get moving." He kicked dirt over their already dying fire. "And you're sleeping in your own damn bedroll tonight."

Chapter Twenty-Four

They didn't talk for an hour, which Vanessa, prone to talking, estimated to last four entire days.

It wasn't that she hadn't tried.

"You know," she began again, for easily the sixth time. "It's not *that* big a—"

"Nope." He kept his eyes straight ahead.

She scowled and kicked a rock out of the path. "You can't go this entire trip without talking to me, just because you're embarrassed. We're buddies. Buddies don't get weird about this stuff."

"I don't have buddies," he reminded her tersely.

"Okay. We're *oath bound mates.*"

He stopped and faced her with an aggrieved sigh. "What am I supposed to say here? That I'm embarrassed that you caught me jerking off?"

"You guys call it that, too?" Vanessa gave a little laugh of astonishment.

He continued walking. His big steps forced her to take a few extra to catch up.

"You don't need to tell me you're embarrassed. I know you are, from how you're acting. The point is, you don't have to be embarrassed at all, or explain anything. I think you just need to hear from me that it's okay. It's not weird." She had no idea ogres were so puritanical. Surely masturbation wasn't a sin in their culture? Vanessa didn't know the old gods they spoke of or what they did, but it would be a bummer to have come to a fairytale world with the same sexual hangups as back home.

She expected him to grumble something or tell her to be quiet. To her surprise, he said, "I'm not embarrassed that I do it. I'm embarrassed that..."

"Yeah?" she prompted when it seemed he wouldn't continue. "Come on. This is me you're talking to. We've been traveling together for days. We're on the run for our lives—"

"Your life," he corrected her.

"Whatever. You can tell me. We're not strangers out here." She didn't reiterate the part where they'd had sex, because it seemed like it would make everything a lot worse for him. "I'm not going to judge you."

He growled in frustration and blurted, "Look, you were all soft and naked and when you sleep you occasionally make these little noises that sound...they just sound nice, okay?"

"Oh. You're freaked out because you were turned on by me, specifically." *Ouch.* "Well, trust me, you're not the first person to react that way."

"I'm not a person. And that's not what I mean," he said quickly. "Why would I be ashamed of being turned on by you? Look at you. You're fat and covered

220

in those stripes and you felt amazing when we were..."

She didn't take offense to the fat remark, not just because he found it a positive. In Vanessa's mind, it was a neutral description, and far less insulting than, "sturdy" or "big" or, gag, "morbidly obese."

And, frankly, the idea that he found her sexually irresistible was a much more interesting idea to explore.

"When we were fucking?" she said, and noted the way his shoulders tensed. "Do you think that slipped my mind? I had the best sex of my life that night. Remembering that occupies about sixty percent of my brain at all times."

He huffed as if in disbelief.

"What if you caught me masturbating because I was turned on by you? Would you want me to be ashamed of that?" she asked.

The words made him flinch like they were bee stings. When he didn't immediately answer, she prompted him with an aggressive, "Huh?" as an impatient follow-up.

He stopped again, turned to her with wide, rapidly blinking eyes, and said, "I would..."

She tapped her foot and held his gaze with strong determination, because in her head she desperately wanted him to finish the sentence with, *"join you immediately."*

Fuck. She was horny for an ogre. An ogre she currently found herself in a forced proximity, fake dating, arranged marriage style survival situation with.

Luckily for both of them, he said, "...not want a conversation about it later."

She sighed, either in relief or disappointment. She wasn't sure which. "Okay. Noted. I just didn't want you to feel bad or assume I was thinking bad things about you."

"No," he said quietly, starting down the road again. "I promise, I'm not worried about any of that."

"Then, let's change the subject," she suggested. "What do you know about giants?"

"Giants?" He gave her a puzzled expression.

"Yeah, we're going into their realm or whatever. Are they going to grind my bones to make their bread?" She hoped he would get the reference.

He did not. "Who makes bread out of bones? They might boil them for stock. But that doesn't matter. We aren't going into their realm."

"You said—"

"The Beanstalk Forest *is* technically a part of the Federation of Giants, but they don't usually come to the ground, and we're not likely to accidentally climb a beanstalk. Besides, as I mentioned before, they're not really much bigger than ogres." This must have been an important point to him, since he'd mentioned it twice now on the same trip.

"So, you could fight them and win, if necessary."

He nodded. "I'm sure I could."

Great, she thought. *Toxic masculinity thrives even in fairytale land.*

"But I won't have to," he went on. "The worst thing we're going to encounter is the terrain. The Beanstalk Forest hasn't always been The Beanstalk Forest. It used to be a city, until there was an accident."

"Jack's mother throwing out his enchanted beans," Vanessa said sagely.

He cast her a sidelong look. "How did you know about that?"

"How did you know about our war?" She countered.

"Right." He looked ahead again. "Watch your step."

Vanessa looked down and avoided the gnarled root poking up and displacing the cobblestones. True to the map, the road really was getting rougher. Chunks of broken stone littered the shoulder, and dips, holes, and puddles became more frequent the further they walked. Her hips ached, her back hurt, and they'd barely covered any ground.

"You're not even picking up your feet," Droguk muttered, and stopped to offer his hand. "Come on. Up you go."

She didn't fight him. He took her pack from her shoulders, slung it around his elbow, and lifted her to sit on his shoulder. The position was easier now that she was used to it. She didn't feel like she was going to plummet to her death at all.

"So, in our story, Jack's mom threw the beans and the beanstalk grew. Then he took a bunch of money, killed the giant, and they lived happily ever after. I'm guessing that's not how it actually went down?"

"You got the stealing part right," Droguk confirmed. "But the giants tracked him down and you can guess how that went."

"Bread," Vanessa answered confidently.

He grunted in annoyance. "Anyway, magic beans are an invasive species, and they grow fast. They destroyed everything. The giants claimed the land beneath their realm once it was deserted, and they won't allow any development now."

"Probably don't want thieving humans to come back," she interjected.

"Exactly. And that's why there aren't any roads. We're going to be picking our way through rubble to get to the other side. The bright side is, there will be ruins we can camp in. Some of them might still have bits of roof left."

"Hey! You found a bright side!" Vanessa patted the top of his head.

"Your human optimism is poisoning me."

If Droguk was joking with her, they were back on good terms. Vanessa decided not to bring up the masturbation thing again, though making everything aggressively weird was her brand.

"I guess that's a real 'good news, bad news situation,'" she said. "Good news, you might find a roof. Bad news, eaten by giants."

"Again with the being eaten."

"Harpy. Vampire. Quaglanterns. Slor," she counted off on her fingers.

"Quaglanterns don't eat humans. They could kill you with their venom, but they won't eat you," he said with the bizarre calmness of a person who could face down a venomous fish pig armed only with a spear. "What I wouldn't give for a big slab of Quaglantern ribs right now."

"Maybe we can hunt something in the beanstalk forest," Vanessa suggested.

"We'll probably have to," he agreed. "Who knows how long it will take to get through it? But as long as we can avoid the elves, I'll be happy."

"What's wrong with the elves?" The one in the bakery had seemed okay to her.

"They're obnoxious. And constantly high. It's impossible to have a conversation with them—" he broke off. "Actually, that's more of your good news, bad news. The bad news is, elves are fucking annoying. The good news is, The Beanstalk Forest is where elf weed grows."

"Oh. Cool." She had a thought. "You know, back

where I live, our equivalent to elf weed can actually help stop seizures, in some people. Maybe we should grab a whole bunch and bring it with us. I'm down to one pill, and I feel like I should save at least half of it for the scientists at the university."

"Smart thinking."

The road changed from frequent holes and puddles in the stone to infrequent stones in the puddles and holes, and Vanessa was glad to be getting a modified piggy-back ride over it. By midday, they ran out of road entirely. Droguk paused at the top of a wind-swept bluff and pointed across the valley below them. On the other side, an impossible wall of green-black rose all the way to the clouds.

"That's the beanstalk forest," he said, and pointed a finger as if she would somehow miss it.

"Where?" she asked, leaning slightly forward.

"It's right—" he stopped. "You're not being serious."

"I am not," she said happily. "Can we stop for lunch before we get there? It still seems pretty far, and my stomach is grumbly."

Droguk turned his head slightly. "What?"

"I said, 'can we stomach stomach pretty far—'" Nope. That wasn't what she'd said at all. "Wait. I mean."

What she meant was, *I'm having an aura that is rapidly becoming a full blown seizure.* She just didn't realize it was happening until it was too late. Her lips were numb and thick. "P'me din."

"Vanessa?" He tried to look up at her, but she was on his shoulder.

And then she wasn't.

She was plummeting headfirst to the ground.

Chapter Twenty-Five

"This is humiliating."

"It's better than the alternative."

Vanessa scoffed. She could think of numerous alternatives that would be better than dangling in a makeshift baby carrier on an ogre's back.

"I'm fine! I can walk!" Her stomach pitched as he took a decline a little too quickly.

"You're not fine. You're post-ictal—your words—and you almost cracked your head open when you fell." That's why he'd taken his knife to her bedroll and tied the strips together into a weird sling that he now wore like a mom volunteering at a god damn Montessori preschool bake sale.

The worst part was bumping her head on the backpacks, which he now wore around his neck.

"You caught me!" she argued. "I wasn't going to crack my head open. I have a big, protective ogre with lightning-fast reflexes that prevents that."

"Your faith in my skill is flattering, but it was a lucky grab. I thought you were going to die." That had been the common refrain throughout her recovery from the seizure that had caused her to topple off his shoulder, and the driving force behind his DIY solution.

"We can't base everything we do on this journey on 'I thought Vanessa was going to die,'" she said.

"The entire journey itself is based on thinking Vanessa is going to die," he reminded her.

She didn't have a retort for that.

"I can move faster this way," he said. "There's a bright side for you."

"Ugh!" She dropped her forehead against his back. "If I get motion sick, I'm puking on you."

"The fact that you haven't puked on me already is astonishing," he said cheerfully. "Hold on, we're going down another hill."

By the time they made it across the valley, the motion sickness was no longer a joke. Not being able to see anything in front of her and getting bounced around like a rag doll while Droguk bounded across the rocky terrain was worse than any long car trip she'd ever taken. She tried to look up to see if that would help, but the stationary clouds above them were a complete mind fuck, way too eerie to focus on for long.

She patted his back. "I need a break."

"When we get into the forest," he said, picking up speed.

"But I have to pee." She didn't actually have to pee. *Is this what I have been reduced to? Empty childhood road trip threats of urinary misfortune?*

Droguk just grunted in response and kept going.

"Seriously, are you trying to catch a plane?" she craned her neck to look around. "Are we being chased by wolves?"

He didn't answer. He probably couldn't hear her over his breath, which thundered through her ear when she laid her head on his back again. What had to be a friggin' massive heart pumped wildly, but even as they reached rising terrain, he didn't slow.

Maybe they *were* being chased by wolves, and she would never see them coming. Vanessa tried to pull up her feet, as if avoiding the snatching jaws of the starving and, as far as she knew, imaginary, animals.

If something is wrong, Droguk's got it, she reassured herself. *Droguk knows what to do.*

Except, maybe he didn't. He had never been to Lua. Maybe the farthest he'd ever been from home was Murkwater, and now he was as out of his element as Vanessa was.

But even that thought couldn't shake her trust in him. Droguk wouldn't let anything happen to her, and if he did, it would be because something had happened to him, first. That wasn't the most comforting thought, but it was what she had.

By the time they reached the edge of the forest, the sliver of ground she could see was moving fast. She wondered if ogres could have heart attacks, because his entire cardiovascular system sounded like the floor of a manufacturing plant that built asthma and loudness. The light dimmed to a weird greenish-gray, and they fell, Droguk landing face first and unmoving with Vanessa piled on his back.

"Are you do—"

"Shh!" he whispered. "Don't fucking talk right now!"

From her vantage point splayed atop him, Vanessa

could see through a window in the crumbling stone wall he'd dived behind. Two black dots moved across the valley, traveling fast.

But it wasn't as if they could hear them from so far away. "Why can't I talk?"

"Because I need to think, and you talking makes that more difficult." He raised himself up on his hands, and Vanessa scrambled to hold onto his shirt for stability. "They're the Baron's men."

"How do you know?" To Vanessa, they looked like two swiftly moving black smears.

"Because they've been following us since the Shinewater gates."

This was brand new information to her, and she didn't appreciate that. "What? Why didn't you tell me?"

"Because I wasn't sure, at first. There were a lot of people on the road. But then I saw them at the inn last night." He grimaced. "I thought we lost them after that."

"Why didn't you tell me?" She thumped the back of his head with her palm. "Teamwork makes the dreamwork, asshole!"

"We can fight about that, later. Right now, I need to decide what to do. Do we keep going and hope we outrun them?"

"What if they're not trying to catch us?" Vanessa suggested. "What if they're just surveillance?"

"In which case, we don't want them to report back." Droguk made a thinking noise. "We could wait here until they catch up and I could try to kill them, but if they're vampires, I'm not sure I can."

"You can't kill a vampire?" She looked doubtfully at the size of the huge hand bracing his massive weight against the ground.

He shook his head. "They're fast, and they're strong."

"Stronger than an ogre?"

His annoyed grumble was a confirmation. Admitting that something was stronger or bigger or scarier than him must have felt like having a tooth pulled before the advent of Novocain.

"What if we worked together?" Vanessa asked. "You could use me for bait and hide behind something, and then pop out and squish them with a rock."

Something pricked her back. Droguk went very, very still.

"Forgive us for interrupting your murder plot," a posh English voice said from above. "But exactly what the fuck do you think you're doing in our forest?"

"Please don't stand up," Vanessa whispered to Droguk. "I think they've got a spear pointed at me."

"We do," the voice confirmed, but the sharpness at her back moved away. "Get up."

"I'm kind of tied to the ogre," she said.

"Both of you." The voice sounded tired of her bull-shit already. That, Vanessa knew, could work in her favor. If she pissed off their attackers enough, they might give up just to get away from her.

Then again, they might just kill her faster.

Tabitha had always reassured her during their true crime binges that no serial killer would ever torture Vanessa to death, because he'd get too annoyed with her constant talking.

Droguk slowly rose to his feet. "I'm going to put the human down."

"No sudden moves," another voice said. The fact that they all sounded like they were from England

painted a picture of their assailants that matched
Robin Hood and his Merry Men. Not the ones from
the cartoon with all the animals, but the Mel Brooks
version.

She was disappointed in the extreme when Droguk
released her from her carrier and she rolled out at the
feet of a guy who didn't look anything at all like Carey
Elwes.

The spear-holder was dressed in forest camo. In
fact, he *was* forest camo. His hair and skin were
both speckly green and yellow, like sunlight coming
through leaves. The tips of his ears stuck up through
his hair in unmistakable points.

The other elf also held a spear trained on them, and
slowly, as her eyes adjusted to the forest, more and
more elves became visible. They blended perfectly
with their surroundings, like chameleons on a polka
dot sweater. It would have been impressive if it hadn't
been so scary.

Droguk held up his hands to show he had no weapons, and Vanessa did the same, though she doubted
she appeared half as intimidating as Droguk did.

"We are travelers on our way to Lua," Droguk said
slowly and clearly. "We're just passing through."

"Travelers to Lua are no longer permitted to pass
through The Beanstalk Forest," the elf who seemed to
be the leader of the group said. "Not since last spring,
when we closed our borders."

"We didn't know that," she said quickly. "See, I'm
from out of town—"

Droguk grunted sharply.

"I'll just let my mate here do the talking," she said,
and cast her eyes down.

"Mate?" The elf's voice rose in surprise.

"Yes. She's my mate," Droguk said. "She has an illness and I'm taking her to Lua for a cure."

"A touching story," the elf said with a laugh, and a few of the others snickered. "But the forest is still off-limits. The Federation of Giants issued that decree several seasons ago. And I've never heard of sick and desperate travelers plotting to, what was it, squish someone with stones?"

That conversation really did sound bad out of context.

Droguk made that noise that sounded like a swear. "We're being followed."

And elf with, frankly, spectacular boobs straining against her beanstalk-leaf bra, stepped from her hiding place behind more crumbled wall and took out a spyglass. She scanned the valley and announced, "Vampires."

"You were right," Vanessa whispered to Droguk.

"Baron Scylas is after my mate," he explained to the head elf. "We would not have led them here if we knew they still pursued us. I beg you to allow us to travel through your lands. We won't quarrel with you—"

"Or squish anyone!" Vanessa interjected.

"—and we will take an alternate route on our return. But it is imperative that we reach Lua and avoid those vampires."

The head elf considered, while the one Vanessa had mentally named Tits O'Houlihan approached him. "There shouldn't even be vampires on this side of the divide, Shanus."

The elf-in-chief nodded in agreement. "There's something they aren't telling us."

"We'll tell you!" Vanessa blurted. "We'll tell you everything. I have no problem talking. Ask him, he hears me yapping all the time. Never gets a word in edge-wise, this one. Just five minutes ago, he was telling me to shut up because—"

Shanus held up his hand and gave her a sharp look.

"We should take them to Elvaneth," Tits O'Houlihan said.

If Elvaneth was far from the vampires pursuing them, Vanessa was absolutely fine with that plan.

Droguk seemed less so. "We must reach Lua as soon as possible. My mate is very sick—"

"The human looks healthy enough." Shanus turned to his busty sidekick. "You're right. Elvaneth will want to speak to them."

The elf leader turned to them both and opened his arms in a mocking display. "Welcome to The Bean-stalk Forest," he said with a chuckle. "You are now officially prisoners of the Elf King."

Chapter Twenty-Six

"Elves are all high and super-duper chill all the time, it's so annoying." Vanessa glared at Droguk. "That's you. That's my impression of you."

"Prisoners don't usually do so much talking," the busty elf said, and gave Vanessa a nudge with her elbow.

"Don't touch them!" Droguk snarled at the elf, who immediately raised her spear.

"Hey, hey," Vanessa said, putting a soothing hand on his arm. "They have weapons. We don't. Why don't you calm the fuck down, okay, buddy?"

"You two have got to be the most annoying prisoners anyone has ever apprehended," Shanus said, not deigning to look back at them. He led them through the forest, on no discernable path, which made Vanessa feel better about being caught. There was no way they would have been able to navigate through the looping vines and man-sized leaves on the ground, not to mention the remnants of a city which, in Vanessa's opinion, should have built their damn roads better. They were completely grown over.

Then again, none of the cities on Earth could withstand an invasion of beanstalks. The things were easily as big as sequoia trees, with vines that spread out across, and sometimes through, obstacles.

And she recognized that she and Droguk would have been fully boned on their trip through the forest. There would have been no chance to navigate by the sun or the stars or any of that outdoorsy shit. Leaves the size of the roof of a house blocked out the sky and acted as a green filter for any light that could manage to make it through.

Vanessa wondered about that. She studied the elf she'd mentally nicknamed Tits O'Houlihan and asked, "Are you wearing camouflage paint, or is that your skin?"

The elf gave her an icy look that suggested death by spear poke was imminent. "It's my skin."

"Oh. That's interesting. I met an elf in Shinewater, and he just looked like a white dude."

"My mate has some kind of defect that prevents them from being silent," Droguk grumbled to one of the other elves.

But her words brought Shanus up short. "You met an elf?"

Vanessa nodded. "Uh-huh."

"In Shinewater?"

"Uh-huh. He was running a bakery. And by the way, he had never heard of Legolas or anything, so if you guys wanted me to give you a brief theatrical retelling of *The Two Towers*—"

"Rathal," Tits said grimly. "It has to be."

"And he's gone completely white?" Shanus asked.

Vanessa sensed she'd created some confusion. "No, I mean. White like Caucasian. Which I am now realizing isn't a concept that you have. I mean... kinda pink and peachy? Like me?"

Shanus shared a look with his comrades and there seemed to be a general air of relief in the party. He addressed Vanessa. "It's protective coloring. If we left the forest, we'd all be one color, also."

"But white is bad?" She clarified.

"Mind your human business," O'Houlihan said, and nudged her again, looking Droguk straight in the eye as if daring him to do something about it.

Please don't provoke the ogre, Vanessa thought, and shot a quick glance to Droguk.

Eventually, their walk brought them to a place where thick beanstalks had been cut and fashioned into primitive gates in a towering wall of leaves. Two elven sentries swung the gates open at Shanus's approach. The group walked through, and Vanessa stopped, causing a domino effect of stumbling elves behind her.

"Fee Fi Fuck me, that's tall," she whispered, staring up at a vertical village stretching far up the stalks. Walkways looped around, through, and between the plants, leading to tree houses stacked around the huge trunks. Rope and pulley—well, vine and pulley—elevators rose and descended, elves strolled along suspended vine bridges, while on the ground, elf sentries stood in a perimeter around the clearing and more elves tended massive cookfires.

"This is just like my Ewok Village playset," Vanessa murmured.

"What are you talking about?" Droguk asked.

"The Ewok Village playset. It was a repurposed version of the Tree Tots. It just had different coloring and stickers." She shook her head. "If I could time travel back and tell little me about this, they would be so fucking hype."

"This way," Shanus ordered.

"As your mate," Droguk said through audibly clenched teeth. "I'm going to advise you to stop talking."

"Why?" She looked around at the elves flanking them. "Because they threatened me with spears? I think I've seen enough movies to know the drill, here. Shanus is taking us to see the king. That means Shanus isn't in charge, which means the rest of these guys definitely aren't in charge. They're not going to kill us because they don't have permission. Is that right?"

Shanus didn't stop walking, but tossed her a terse, "You're correct."

"We can't kill you until Elvaneth gives us permission," O'Houlihan muttered.

Elves stopped and stared as they walked through the village. Vanessa assumed they probably didn't see many ogres. Maybe not even people. But none of them seemed to be afraid or alarmed. Nobody grabbed their little elven children and hurried them away. Nobody shouted, *Oh my god, an ogre and/or a human!* They just stopped to watch with interest before going back to their own elf business.

Shanus led them to the stump of an enormous stalk. Two huge, pointed doors were carved into it, between two big, gnarled, dead roots. The broken stalk was brown, but its jagged top was roofed with verdant leaves. Smoke rose from it, and it smelled unmistakably like...

"Dude, who's holding, am I right?" Vanessa said with a snort.

Droguk made a low growl.

The doors opened and Shanus led them inside. Droguk didn't even have to duck to enter.

Inside, a fire burned in a center pit. Scantily dressed elf maids tossed handfuls of elf weed into the flames now and again. The whole place was a mystical forest hot box. Beyond the flames, on a throne of beanstalk wicker, lounged an elf with long, silky white hair.

"King Elvaneth," Shanus said, leading them around the fire pit. "Intruders from beyond The Divide."

The king made a face and sat up with a groan. "Really? Still?"

"They had no knowledge of the ban," Shanus explained. "I really think we need to revisit our advertising strategy. Our current campaign is obviously not working."

"There were more behind them," O'Houlihan said. "These travelers believe they're being pursued by vampires."

Elvaneth made a face. "Vampires? Really?"

"Baron Scylas's men," Droguk spoke up, and added, "Your Majesty."

"Oh, please, none of that." The king waved an impatient hand. "Call me Elvaneth."

"We left a few scouts behind to trap them," Shanus said. "They'll escort them through the forest."

"Wait, you're going to escort the vampires, but not us?" Vanessa protested.

"This works out for us," Droguk said. "The vampires will be ahead of us, thinking they're still following us. This elf has done us a favor. But I want to know why."

He directed the last sentence to Shanus.

It was Elvaneth who answered. "Faeries do favors. Elves do as we will."

"The vampires are pursuing you, so you must be important to the Baron."

"Okay, can I ask a question here?" Vanessa put her hand up. "Who is this Baron guy? Like, I know everybody in the Mire was afraid of him, but even you all know him?"

"The Baron is one of the, if not the, most powerful beings in all of Fablemere." O'Houlihan's voice was coated in disbelief. "They're playing stupid, Elvaneth. This is a trap."

Droguk was quick to step in. "My mate was born in The Baneful Wood. She has been entirely cut off from the rest of Fablemere for most of her life."

All of the elves seemed to understand this, which made Vanessa pretty sure they now all thought she was a freak.

"The Baneful Wood?" Elvaneth's non-existent brows rose in surprise. "I thought no one left The Baneful Wood."

"Well, we do," Vanessa said cheerfully.

Droguk spoke over her. "Her family lived on the edges of the forest and traded in the Springlands. It's not so unheard of, locally."

Vanessa tried to commit those details to memory, but she wished they'd created this cover story a long time ago, so she could have practiced it, and also so she could have explained to him just how disastrous she would be at keeping up a cover story in the first place.

"All the way from The Baneful Wood to... where is it you intend to go?" Elvaneth asked.

"Lua," Droguk answered. "She has a terrible condition that we hope the physicians at the university can fix."

The air in the throne room was hazy, and Vanessa took a deep breath of it before saying, "Elf weed helps, though. If you can spare some."

A laugh rippled through the room.

Droguk wasn't laughing. "All we ask is safe passage. We would never have entered your forest if we'd known it was off limits. And we certainly would never have led the Baron's men to you."

Elvaneth lifted his hand and let it fall lazily to the arm of his throne. "We really do need to put up signs. I thought distributing pamphlets through Shinewater would do the trick."

Vanessa tilted her head. "Wouldn't signs just alert people to the fact that you're here? I mean, the camo and the big gates kind of suggest that you're not interested in being found by outsiders."

Elvaneth sat up straight, his face going intense and serious. "That is exactly what *I* said, and no one agreed with me."

"Consider, my king, that the source of this agreement is a human from The Baneful Wood," Shanus said, and it got a big laugh from the other elves.

But Elvaneth didn't laugh. He leaned forward and beckoned Vanessa closer.

She walked toward him, and every step she took away from Droguk felt a little bit less safe.

"Do you have any ideas, perhaps, for how to relay the message without signs?" the king asked.

Vanessa held up her hands in a defensive apology. "Oh, no, I'm not... That wasn't my..."

"Her family homestead is protected by a thicket of

thorns," Droguk supplied for her. "You'd never believe that someone lived beyond it, because it looks impossible to pass through."

"There are no thorns in The Beanstalk Forest." Shanus shot the idea down testily.

"No, but there are all sorts of vines and things," Vanessa pointed out. "What if you made the roads into the forest so impossible to traverse, people didn't have a choice but to stay out? It's what we did in The Baneful Wood."

Lying to elves just seemed wrong. All they wanted to do was help people make shoes and Santa's toys. And, with one notable exception, to go into dentistry.

"The Baneful Wood's reputation helps keep people out, too," Droguk said. "Perhaps if you catch some travelers, who are not us, and you skinned them or hung their heads up, it would discourage travelers."

The elves recoiled in horror, and Vanessa was grateful for that. She would have to have a serious discussion with Droguk about recommending skinning as a solution in situations where they could be the ones getting skinned. They were lucky that this time, the creatures around them weren't into that sort of thing.

"Maybe not skinned," Vanessa jumped in. "Maybe like, you could take some clothes and hang them up as a warning."

"Again, not our clothes," Droguk specified. "We need them."

Vanessa's brain lit up with a plan. "I have some really gross, nasty, shredded stuff in my backpack. I could give you that and you could, I don't know, find some animal bones or something and make it seem like you left a body out there to rot. That would keep me away."

"The human makes a good suggestion," Elvaneth announced. "All right. In exchange for this advice and your materials, we can provide safe passage through the forest."

"Oh, great! Honey bear, get the clothes," she said. She noted two elves leaning their heads together, one of them mouthing, *"Honey bear?"*

Droguk dropped her pack to the ground, pulled the ratty t-shirt, jeans, and jacket out, and tossed them down in a pile.

"This is how the humans of The Baneful Wood dress?" O'Houlihan observed with a sneer.

"Yeah." Vanessa shook her head fervently. "Exactly like this. All of us."

Another elf picked up the t-shirt, then held it far away from his body.

"And we like smelling like that, so it's pretty xenophobic of you to critique my cultural norms," she added.

"It's too late in the day to try to traverse the forest now," Elvaneth said. "Find them somewhere to camp and... take them to the faery baths. Goddess knows they need it."

The word "bath" perked Vanessa up immensely.

"After that," Elvaneth went on, "you'll join us in our ceremony."

"Ceremony?" Droguk clenched his fists. "If you plan to sacrifice us, I strongly encourage you to rethink those plans."

"Of course, we're not going to sacrifice you." Shanus sounded disgusted by the notion. "It's the celebration of the living essence."

That still sounded creepy, but Vanessa had to find a bright side somehow. "Hey, as long as we're not going to end up on a spit roast and served with apples in our mouths, I'm happy."

"Again, with the being eaten," Droguk grumbled.

"You've never seen *Return of The Jedi*," Vanessa snapped. "It's possible with tree people."

As they were led out of the royal hot box, Vanessa weaved on her feet. "You know, I never believed in contact highs before now."

"I don't know what that means," Droguk replied.

"Do you know what 'living essence' means, though?" Vanessa asked. "Because that would be helpful to know."

"You're better off not knowing," Droguk said.

"Why?"

"Because this is going to be truly disgusting."

Chapter Twenty-Seven

The "faery baths" turned out to be a sandstone cavern with bubbling hot springs of opaque blue water. It reminded Vanessa of those travel documentaries about Iceland. Except in Fablemere, the springs were enclosed within the dome of rock. Light emanated from something, giving the entire place a warm glow, but Vanessa didn't see any torches. Glittering motes drifted through the air and the slightly sulfurous smell of the bubbling water brought to mind her childhood trip to Yellowstone.

"Places like this exist where I'm from," Vanessa said, looking out on the numerous little pots and cauldrons around them. Some rose in columns high in the air and spilled water down their sides. Others, she could look down on and feel the steam against her face. "They have something to do with volcanoes."

Vanessa had mentally nicknamed the elf who'd led

them there Short Stuff. Not due to his height, but the fact that, unlike the other elves, he wore pants that were cut high on his legs like those tragic gym shorts from the eighties. He listened to her without interest and replied dryly, "Well, here they're something to do with faeries. Enjoy."

He left Vanessa and Droguk standing there inside the cavern.

She looked all around for a sign like one at a hotel pool. Something to tell her what the rules were, so she wouldn't commit any weird faux pas. So far, the elves were not the easy-going stoners Droguk had described.

"Did he seem a little sassy to you?" Droguk asked, watching the mouth of the cave.

"What? Did the Lieutenant Dangle shorts give it away?" Vanessa snorted, then subdued. "Right. Another reference you wouldn't get."

"I got volcanoes, though," he said, and clapped her on the back gently. Still, it was ogre-gentle, so she staggered under the force. "Come on. Might as well make use of these."

To her surprise, Droguk started stripping off right there.

"Wow, somebody's eager." She carefully unlaced her new boots.

Droguk tossed his shirt aside and shrugged. "Ogres like to be clean. We're not as pathological about it as you are, maybe—"

"It's not pathological to not want to smell my own crotch from two feet away," she interrupted. "Speaking of, I'm taking these pants off, so hold your breath."

He laughed and kicked off his boots. "Tell me about the faery baths where you're from."

Droguk was encouraging her to talk? That was new. Maybe the elf weed smoke from the king's royal bonfire had given him a much needed chill-out effect. "We don't call them faery baths. There's this area of land that's on top of a massive volcano, and it creates springs and geysers. It's famous for it."

"But you can bathe in them?" he asked, stepping out of his pants. "Like these?"

Vanessa averted her gaze and finished undressing. "Not unless you want to be dissolved in acid. They're not friendly."

"Your world sounds terrible," Droguk announced, and took the steps hewn into the rock down to the largest of the pools. He climbed into the scalding water without hesitation and sank until he was submerged up to his chest.

"I'm weirdly not missing it." It was a shock to realize that. "Somehow, being chased by vampires and captured by elves is preferable to going to my job and paying my bills."

"Surely, you have people you love."

She tested the temperature with her toes before stepping in fully. "Yeah. I love Tabitha, for sure. She's my best friend."

"What about family?" he asked.

It took a lot of restraint not to snap at him that he didn't need to know all of her personal details. "Um. Not really. Wow, this water is super hot. Is it super hot to you?"

"Ogres run hot," he reminded her. "What happened to your family? Were they killed in a raid or something?"

"No, not a lot of raids in my neck of the woods." She hated talking about her past. It lived in her head all day, every day, any time she felt like she wasn't good enough, or she was being annoying. If a cashier was snippy, if a waitress was curt, Vanessa took it upon herself to work backward from that incident and figure out which of her abhorrent personality traits had caused the stranger such harm. Then, she walked around feeling like shit about it for a full week. "My parents were kind of estranged from their families, so I didn't see my aunts or uncles or cousins very much. I barely remember my grandparents."

"And your parents?" he pushed.

She sighed. "Imagine you have a kid, right? And then the kid turns thirteen and suddenly, out of no-where, they have this awful medical condition—that you're pretty sure they're faking, by the way—and you have to take time away from your job to drive them to medical appointments. Appointments that are expensive, where the doctors prescribe medication that's expensive, and you're not really thrilled with how that kid is turning out, in the first place, so it's starting to feel like a sunk cost. Oh, also, you belong to a religion that massively distrusts medicine and sees any failure to pray disease away as a sign that you're secretly doing something shady in the Lord's eyes. Then, the kid grows up, drops out of the nice, Christian college you sent them to, shaves their head, pierces their belly button, and starts showing up at rallies screaming, 'We're here, we're queer, get used to it.'"

"Much of that is difficult to imagine, owing to our cultural differences," Droguk admitted. "But I am willing to learn, if you want to teach me."

Her ribs ached. Probably from all the walking. "No, it's fine. there's nothing worth learning in that sentence. Well, aside from civil disobedience. I have a feeling that's universal and not just confined to my world. But to answer your question, no. No parents. They're alive. They would just prefer it if I wasn't."

"Vanessa—" Droguk began, looking utterly crestfallen.

She couldn't have that. She couldn't stand to be pitied. "It's fine," she said, and stepped into the water.

She plunged in, way over her head.

Fuck.

The bottom of the pool was uneven; it was much shallower where Droguk had gotten in, and she hadn't thought to test the depth, herself. That was the first problem. The second was the shock of all that hot water hitting her everywhere at the same time. She was very much an "enter the hot tub in stages" person. First, calves while sitting on the edge. Then, carefully lowering oneself onto the step. Then, after more adjustment time, onto the seat.

Only a total maniac would cannonball into a near-boiling pot.

Droguk caught her with his big hand around her neck, as if picking up a kitten by its scruff. She spluttered and flailed, ultimately turning in his grasp to clutch at his shoulders. He brought them both to the shallower spot, patting her on the back. "Are you okay? Vanessa?"

"Yeah, if you don't break my spine trying to get me to cough up water I didn't swallow, I'll be fine." She leaned back, her hands still on his shoulders.

"I didn't realize..." Droguk gestured to the drop off. "I should have made sure it was safe for you."

"I could have checked it out. I didn't." She pushed her dripping hair back from her face. "No harm, no foul. I'm just wet, is all."

His yellow eyes narrowed. "You're sure?"

"Yeah." But she didn't want him to release her. He didn't seem to want to, either.

"If you're fine, I should probably let you go." His gaze fell to her mouth.

She nodded in slow motion. "I'm fine."

"Yeah. It was just a little slip. Nothing to worry about." His hand slid down her back.

"More embarrassing than anything." Her fingers curled against his skin.

His wet, bare skin.

He shifted a little, and the water rocked. It was like silk slipping between her thighs.

"The water is nice," she said, her voice a little strangled.

He nodded, his hand idly stroking up and down her spine. "Very relaxing."

"Yeah." But she didn't feel relaxed. She felt all kinds of tension. The cavern fairly vibrated with it.

What was she doing, thinking of vibration?

Because you haven't had an orgasm in a while. Sure, she'd had way, way too many with him on their wedding night, but that was the thing about orgasms. They were addictive, and she hadn't exactly had time to get her fix.

Then again, neither had Droguk. She'd interrupted him. It was only fair to get squirmy with him, wasn't it? Didn't she owe him that?

Droguk swallowed audibly and said, "I want to kiss you."

They didn't have to do it. She knew that. Physical intimacy was no longer required between them. The ritual was over. But they were both naked and pressed together and probably the water had some kind of horny elf magic in it. That totally explained why she wanted to fuck an ogre again.

Yup. That *had* to be the reason.

Chapter Twenty-Eight

His eyes never leaving Vanessa's, Droguk took a deep breath, as if summoning up courage. "I'm going to kiss you."

Not *"I want,"* anymore. *"I'm going to."* That should have infuriated her and prompted a long lecture about consent, but she would let it slide this time, because she consented. Oh, she consented big time.

His mouth covered hers, his tusks pricking her cheeks, and she squirmed a little in his arms until they found a better angle, one that wouldn't require facial reconstruction surgery when they were finished. He hadn't forgotten how to do it, otherwise; his kiss turned her knees as weak as it had that first night together.

Without the newness and uncertainty of that night, everything was less awkward. Vanessa let herself fall away from the rest of the world and all its weirdness.

Outside of Droguk's arms, things were scary and confusing. She didn't realize how unsafe she felt when he wasn't touching her.

"Fuck," he growled, breaking his mouth away for breath. They stared into each other's eyes, their rasping inhales audible above the water sounds echoing through the cavern. "I can't believe how good that feels."

"You can take that knowledge back to your people," she said with a laugh. "Teach them the ways of the tongue."

"We know how to use our tongues." He stuck his out and Vanessa swallowed hard at the sight of the forked appendage wriggling playfully at her. "Is that something humans do? You know...use their tongues..."

"Yup," she said, but it came out as a high-pitched squeak. She cleared her throat. "But not generally when we've been without a shower for over a week."

He looked around them. "Well, we're in a faery bath. Can't get much cleaner than that."

The water seemed to have magically erased the grime from her skin. Her hair was, for once, not just a jumble of tangles.

Maybe they could take some of it on the road.

He grabbed her around the waist and boosted her onto the lip of the pool. But even without hygiene concerns, she was self-conscious.

She placed her palms on his chest and pushed him back a step. "Okay, but wait. What if... you don't like it."

He blinked at her, then glanced between her spread thighs and back to her face. "I'm pretty sure I like it."

She rolled her eyes. "I know you liked *that*. But what if you get up close and personal with it and it grosses you out? What if I taste like wet garbage?"

"I don't think you will," he said doubtfully.

"Right, but you don't—"

He straightened to his full height, looming over her a moment before cutting off her words with a crushing kiss. Rude. But he swept every thought from her mind, and if his tongue could do that in her mouth, she had a moral duty to find out if the effects would be the same downstairs.

For science.

He lifted his head. "Give your mouth a rest and let mine do some work, okay?"

"Oh." Well, that certainly was not a sentence Vanessa would have ever let a human get away with, but in fairness, she didn't know any with forked tongues.

He dropped to his knees in the pool and slid a hand beneath her hips. There was room on the ledge to lean back on her elbows; it wasn't a flattering position, but Droguk didn't seem to mind. He looked up at her, eyes roving over every squished roll of fat, taking her in with that heart-crushing wonder she'd seen that first time.

"You are..." He stopped himself. "Maybe you don't want to hear it."

"You're about to stick your tongue in me," she said, letting her palm slap the stone beneath her. "Kind of silly to be shy now."

His gaze held hers, and it shocked her to realize that she hadn't just gotten used to his strange yellow eyes. She found them legitimately gorgeous.

When had that happened?

He let out a frustrated breath, and his words spilled out as if they caused him pain. "It's torture to be around you."

"Oh. Not what I would have gone with, if I were try-ing to get someone in a sexy mood—"

He wasn't finished. "I constantly want to toss you on the ground and fuck you until we have to sleep for three days just to recover. I try to be respectful and not stare at you or think about you and what you feel like, but all I can think of, every second of every day, is how you looked bathed in sweat and screaming while my cock was buried in you."

Aaaaand gush. Niagara god damn Falls.

"And what's terrifying," he went on, wetting his lips with that amazing tongue, "is that even if I had you every single night, even if all I ever did for the rest of my life was fuck you senseless, it wouldn't be enough."

She opened her mouth to speak, but her lungs couldn't work anymore. Probably because every part of her brain had united to focus solely on her stiff, throbbing clit.

He didn't give her time to collect herself. He parted her labia with two thick fingers, spreading her wide to study her. He let out a rumbling moan at just the sight. "It's like a flower."

A flower. No one had ever compared her to anything dainty before. That was new, and oddly comforting. Of course, the ogre that was attracted to her to the point of distraction wouldn't be turned off by seeing more of her. He'd made it clear how badly he wanted her. Any doubt that remained was her own traitorous brain telling her that she didn't deserve to like sex, to feel wanted, until a specific number on the scale gave her permission. That she should be ashamed to want this kind of intimacy, that reveling in it was disgust-ing if she couldn't pull off sexy, Bowie-like androgyny to perfection. That her very lack of gender made her something unfuckable by default, and that her fatness only compounded the issue.

Droguk had none of those hangups. She probably couldn't have explained their existence if she tried, because he held her in such abject adoration and debilitating horniness.

He leaned forward, his tusks pricking her thighs, and he cursed. "Sorry. Ogres have thicker skin. I guess I need to adjust—"

Vanessa spread her legs wider for him.

"Just be careful not to like, impale my butt cheeks or something," she said with a laugh, because it was such a strange thing to have to ask someone.

His flat, broad nose nudged her folds, and he took a deep inhale. He didn't need to tell her what he thought; his groan was enough to express his approval.

Then, his tongue touched her, traced along her inner labia in a wide, wet stripe ending at her clit. She bucked her hips.

"So, right there?" he asked, never bothering to raise his head.

He pressed the pad of his thumb to the hard nub and rubbed it, and she moaned, "There, yes. Exactly."

He touched the tips of his bifurcated tongue to her, probed around her sensitive flesh until her thighs shook. Then, he slid her clit between both forks and—

Oh, fuck. The two prongs of his tongue moved independently. One stroked up one side while the other licked down, tugging her hood back and forth over the nerves beneath. She jolted up and grabbed at his head.

He immediately stopped. "Did I do something wrong?"

"No! Get back in there!" She laughed breathlessly,

and those laughs turned to little yelps of pleasure as he returned his tongue, cupping and squeezing her clit with both muscular halves while stroking up and down at the same time. They curled and unfurled around her and set up a delicious suction, drawing at her as he relentlessly licked. She locked her thighs around his head, pulled him in closer, his tusks pressed hard against her mound.

If he ever wanted to throw her on the ground and have his way with her again, she would allow it. In fact, if he said that he'd rather not go to Lua at all, that he'd rather stay right there with his head between her legs until it was orgasms and not seizures that killed her, she would have happily agreed.

When she grabbed a handful of his hair, he grumbled against her. She drummed her heels on his back and arched into him, babbling, "Don't stop!" as he pushed her nearer and nearer her climax. She practically sat up, grasping at his head, and with a growl, he lifted her completely off the ledge. He tipped his head back and her knees hit his shoulders while he grasped her ass and held her.

It was the first time she'd ever sat on someone's face. Past partners had wanted her to, but the threat of suffocation had, in her mind, been too great. With Droguk, she had absolutely no fear of having to provide a humiliating explanation to the paramedics.

Kneeling on his shoulders, firmly straddling his upturned mouth, she held him by two handfuls of his hair and simply hung on, her cries echoing through the cavern with his groans of pleasure and appreciation. Her thighs trembled, her muscles tensed, and she managed to shriek, "I'm coming!" just as he pushed her over the edge. Vaguely, she felt her juices bathe his cheeks, and he practically roared against her. His tongue released her clit and dove down to push into her cunt. It really was an impressively long tongue, when fully extended, and he lapped every drop from her until she squirmed and squealed in his hold.

She was still shaking all over when he lowered her into the pool with him, his face shining with her wetness.

Reaching beneath the water, she grasped the thick length of him. He hissed that word that sounded like cursing as she stroked. The natural lubrication on his skin was more slippery than the water.

"Fuck me," she pleaded, squeezing him. She'd never felt so empty in her life, that she could remember. The memory of their night together taunted her. It was so much worse, wanting it when she knew what it felt like. When she knew how impossibly huge and thick he was. When she knew about the magic cum that would make her eventually black out from too much pleasure. "Please. I'm begging you."

"Wait." He stopped her hand. "Not here. We can't."

She knew what all those words meant on their own, but together in those sentences, in that moment, they seemed like gibberish.

He slowly disentangled from her. "We don't have time."

"What if we didn't do the bulb thing?" she whined, vaguely aware that she was engaging in just-the-tip coercion. "I promise, I'll be good this time."

He dropped his head, shoulders shaking with a shiver. "Vanessa. I need you to be the one with self-control here. We both know that once I'm inside you, we're not going to be able to resist."

He was, unfuckingfortunately, absolutely right.

"And if any of my 'magic cum' gets in here," he said with a grim huff at Vanessa's term, "then whoever visits next is going to accidentally have a really weird time."

That was enough to sober her up, a little. The last thing she wanted to do was commit assault in absentia on some poor elf who would never, no pun intended, see it coming.

"What are you going to do, then?" she asked, taking a few steps back. "You were grouchy enough when you didn't get to finish jerking off—"

"Oh, I'm going to finish," he said, climbing out of the pool.

She frowned at him. "In here? Where you just said you wouldn't fuck me because of the possible consequences?"

"No, in the woods." He pulled up his pants and didn't bother lacing up the fly. He probably wouldn't have been able to stuff his huge erection into them, anyway. "Just give me a little time. Wait here for me, and I'll be back."

"Okay. Don't—" She'd almost warned him not to get eaten by something. "Get lost. And don't leave me to deal with the ritual on my own. You said it would be disgusting."

"I promise. Now shut up and let me get out of here before I get really grumpy," he warned.

Understandable, Vanessa thought. *Totally understandable.*

Chapter Twenty-Nine

With the exception of the potentially disgusting ritual they were going to be forced to observe, the world felt a lot lighter to Vanessa. Her feet didn't hurt for the first time in what seemed like forever, her ribs didn't feel bruised, and she had enough energy to hop over the occasional beanstalk root in their path back to the village.

"That was exactly what I needed," she said with a long, happy sigh. "I know we're running for our lives from a vampire, but we can't keep underestimating the importance of self-care."

Droguk chuckled in agreement. "I do hate you a lot less now."

She elbowed him. "Where did you go? I mean, since you couldn't poison the faery bath with your magic—"

"It all worked out," he said. "Let's leave it at that."

"Okay," she grudgingly conceded. "But I do have a

question."

"Thanks for the warning."

She stopped walking to face him. "If you couldn't do it in there, why were you going to do it in the stream? Wouldn't that have just created miles upon miles of horny turtles?"

"What? No." He scrunched his eyes shut and shook his head. "The faery baths are like... bowls of soup."

"Please don't make me imagine you jacking off into a bowl of soup," Vanessa interjected, but it was too late the moment she said the words.

Droguk paused a silently recriminating pause at the interruption before continuing. "But a stream is like a river of soup. Someone keeps ladling more and more in, and eventually everything that was in the bowl before has sloshed over the sides—"

"That's not how soup works. You're saying it gets diluted," she supplied for him. "I get it. Let's not talk about cum and soup in the same conversation ever again. Unless I'm about to eat a bowl of soup and you happen to know there's cum in it. Feel free to bring it up then."

"Fine. I won't bring up soup," he said, holding up his hands. "Or the living essence."

That was what the elves meant by *"living essence?"* Vanessa very much didn't care for that bit of news. *"That's* what the ritual is about?"

Droguk shrugged and started down the path again.

"Whoa, whoa!" She hurried after him and grabbed his arm. "Tell me everything you know about this ritual."

"If I do, will you stop hanging off my elbow like a yellow-tailed skin slug?"

Vanessa let him go, lest he describe the horror of a

yellow-tailed skin slug, as well. They slowed their pace while he explained.

"Brentan has seen the ritual before, when he visited the Court of Seasons." Droguk paused. "A court is—"

"Fairies, I got it. We have fantasy novels on Earth." She made a speeding-up motion with her hands.

"He said that some fairies volunteer to be chained to standing stones and magically..." He made a frustrated noise. "What I did. Into cups. And then everybody—"

All the blood drained from Vanessa's face, replace by a numb and tingly dread. "Don't say it."

He looked like he couldn't wait to say it. Like he delighted in saying it. "They drink it."

"I am not drinking elf cum!" she shrieked.

He shushed her through his laughter. "They probably won't ask you to drink it. It's bad enough that we have to stand there and watch while they fill up the cups."

"You're joking." Her eyes widened. "Please, tell me you're joking."

He held up his hands in an open posture. "I'm just repeating what Brentan said he saw."

"Well, these are fairies," she said. "Not elves. They might do things differently."

"They might," Droguk agreed. "But elves and fairies aren't that different. Don't ever say that in front of them, though."

Great.

The adults of the village were already gathered in the clearing when Vanessa and Droguk returned. Vanessa's jaw dropped at the sight of them. Before, they'd been dressed in leaves and woven vines, tending their primitive little business in their beanstalk cottages. Now, they were all robed in long vestments of phosphorescent, sheer material that floated around them like silk.

"Those must be made from the webs of stalk-spiders," Droguk said, as quietly as he could say anything in his deep, rumbly voice.

"Oh good. I love spiders," she said with an irrepressible shudder.

"You do?" Droguk gave her a *"fair enough"* shrug. "Look up. You'll be thrilled."

Her skin crawled as if she were already being touched by millions of skittering legs, but horrible curiosity drew her gaze to the beanstalks above them. There was nothing but blackness. She was about to shove Droguk for teasing her, but then six bright green headlights swiveled toward her, and it took a single, horrible second to realize that they were eyes on a spider as big as a Dodge Ram.

It wasn't her proudest moment, but she cringed and wrapped herself around Droguk's arm, practically climbing him in her horror.

To her astonishment, he pulled her in with that arm and held her. He didn't have to say a word to convince her of her safety, and that was even more astonishing.

She supposed a new level of trust was unlocked with a person when you let them go down on you despite them having tusks.

The mass of elves thickened the closer they moved toward the royal hotbox. Vanessa looked around for anyone marked out to fulfill the cock milking fetish portion of the evening's program, but no one seemed immediately apparent. Maybe Droguk had made all that up.

If he did, it was certainly an interesting insight into

his psyche.

Somewhere, a chime tinkled, and the assembly fell silent. Both of the massive doors in the stalk stump opened, and with a truly flesh crawling *click-clickety-click*, Elvaneth appeared, standing on the back of a stalk-spider like it was a chariot, holding reins in one hand.

Oh good. It's not just elf bukkake. There are also giant spiders.

Worst party ever.

The glowing, cobweb covered elves fell into two lines behind Elvaneth and his ride. Silently, they moved through the forest and into a tunnel of glowing green web.

Vanessa was going to throw up. The only thing that kept her from screaming and freaking out was the newly acquired knowledge that if they were cast into the forest now, they would almost certainly die by giant arachnid, a fate she had feared ever since one particularly horrific episode of *Punky Brewster* that had traumatized her in childhood.

Droguk kept her in front of him, propelling her forward with a huge hand on each of her shoulders, as if knowing instinctively that her legs would not move her on their own. As they neared the end of the tunnel, more of it appeared, the snick-snick-snick of spinnerets working as the spiders happily knit to light the way. Vanessa could see Elvaneth at the head of the column, nodding respectfully to the spiders they passed. Finally, they reached a place where the web stopped, and the elves glided out into an eerie, dimly-green clearing.

The light, Vanessa realized with nausea, came from huge, pulsating egg sacks tied high in the trees.

"If those hatch, I'm out of here," she whispered, and Droguk shushed her. He steered her toward the thick roots of a beanstalk trunk, separating them from the group to observe.

Then, he uttered a soft, "Oh no."

"Oh no?" she whispered vehemently. "We are surrounded by giant spiders. This is not the time to say, 'oh no!'"

Elvaneth's spider stopped before a broken stone cylinder in the center of the clearing. As far as Vanessa could tell, there were no standing stones. Nobody had started jacking off yet, so that was probably a good sign that Brentan's story was absolute bunk.

"We gather here beneath the apex of the full moon to give thanks for the gift of the living essence," Elvaneth began. "It is only by the grace of our sacred well that we are given new hope for our future. It is only by the sacred waters that we are granted the gift of our children, fully born into flesh."

"Um..." Droguk said, his voice unusually high. Vanessa looked between him and the four elves that came forward with gleaming silver chalices, noting the look of dawning alarm on the ogre's face.

And then she got it.

"What did you do?" she whispered, tracking the movements of the cup bearers as they dipped into the well and took up places around it. Elves filed forward, bowing their heads.

Droguk stared in increasing horror as the first of the elves drank from the chalices. He turned his mortified gaze to Vanessa. "Soup."

The first four elves moved aside, a second group taking their place to drink.

"In their sacred well?" she hissed. "You masturbated

269

into someone's sacred well?"

"I didn't know it was sacred," he whispered back in a panic. "The place wasn't covered in spider eggs and religion at the time. I thought it was just abandoned!"

A loud, lusty moan broke the respectful silence, then another and another. Elves at the back of the lines craned their necks to see what was happening at the front. Another elf fell to the ground, crying out in unmistakable sexual ecstasy, his back bowed as he humped the air.

Still perched atop his spider, Elvaneth chugged down a massive amount of sacred well water. The effects of it didn't stop anyone in the lines from dutifully stepping forward and imbibing, either.

Two elves tumbled to the ground, pawing at each other's spiderweb robes. Shouts and moans filled the air as the clearing slowly turned into a writhing mass of frantically fucking bodies.

Droguk took her by the hand and slowly backed into the darkness of the stalks. "I think this is a good time for us to run."

Chapter Thirty

"Our stuff!" Vanessa cried. Leaves and vines whipped past her as she bounced upside down over Droguk's shoulder as he raced through the forest.

"We'll get more stuff!" he argued, but his steps slowed as reason, Vanessa hoped, set in.

"Put me down, please," she said, and he complied. He was a lot easier to deal with now that he'd had a good crank, but he wasn't thinking logically. "There's no place on that map to get more stuff. We need our packs. I need my pills. I've got one and a half left."

That was three days. Six, if she skipped every other day. She might make it to Lua before things got dangerous.

"There are probably guards," he reminded her. "And they're probably not going to be happy that I... souped in their ancient well."

"Stop ruining soup for me!" Vanessa pressed her

fingers to her temples. "Okay. If there are guards, we deal with it then. The packs are in the tent. For all they know, we came back to get something. If we run into anybody, don't get aggro. Let me do the talking and just go with it."

To her shock, he didn't argue with her.

They returned to the clearing, where their temporary quarters had been erected earlier. It was a simple tent of woven beanstalk fiber, but Vanessa had really looked forward to sleeping under some kind of shelter.

Droguk kept watch while she crawled through the flap and chucked their packs to him.

"I don't see anyone around," he said cautiously.

"Good." She poked her head out. "Then we can steal the tent, too."

"We can't steal from them!"

"Keep your voice down!" she hissed, climbing out and brushing her knees off.

"It's not stealing. It's survival. We don't know when we'll need shelter again and if we'll be able to find it. We've already made enemies and we have exactly zero allies on this side of the divide, so it's every ogre and they/them for themselves."

He growled and ripped the tent off the ground, stakes dangling from each corner. He wadded the whole thing up around the center pole and tucked it under his arm. "Let's move."

Vanessa struggled her pack onto her back and trotted after Droguk toward the path from the village.

"We came in from the north, so if we keep going this way, we'll end up south," he said.

Vanessa wished he would keep his voice down; they had no idea where guards might be stationed, and the

elves had already proved themselves adept at camouflage. Her nerves were wound too tight to scold him,
though. Every step they took, she felt like they were
being watched, even when they'd moved swiftly away
from the smoke and fires of the village.

Something skittered in the canopy.

*Don't think about it, don't think about it, don't think
about it,* she chanted to herself, eyes fixed firmly on
the ground.

"It looks rocky up ahead," Droguk said.

"I'll be careful." But there was a loud *whoosh*, like
a broken cable fleeing its pulley, and a *whump* as
Vanessa hit the ground. Everything was dark for a
moment, and then she was on her back, gasping for
breath, as Droguk's roar of fury shook the forest. She
scrambled back on her hands. Droguk grappled with
one of those terrifying, truck-sized spiders, his massive fists gripping the creature's enormous fangs. He
buckled under its obvious strength, his feet sliding in
the dirt as the monster pushed back.

Time slowed until even her pulse was nothing but
an occasional, troublesome thunk in her ears. Droguk
was big and strong and scary. He could fight anything,
couldn't he?

She thought about the moment they first met, when
he'd been so terrified of the gargoyles.

There were things in this world that could hurt
Droguk as easily as they could hurt her. Vanessa had
known that, logically, but she'd never really grasped
the truth of the fact, because she'd always felt so safe
with him. Everything he'd done, from the second
they'd collided in the woods, he'd done to protect her.
She had no doubt that he would keep doing that, or
die trying.

She owed him no less.

But what help could she possibly give him? She had no weapons, she'd never been in any hand-to-hand combat, and even if she had, whoever she would have fought wouldn't have had eight arms.

They were both going to die by spider.

Droguk roared again, a pained, desperate sound. Even in the utter darkness, Vanessa could see the fear in his eyes when he yelled, "Run!"

Run, and leave him. That's what he was saying. Vanessa wasn't willing to abandon him, but she wasn't sure what she could do. *I should have done CrossFit.*

The tent lay in a messy pile beside her, its ropes and stakes splayed out like the tentacles of a dead octopus. She stared at it, an idea forming in the space between firing synapses. A bad idea, but an idea.

If they were both going to die, she was going to die trying.

She pulled one of the ropes free, smacking herself in the face with one of the heavy pegs. Her eye squinched shut involuntarily and her nose dripped what was almost certainly blood, but she got to her feet and raced toward the spider, which had very nearly gotten Droguk beneath it.

"Don't think about it, don't think it about it," she muttered aloud as she gripped a handful of the monster's coarse fur. *I should have gone rock climbing, too.* What she lacked in upper-arm strength, she made up for with pure, terror-fueled adrenaline, pulling herself hand-over-hand up the beast's back until she was splayed atop its head. Its hubcap-sized eyes swiveled upward, and Vanessa used that moment to swing the rope down.

"Catch it!" she shouted to Droguk, but he'd already

done so, slipping the makeshift reigns under the deadly fangs and scrabbling clear. With the stakes in her hands, Vanessa pulled, and the creature reared back, nearly toppling her. The rope held, though, and the monster's shrieks of fury stopped with its struggles as it realized it was truly caught.

Droguk, still sprawled in the dirt, looked up at her in frozen confusion.

"Well, don't just stare at me." She was completely out of breath and quite pleased with herself. "Hop on."

* * * *

"My mate wrestled a giant spider. And won." Droguk laughed proudly. "My mate defeated a giant spider."

"Your mate doesn't know what they're going to do with a giant spider when they get out of this forest," Vanessa said, but it was difficult to be pessimistic in the face of his pride. "It's hungry, I assume, since it tried to eat us. I don't know how to let it go without becoming its next meal."

"We'll figure that out when we get where we're going." Droguk sighed happily behind her. He rode cross-legged, with Vanessa in his lap, while she held the reins. He didn't try to drive even once. "My mate captured and rode a giant spider."

They'd been riding for a while, and the forest around them began to lighten. The spiders appeared to be nocturnal; they saw fewer and fewer the closer dawn came. That was fine by Vanessa. One spider, it turned out, she could handle, and that had been mostly luck. She didn't want to take a chance with spiders, plural.

"Just wait until we get back to the Mire. Nobody will believe this," he said. "We'd better take something off

276

it. One of its fangs, maybe. Just so we have proof."

Vanessa's stomach soured. Not just because she didn't want to hurt the creature, which had only been doing what it needed to do to survive, but because she hadn't thought about what would happen or where she would go after Lua. They were headed there to treat her medical condition. She had no idea if they could get her home.

"We're not taking its fang," she said, sharper than she intended.

"Okay," Droguk said, and she felt his movement as he held up his hands in defeat. "It's your spider. I'm merely the passenger. But we could turn it into a nice axe for you. Or a spear. At the very least, you could add this to your name."

"My name?" She shook her head. "I have a name."

"You could have a better name. 'Vanessa the Spider-Slayer.' 'Vanessa the Fangbane,'" he suggested.

She had to admit, "Vanessa the Fangbane" did sound pretty cool, even if she was guaranteed to accidentally say "gangbang" instead. But she didn't like thinking that far ahead. "I think I'll stick with Vanessa, thanks. I mean, you only have one name."

"I just haven't done anything notable enough to get more of one," he explained.

"Even when you were working for Vikthor?"

"I suppose I could call myself 'Droguk the One Of Many,'" he joked. "If I'd done anything in his service that deserved a title, he would have given me one."

"What about now, though?" Vanessa asked. "You're doing something brave, now."

"Protecting my mate isn't brave. It's what I'm supposed to do," he said.

"Then I don't deserve a name, either." Afterall, that's

what she'd been doing, too. "I was just protecting my mate. Like I'm supposed to."

He didn't have an answer for that, and they rode on in silence broken only by the chittering of their mount.

Thirty-One

Riding a spider wasn't even that hard.

It was easier to pretend it wasn't a spider, of course; that part still freaked Vanessa out greatly. A few times, it seemed like the beast might try to scuttle up a stalk, but a tug on the reins was all it took to put it back on track. It made travel delightfully easy on a journey where a car would have been handy.

They reached the edge of the forest at midday. Vanessa pulled the reins to halt the spider, but she wasn't sure it was the action that brought the creature to a stop or if it was just shrinking from the sunlight. There was a marked difference between the gentle, dim light of the forest and the blinding white beyond the stalks that even made Vanessa long for sunglasses.

And she only had two eyes and not eight.

The spider's aversion solved their big problem of how to release it without getting eaten, though.

"I don't think he'll follow us out, if we get off now," Vanessa said, trying to urge the spider forward with a slap of the reins and a cowboy worthy, *giddup*. "See? He doesn't want to go out there. I don't think he likes the light."

"Let me go first. If it tries to eat me, steer it the other way." Droguk hopped down from its back and put out his arms to catch her. "Come on."

Vanessa held one end of the improvised reins by the stake tied to it, held the rest of the battered tent to her chest, and jumped down. The moment she landed in Droguk's arms, he ran to put distance between them and the monster. The rope slid from the spider's fangs, and the creature scuttled up the trunk of the nearest beanstalk.

Droguk set Vanessa on her feet, and they both watched, relieved, as the spider fled rather than attack.

"Sorry we rode you," Vanessa called after it. "You were kind of a dick, though!" She turned to Droguk. "See that? Team work makes the dream work."

Beyond the edge of the forest lay a rocky, windswept plain of white stone dotted with splotches of green. The thick roots of beanstalks broke through pulverized chips on the ground that made walking surprisingly slippery. They picked their way past the reach of the curlicue roots, their feet sliding. It was only Droguk's grip on her arm that kept her from going ass-over-tea-kettle.

When they were out of spider range—Vanessa hoped—Droguk stopped to take the map from his pack. "I would rather that had all gone a lot differently, but the spider really cut down our time."

"Right?" Vanessa said. "I had no idea they could be

so fast. If it would have come out here, I would have kept it."

Then again, the more she looked around, the more devoid of life the area seemed to be. They would have ended up a spider meal for sure.

"We'll probably reach Lua in two more days. Maybe three." Droguk looked over his shoulder. "I don't know how long it will take us to get home, though, because we can't go through elf country again."

She hadn't been thinking of the return journey. Maybe because she'd thought she would die on the way there. If they couldn't help her in Lua, she still might die. And if she survived, her next quest would be getting back to Earth.

"Do you think they'll still be mad by the time we get back? They looked like they were having a good time," she said.

He folded the map and tucked it into his pack. "They could make me the king of Bean Town and I still wouldn't be able to show my face there."

Vanessa snorted. "We have a place back home called Beantown. No stalks though. And the Giants are in San Francisco."

Droguk picked up his pack and shrugged it on. "I'm not going to fall for that. I know you don't have giants in your world."

"You caught me."

They started across the stone field carefully; without a road, they had to plan several steps ahead to find the least obstructed path.

"What happens after this?" Droguk asked, looking at his feet.

"You're the one with the map." But Vanessa knew what he was asking her, and she felt dishonest pretending otherwise. "I don't know. I wasn't thinking beyond Lua. I mean, if they can't help me, I don't know how long I'll have. I could live for years, potentially, but seizures can damage your brain. They can kill you. When mine were really out of control, I was having seven a day."

"And there would be nothing I could do to help you," he said. "I would just have to watch you go through them and wonder every single time if that was the one that would…"

He stopped as if he couldn't bear to actually say the words.

"That's only if they can't help you, though," he said firmly.

"Yeah. In that case, the only option left to save me would be to go back to my world. But I'm not sure if I can even get back there." That had become a little less important every day. "Don't worry. I don't expect you to take care of me forever."

"Why wouldn't I?"

The question made her stumble. "Well… because that wasn't part of the deal. You're taking me to Lua for help. We didn't agree on anything beyond that."

"I did, when I took the binding oath." He sighed the sigh of someone who didn't actually want to say what they were about to say but couldn't avoid it any longer. "I never believed you would get back to your world. I knew that my oath to you wasn't temporary."

Something in her chest eased and opened, like her ribs could finally stretch their legs after being balled up for over a week. "You barely knew me."

"It was the right thing to do."

Was it? Because to Vanessa, it felt more like an above-and-beyond thing to pledge one's entire life to someone one had just met.

Her ribs retracted again. "You know, I won't hold you to it. I get that you felt responsible for me, but you shouldn't have to be saddled to a stranger for life."

"You're not a stranger, anymore." He paused at a wide, flat rock shelf too high for her to step onto. He lifted her up and set her on her feet on the ledge, bringing them eye-to-eye. "You're my mate. After they find a cure for you in Lua—and they will find one—we're going back to Mudholme together."

He ruined his forceful declaration by adding, "Unless you don't want to."

She thought of a life in the muddy swamp, in a crumbling castle, surrounded by creatures with big teeth and under constant threat of bandit raids because there were no laws.

And then she thought about life here, in this strange place, without the one friend she'd made so far. It was unbearable to imagine being on her own, in a weird place, trying to survive. Shinewater hadn't been too bad, but she hadn't seen many "Now Hiring" signs in the windows. And it would be awfully lonely with no one to talk to at the end of the day. What were the chances that anyone else, in all of Fablemere, would tolerate her nonsense the way he did?

"Just to be clear, in this scenario I am no longer sleeping on the floor at the foot of your bed like a dog, right?"

"I'll build a bigger bed," he promised. "I'll even build you your own, if you want me to."

"What I want is to not be alone," she admitted. "I'll come back to Mudholme with you. If that's okay."

"I wouldn't have offered if it wasn't okay," he said. "Plus, you're still going to need protection from the

Baron, until he loses interest in you."

"Fair. It's not like I can prove that I don't have 'visions' just because my seizures went away." But that opened up an entirely different set of problems that she didn't have the energy to worry about. "Won't he target you and your family, then?"

"Probably. But do you think you'd fare better here on your own?"

"Touche."

He raised an eyebrow.

"That means you have a good point." She was tired. Way too tired to argue against a good future for herself. The thought of being wrapped up and cozy by the fire at Mudholme was enough to make her want to cry with longing, after the night they'd had.

"And if something happens that you can get back to your world someday, I won't stop you." His gaze fell to her mouth, then flicked guiltily away. "I'll want to. But I won't."

"You would want to?" She took his face in her hands.

"Of course, I would." He finally looked at her. "We're buddies, remember?"

He stepped up onto the ledge with her and scanned the horizon. "I'd like to get over that next rise before dark, but then I think we should camp early and rest up."

She could have sobbed with joy at the suggestion. They'd been awake all night, and her legs were impossibly heavy. "Are there any animals out here that we could ride? Because I'm exhausted."

"Just one." He held out his hand.

"You're tired," she protested, but when he extended it further, she gave in and let him pull her, pack and all, onto his shoulder.

Maybe he'd forgotten the makeshift baby carrier. She wasn't about to remind him of it.

Once she was comfortable on his shoulder, she leaned her head on the top of his. "I knew I would win you over."

"Yeah," he said with a chuckle. "I knew you would, too."

Chapter Thirty-Two

It took three long days and two cold nights to finally see the towers of Lua shimmering on the horizon.

"There." Droguk pointed at the onion-shaped domes that blended almost seamlessly into the clouds. The spires and turrets reached toward the sky like cheerful phantoms, and the waving grass sea that stretched between them and the city was so vibrant, it seemed painted.

"Very Studio Ghibli," Vanessa breathed, her eyes roving everywhere as if she could devour the whole countryside.

"Is that something that doesn't translate?" he asked, gently lifting her off his shoulder to stand beside him.

"It's a type of story we have. It's painted in a specific style and the images move." She turned to face him. "I wish I could show you. There's a lot of things I wish I could show you."

"Your magical moving paintings? We know about those from our stories." He paused, a look coming over his face that she had never seen before. Not regret, but a close cousin to it. A cousin who was chronically depressed. "You're really from that place, aren't you?"

She frowned. "You said you believed me."

"I do believe you. It's just... impossible to comprehend. Finding out all those tales are real, that all the fantastical things in them are true..." He gave up trying to explain with a huffing sigh.

"Imagine how I feel. You're just hearing about this strange other world. I ended up in it." The direction of the wind changed, blowing the faint scent of cotton candy toward them from the waving grass.

He turned to her, a smile touching the corner of his mouth. "Do you really have carriages that run on fire and the bones of ancient beasts?"

"That description makes cars sound way cooler than they are, but yes." And while one might have been handy during parts of their journey, Vanessa couldn't imagine four tires trampling a path through the peaceful, sugary-smelling field before them. "But they're dirty. They cause pollution. My world is actually dying because of that kind of thing."

Visibly horrified, Droguk said, "Then you should be glad that you're here, instead of there."

"You know what? I kind of am." She took his huge hand and tugged him forward. "Come on."

They walked down the last of the rocky slope hand-in-hand, though it turned from affection to necessity as she clumsily slid on the loose pebbles and pulverized sand. The boots he'd bought her were pretty, but not necessarily all-terrain.

He paused at the edge of the field and gestured to his shoulder. "Up again. You're short. I don't want to lose you."

Indeed, the grass reached far over her head. It came up to Droguk's nose, which twitched and exploded with an ogre-sized sneeze.

"Oh my god, do you have allergies?" Vanessa laughed in disbelief.

"No," he said, and sneezed again. He wiped his nose on his sleeve—*eww*—and grimaced. "Up you go."

"No. I don't feel like being launched when you do another one of those full-body convulsions. I'll just follow you." *And not get near the shirt you just snot- ted on.* In his defense, he hadn't had many options for clean-up.

They started through the field, Droguk cutting a path ahead of her.

"Do you think there are any monsters in here?" she asked, glancing around. While the whole thing seemed very pastoral and pleasant from the outside, now that she was immersed in the green sea, it seemed slightly sinister. She couldn't help but imagine weird lion-like beasts bursting through the grass and dragging her away bloody and screaming.

"So, what if there are?" Droguk responded, every consonant slightly softened by his increasingly stuffy nose. "You've already beaten a giant spider. And you have me."

"That's a very positive outlook you have there," she responded. "I wonder where that's rubbed off on you from."

He grunted and pushed the grass aside more aggres- sively as she grinned to herself.

"What happens when we reach the city?" she asked,

eyes on her feet as they sunk slightly into the rich black soil. "Do we just ask, hey, where are all the good doctors at?"

"That was my plan, more or less." Droguk stopped for another mighty sneeze.

Vanessa hadn't given a lot of thought to how they would proceed once they arrived. Somehow, despite their days and days of walking and sleeping on the ground, their goal seemed further away when faced with the reality that they didn't know anyone in the city. No one knew they were coming. What if they couldn't even access these physicians who might or might not be able to help her?

"If we can't get an answer," Droguk went on miserably, "We'll just wait around outside the citadel until we find one."

"And then?"

"And then I beat him into submission until he'll help you."

That was a very ogre solution to what was a less ogrey problem.

"Don't do anything that extreme without warning me," she said, in the hopes that she would be able to dissuade him should the time come.

Crossing the field turned out to be the easiest part of their journey so far. No one kidnapped them, trailed them, or tried to eat them, and no accidental orgies sprung up. It was just a pleasant stroll with a violently sneezing ogre through a quaint countryside. She wasn't even winded by the time they reached the shining crystal road to the gates.

"Huh." She looked up and down what should have been a very busy thoroughfare. "I thought there would be more people."

"Me too," Droguk said cautiously, though the gravity of his statement was somewhat impaired by the fact that he sounded like a sick preschooler.

"I see guards, though," Vanessa said as they followed the road. The sight of the personnel stationed there in their gleaming suits of armor somewhat eased her mind. She'd instantly and involuntarily envisioned an entire city of corpses, decimated by a plague.

The road rose in a bridge over a ravine and ended at the base of an impossible amount of stairs. By the time they reached the top, her butt and thighs ached, but Vanessa plastered on a smile, wiped sweat from her probably fire-engine-red brow, and greeted the nearest guard. "Hello! We have business at the citadel. Is it cool if we go through that gate there?"

The gate was more like a door. A giant, gleaming silver door with bas-relief scenes depicted on it like a very fancy comic strip. It wasn't open, but it wasn't closed, either. Pale light spilled from a gap that was comparatively narrow relative to the entrance's size, but still wide enough that anybody could just walk on through.

And Vanessa would have, if not for the armed and very serious tin can men assembled around it.

The guard didn't answer. She tried to peer through the slits in his visor. "Are you asleep? Hello?"

"Vanessa..." Droguk said in a wary tone.

Dread turned her heaving, hot breath to cold wind that chilled her from the inside out. Droguk gave one of the guards a slight push. The suit of armor collapsed in a jumble of metal and sticky bones.

"Fuck this." Vanessa turned on her heel and was down six whole steps before Droguk caught up to her.

"Wait! Wait," he said, gripping her by one shoulder.

"This is our only chance, remember?"

"I remember that the guy who sold you the map said that people weren't returning." Her gaze flicked to the collapsed corpse at the top of the steps. "Look around. This is supposed to be a major city, but nobody is on the road. The gate is wide the fuck open and the only thing stopping anyone from entering are a bunch of corpses. Something bad happened here."

"It did. But whatever it was, it happened so long ago that these men are skeletons now." Droguk turned his grim gaze back to the gate. "We came all this way."

It was his helplessness that convinced her, even though she knew they were probably going to get killed by whatever horrible thing had befallen the guard. She could brave whatever that was if it would erase the desperation in his expression.

"Fine." She glanced down at the fallen pile of guard. "But I'm taking his sword."

Not that she knew how to use one. When she retrieved the weapon, it was shockingly heavy. It wouldn't do her much good if she couldn't swing it, but she dragged it along, anyway. Droguk took another guard's poleaxe; it looked like a toy in his huge hands.

"Do you know how to fight?" she whispered as they moved toward the open city gate.

"Not really," he answered, his gaze firmly focused on the gap as they approached.

"You were like, a soldier or something, I thought," she hissed in alarm.

"You'd be surprised at how little force is required to convince the general populace to not fuck with a group of ogres." He gave the door an experimental push. It didn't budge. Vanessa walked through, and

Droguk managed to squeeze in sideways.

The city was as still and empty as the basement of a deserted mall.

"It was a plague," she said, and pulled the collar of her coat over her nose. "I was right. We're going to die from flesh-eating plague."

"Then we're already infected. Keep moving."

They crossed an abandoned square still ringed with merchant stalls. Nothing hung from them or filled the baskets around them.

"It doesn't look like anyone left in a hurry." She put a hand on her hip and frowned. "There would still be stuff."

"And if they all died, nobody would have cleaned it up." Droguk's gaze moved steadily up as they passed into the shadow of the towers. "Why would they abandon this place?"

"Because of whatever killed the guards, I guess?"

"The guards were dead when I put them there."

Vanessa and Droguk whirled to face the voice behind them. As they did, the huge door shut with a ground-shaking clang.

Vanessa had only ever seen his face, but it had been stamped on her memory like a nightmare ever since her first day in Fablemere. The Baron stood in the shadow of the doorway, flanked by six hulking, winged figures. Their gray skin glittered with flecks of minerals as their stone muscles flexed. There was a faint ceramic clinking as their chests rose and fell with breath.

She felt Droguk tense beside her, caught his hand tightening on his weapon. He'd been afraid of the gargoyles in the woods, which signaled to Vanessa that there was no way he could beat one, let alone six.

Before he could do something foolish, she stepped forward.

"Baron Scylas." She bowed at the waist. "I believe our conversation was interrupted when last we met."

His bloodless lips parted in a needle-tipped grin. "I believe it did. When this ogre absconded with my property."

"The chest is still in the woods," Droguk growled. "You're free to retrieve it. Though what's inside flew off."

The Baron clapped his slender hands in delight. "How audacious of you. Opening a stolen chest and complaining about what's inside. The chest is no matter. Simply hand over my property and I will leave."

"I'm not your property!" Vanessa snarled.

"Well, I say that you are. And I have all of these gargoyles..." His voice trailed off with his gaze as he looked around the square. When his eyes settled on Vanessa's once again, he tilted his head. "You do still have time to change your answer."

"Or what? You'll kill me? Fat chance." He'd gone to what appeared to be fairly fucking drastic lengths to catch her.

"Of course not. Why would I have gone to all of this trouble to find you, just to kill you?" he echoed her thoughts. Then, he motioned to his gargoyles. "They'll kill him."

It happened so fast. One moment, Droguk stood beside her. The next, he'd been yanked into the sky.

"We should move," Scylas said. "An ogre his size will likely make a huge crater."

"No!" In a move of pure instinct she couldn't have anticipated or planned, she threw herself at the Baron's feet. "I surrender! Don't kill him!"

There was a loud, grinding woosh as stone feet touched the ground beside her. Droguk stumbled away from the gargoyle, but they were surrounded by them, caged into the center of a ring with the Baron.

"Don't hurt him." Vanessa clung to the Baron's ankles, fully aware of how pathetic she looked and not caring one damn bit.

All the Baron said was, "Interesting."

Vanessa kept her eyes squeezed shut tight, resolved to continue pleading for as long as it took to assure Droguk's safety. She wouldn't let go of the vampire even if he killed her. She would just lock her rigor mortis arms around him and he would have to hop everywhere with her corpse attached to him like a Skip-It for the rest of time. *Good luck looking like a cool scary vampire then.*

Finally, Scylas spoke again. "Your pity for the beast has intrigued me. Bring them inside."

A gargoyle snatched her in one impossibly strong arm. Another took Droguk.

"I will spare your pet, human..."

The Baron's voice split through the inside of her skull.

"...if you tell me how you crossed the barrier between your world and Fablemere."

Chapter Thirty-Three

"I wish I could offer you some refreshment." The Baron looked around the dim, empty room. The candlelight playing off the sheen of his ruby red velvet robes cast a light flush across his pallid face, and Vanessa could almost mistake him for a human. He gestured with one elegant hand. "But as you can see, there is nothing left in the whole city."

"That, and we're tied up," Vanessa snapped. The first thing the gargoyles had done when they'd dragged them into the abandoned tavern was cover the windows; the second thing was to bind Vanessa and Droguk with their hands behind their backs.

Some of us are more tied up than others, Vanessa thought. There wasn't a doubt in her mind that Droguk could get free any time he wanted to. But what good would it do? The gargoyles would just fly him to the tippy-top of the gleaming towers and drop him.

She'd almost gotten him killed. Her stomach burned with bile. She couldn't stop herself from imagining the horror that hadn't befallen them, and how it would have been her fault.

And how it would have hurt to lose her only friend in this strange world. A best friend, who made all of the impossible nonsense of the past weeks make sense.

"Yes, that does seem a bit like overkill, doesn't it?" The Baron nodded to his henchmen. "Untie them. They're not going to flee. And even if they tried, they wouldn't succeed."

"I wouldn't have questioned it," Vanessa admitted. "I've never been taken hostage before, so I just assumed the rope was part of it."

They untied Droguk first, and he put his huge fists on the tabletop.

The Baron arched an ink-black brow. "You're oath marked."

Droguk covered the mark with his hand. "I am."

"This one, too," the gargoyle untying Vanessa said, his stone hand grasping her wrist and pulling it up to display the lines on her forearm.

The Baron's eyebrows made an acquaintance with his hairline. "You're bound to this ogre?"

"She is," Droguk answered for her. "She is my mate."

"And is that what drove you here to Lua?" The vampire motioned for them to display their marks. "You were looking for a more enlightened society to accept you?"

"No one has had any issue accepting us, so any prejudice you're thinking we've been subjected to is likely a projection of your own feelings." *Careful,* she warned herself. There was no need to bait a guy who could have them both ripped apart in seconds.

But the Baron agreed with her. "You're right. I do feel a certain disgust at the notion. But if that's not what brought you here, what did?"

"I think you know that the ogres believe I have 'visions.'" She made air quotes around the word. "I hate to disappoint you after you traveled all this way, but I don't. I have a neurological condition that makes me fall on the ground and violently shake. If it's bad enough, I sometimes pee myself. Maybe that's what you're into?"

The Baron laughed. It was the sonic equivalent of a guillotine blade dropping. "You're amusing. I've forgotten how amusing humans can be. Perhaps I should spend more time in their company before I drink them."

A low growl rumbled from Droguk's chest. Vanessa laid her hand on his arm to silence him.

"Don't worry, ogre. I won't be dining on your mate." The Baron turned his attention back to Vanessa. "Your mate's associates did tell me that they believed you had certain powers, but I didn't believe them."

"If you didn't believe it, why did you follow us here?" Droguk asked.

"The human knows why. The question I find most important is why this condition would lead you to flee The Mire. Ogres aren't known for their lust for travel."

In Vanessa's brain, the Baron said, *"I knew you were not of this realm the moment I saw you. Does your mate know?"*

She nodded, the smallest possible motion, not wanting it to catch Droguk's attention.

"I don't wish for my guard to know. Not yet. Don't speak it aloud."

Don't speak in my fucking head, she thought, and to her horror, the vampire smiled. Shit. He could read her mind.

"I don't read minds. I hear thoughts directed at me. For example, your mate is having astounding visions of ripping my head off with his bare hands. I would dissuade him from such an action if I were you."

She cleared her throat. "My mate brought me to Lua in the hopes of finding a cure for my condition. If we'd known that you'd taken over the whole city, we wouldn't have bothered."

"You think I'm responsible for all of this emptiness?" The Baron tilted his head. "My reputation not only precedes me, but it's become wildly outsized. I had nothing to do with whatever caused the citizens here to flee."

"We thought it was a plague. But there isn't any sign of one," Droguk said, sounding surprisingly rational despite the images the Baron claimed to have seen.

"Not a corpse in the place," the Baron confirmed. "Except for those four at the gate. We found those when we arrived."

"And you used them to make a trap." Vanessa's lip curled in disgust.

"They weren't serving much of a purpose decomposing in the square," the Baron said. With a sigh, he went on. "I'm afraid, human, that you will not find relief from your condition here. The university is bare. They didn't leave a single stick of furniture behind."

"None of this news has reached Shinewater. The elves didn't seem to know about it, either." Droguk seemed to have shifted from angry protective mate to amateur true crime investigator within seconds.

Vanessa put her palms on the table. "Before this

turns into a season of Only Murders In Lua, can we circle back to why I'm your prisoner? And allegedly your property?"

"Of course." He gestured to his guards. "Leave us."

They filed out of the tavern, shutting the door behind them.

"Ogre," the Baron said, turning to Droguk. "You know where your mate comes from, do you not?"

Droguk hesitated, but said, finally, "I do."

"I know of only one other who has ever successfully walked between worlds. An old enemy of mine." The vampire's already chilling expression hardened with true hatred.

"Merlin," Droguk said.

Scylas slammed his fist on the table, cracking the wood. "Never speak that name in my presence!"

"We won't. Jeez." Vanessa took a deep breath. The tension had already frayed her nerves down to their last, creaking strand. "If you're looking for this guy, I can't help you. I promise you, I don't know anyone by that name. In fact, in my world, he's just a myth."

"In my world, he is a scourge." But the Baron relaxed some, sitting back in his chair. "Whether you know him or not, you have a skill that is useful to me. You'll return with me to Palat Scylas."

"They won't." Droguk's voice was deathly calm. "They're my mate, and she's leaving here with me."

"With you, yes. And with her condition, which must be very serious, considering that you've traveled all this way." The Baron spread his hands. "And yet, you've found no cure."

The reality of that hadn't quite sunk in yet. It chose a piss-poor moment to do so.

There was nobody in Lua to help her. No chance of

a medicine or a cure, magical or mundane. It didn't matter if the Baron took her away from Droguk, because after the half-life of her medication ran out, she had no idea how long it would be until she had her very last seizure of all time.

Droguk covered her hand with his on the tabletop. He didn't have the Baron's talent for speaking directly into her mind, but his touch got the point across. *"I won't let anything hurt you,"* he seemed to be telling her. *"I won't let you die."*

And while she wanted to believe that he could protect her from anything, even in a fairytale world, she couldn't believe there was a fairytale ending in sight for her.

"I know a way that you might be cured," Scylas went on. "But I don't do favors. Not since that wretched mage betrayed me. Help me find him, and I will give you the cure you seek."

Droguk's hand tightened on hers.

"I don't know where to find him. This is the first time I'm even hearing about his existence outside of stories," she protested.

"You crossed the threshold. He'll know. And he'll come to you."

"So, you're going to use me as bait," Vanessa said.

"Exactly. All you need to do is return to Palat Scylas with me and live in comfort until that fool magician comes to find you. And he will find you. You've used magic as powerful as his own. He can't let such an insult stand." The pure satisfaction on the Baron's face made Vanessa's spine recoil.

She looked to Droguk and saw only defeat in his eyes. It gave her the resolve to speak her fear aloud. "I don't think we have much of a choice. We have to go with him."

"We?" The Baron scoffed. "I've been speaking only about you."

"Ogres can't go into the Sorrowlands," Droguk said, more subdued than she'd ever heard him before.

Vanessa snorted. "This dude sounds like he's the king of the place. I'm sure he can bend the rules."

"The ogre is correct," Scylas said. "It isn't a matter of policy, but nature. Most creatures in Fablemere can't survive the Sorrowlands, and ogres are among them. The soil, the water, even the air would poison him were he ever to step foot there."

If it could poison an ogre, what chance would she have? "Then how will I survive there?"

"You won't," Droguk said. He held the Baron's gaze boldly. "That's the cure, isn't it? You'll make her a vampire. Like you."

That was preposterous, obviously. Vampires were skinny and gorgeous and exuded sex appeal. They could pull off a smokey eye look without a raccoon effect. And they had cool names like Dracula or Lucien LaCroix. The thought was so absurd, it made her laugh.

Droguk wasn't laughing. Neither was the Baron.

"Wait, what?" she looked between them. "Are you serious?"

The vampire shrugged one shoulder. "It's better than death, isn't it?"

"It is death," Droguk corrected him.

"It's living death," the Baron said. "And it isn't a step to be taken lightly. My time is valuable, and I don't offer it generously, but due to your usefulness and the nature of my offer, I can give you and your mate one night to decide."

"A whole night to decide, huh?" A whole night to decide on something as important as becoming a vampire. *It was more than Spike or Drusilla got.*

"As I said, I'll give you a night to decide. And then, should you choose not to help me, my gargoyles can administer the ogre's sentence in the morning." He whistled, and the creatures entered the tavern once more.

"His sentence? So, it's join you or my mate dies?" Vanessa had the distinct sensation that all of her internal organs were crowding into her stomach.

"I'm offering you a choice, am I not?" The Baron looked to his men. "Find them suitable accommodations for the night. Somewhere they can't escape."

"Yes, Baron," one of the stone monsters said, and they moved in on Vanessa and Droguk.

"I have a question," she said quickly, and the gargoyles halted. "What happened to your agents who followed us here? The ones we lost in The Beanstalk Forest."

The vampire's forehead creased. "I don't know what you're talking about."

"Oh, come on." Vanessa rolled her eyes. "We saw them. Two people in black cloaks trailing us?"

Infuriatingly, the Baron shook his head. "If someone was following you, it was for their own purposes, not mine. I didn't send anyone after you past The Mire."

Chapter Thirty-Four

Tabitha had just ducked back into the building through the service door when she heard her best friend's voice from the front of the shop.

"Hey, Art. Didn't see you there behind your latest ADA noncompliance."

Half-laughing, half-choking as the last hit from her vape pen exited her lungs, Tabitha went back to the folding table that served as the management office. She bumped the leg by accident when she sat down, and the whole enterprise swayed precariously, laden down with years upon years' worth of unfiled tax returns, balled up receipts, and threatening IRS letters. Here and there, scattered crystals of different types poked up through the paperwork.

She flicked aside a red-black stone. Garnet for wealth. Aventurine for prosperity. Jasper to—and Tabitha had absolutely lost her shit at learning this piece of information—*facilitate organization*.

None of that appeared to be working, but he clearly had some kind of spell on the place that made it invisible to the Treasury Department.

She heard Vanessa ask, "What's the strategy here? Does the fire marshal accept bribes?"

Tabitha would have worried that they were going to get her fired one day with a smart remark, if Arthur hadn't always referred to her as "indispensable" and "the most reliable employee I've ever had."

She tucked her vape into her bra and considered how sad that statement was.

"Tabitha's in the back. I'll get her." The shower curtain rings on the tension rod in the door frame rattled as Arthur entered. "Your delightful and pleasant friend is here."

"Thanks, Art." Tabitha collected up the day's receipts. "Here you go. All six purchases."

"Six?" His lined face split into a wide grin. "Watch out, Amazon. Merlin's is on your tail."

Tabitha had long ago stopped worrying about how the store stayed afloat. Vanessa had once suggested Art might be independently wealthy and didn't mind sinking all his cash into a dying business. Tabitha suspected for a while that the place could be a mob front, although she wasn't sure the mob had a huge presence in Kalamazoo.

Maybe it really was just the energy from the crystals.

She reached for the ancient calculator with its big, worn-down keys. "Okay, read them off to me."

"Vanessa seemed like they were in a hurry." Art scratched the top of his head, scrunching his fluffy white curls. "You should get out there."

"And you seem like you just don't want to deal with

numbers." Which wouldn't come as a huge surprise to anyone looking at his filing system.

From the shop floor, Vanessa shouted, "Hey, we're gonna miss the previews!"

"Go. I promise I'll tally these up before morning," Arthur assured Tabitha.

She gave him a silent, dubious stare.

"Not right away," he admitted. "I'll lock up, make a cup of tea, but right after that, I'll be sure to add up those blasted receipts."

She grimaced, tight-lipped. "Send me a text with the total."

His shoulders slumped in defeat. "Fine. Yes. All right. You're a real ball buster sometimes, do you know that?"

She rose from the creaky, ancient folding chair that still had "Property of St. Augustine" stenciled in spray paint on the back. She hoped he'd bought it at a rummage sale and hadn't just stolen it from the cathedral. With Arthur, it could have gone either way.

"Okay. See you tomorrow. Try to be here before opening? It's getting too chilly in the mornings to stand around waiting for you to arrive." She grabbed her hoodie off the coat rack near the door and headed onto the sales floor.

It was empty.

"Vanessa?" she called. It would have been unlike her friend to wander into the stacks. They always talked about what a hazard the place was. "Hello? Did you abandon me?"

Silence. As unlikely as it was for Vanessa to be browsing the shelves, it was even more unlikely that they'd actually be mad enough to leave, no matter how late Tabitha had been making them. And she and Art would have heard the chimes when the door opened.

A stack of books had toppled to the floor, and Tabitha bent to pick them up, sighing. "You've really got to sort these new acquisitions, Art!"

He emerged from the back room. "Where's your friend?"

Tabitha stood with an armful of books. "I have no idea. I guess they left? I'm going to call them."

A basic tenet of their friendship was the reservation of phone calls for only the direst of emergencies. Usually, it was texts only. That was how weird it was for Vanessa to run off without a word. It merited a phone call.

"It's like they disappeared out of thin air." Tabitha deposited the books on the counter. "Shelf these. I almost tripped and died."

Art's gaze dropped to the pile, and then everything else dropped, too. His face went pale and long as he stared at the heavy, leatherbound monstrosity on the top of the stack.

"Hey," she said, waving her hand at him in alarm. "Are you having a stroke? Smile for me."

His gaze met hers. He didn't attempt a smile. "I'm not having a stroke. No, no, I'm fine. I just... You should go and find your friend."

Prickles crossed the back of her neck. "What's wrong?"

"Nothing's wrong." He snatched the book to his chest and turned to the curtained doorway. "Run along. Enjoy your evening."

Absolutely not. There was something about that book that Art didn't want her to see. Had he spent the shop's money on some expensive first edition for his own collection, then forgotten it? That would be extremely on brand for him, but curiosity was on brand for her. She followed him through the curtain and blocked the doorway, her hands on her hips. "I will not allow a man in a flowered shirt and hemp bracelets to tell me to run along, old timer. Explain yourself."

"Explain what?" he asked, turning to show her his empty hands.

She looked around. There was no sign of the book, but there hadn't been any time at all for him to effectively hide it. "Where did it go?"

He blinked at her. "Where did what go?"

"Um, the book you just ran back here with like it was stolen property on fire." She waved her arms. "What is it and where did you hide it?"

"I don't know what you're talking about," he said, holding her gaze as if daring her to question him further.

The truth was, she didn't have any right to keep questioning him. It was his store, the inventory belonged to him. She was just an employee who helped customers—on the rare occasion they had any—and tried to make a dent in the decades of fiscal neglect littering the office. But his reaction, especially on the heels of Vanessa's disappearance, was so odd. And unless it was "Everyone React Bizarrely Out Of Character Day," it was a little too much of a coincidence.

Tabitha held up a wait-a-minute finger to Art and pulled her phone from her pocket, breaking eye contact with him only long enough to unlock the screen and pull up Vanessa's number.

A robotic voice greeted her. "The number you have called is not in service."

It absolutely was in service. They'd just been texting

not an hour before.

She tried again and got the same message. All the while, Art watched her like a kid waiting to get into trouble.

"Maybe they went back to their car," he suggested. "Why don't you go check?"

It was a good idea, but it felt like a trick. She gave him a mistrustful glance and headed out to the sales floor. When she stepped out the door, she kept hold of the handle and placed one foot firmly on the threshold. There was Vanessa's car, parked at the curb. But Vanessa wasn't inside it.

When Tabitha stepped back, she bumped into Art.

"Jesus!" she shouted, pressing a hand to her chest. "Can you at least attempt to make sound when you walk?"

He ignored her jab. "Maybe they went for a walk in the park. You should go check there."

"We were running late for a movie. They wouldn't have gone to the park," she snapped. "You should stop being so cagey. How about that?"

He stepped closer, almost forcing her to move her foot from the door. "Then check the juice bar. They might have been thirsty."

"I know you've heard them rant about that place and its suspected MLM ties." Tabitha didn't back down. She pushed her way through the door again and closed it behind her. "What the hell is going on? Why are you trying to run me off?"

"So you're not late to your—"

"That's not why!" she shouted. The distinct feeling that something wasn't right made her heart pound and her chest ache. Usually, she would talk herself out of a panic attack, but at the moment, panic seemed perfectly reasonable. "Tell me what's going on!"

Art's expression softened into one of despair. "I want to. But you won't believe it."

"You don't know what I will or won't believe. I tolerate your crystal nonsense, don't I?" she protested.

"Tolerate. You don't believe." He cursed under his breath. "In order to explain, I have to tell you things that you'll never be able to forget. Things that will seem utterly preposterous. Far beyond my 'crystal nonsense.' And once I tell you, you'll be in danger."

"Oh god," she whispered. "It's drugs. You and Vanessa are dealing drugs. They hid them in that book, didn't they? And they got spooked and ran off to avoid getting caught. That's what's happening, isn't it?"

Art looked totally offended. "I don't sell drugs. I take drugs. There's a huge difference."

"Then what is it? Where is Vanessa?" she demanded. "Look, I'll believe whatever you tell me. I swear. I just want to know what's going on."

He studied her for a long moment, his brows drawn together in sorrowful consideration. Finally, defeated, he pulled the book from the air.

From the air.

The book appeared from the fucking air.

She leaned back on the door for support.

"That wasn't a magic trick," he said calmly. "It's real magic."

"Fuck you," she whispered in disbelief.

"You promised you would believe me. This should be evidence enough, right?" he asked. Then, slowly, he reached for her hand and drew her away from the door. She followed him on legs made of get-the-fuck-out-of-here magnets.

He placed the book on the counter. "I'm not from

this world."

A sharp, hysterical laugh burst from her throat.

He ignored it and continued. "I came to this one a very long time ago."

"I figured you were about seventy," she said.

"First, how dare you. Second, no. I'm not seventy. I'm much, much older." He laid a hand on the book. "I came to your world in four-hundred-fifty A.D. And I've been here ever since."

She tried to mentally calculate how long that was and gave up immediately.

"My name isn't Arthur. You would know me as..." He took a breath and closed his eyes, like he was summoning up courage. "Merlin."

"Merlin?" The name rode up on a wave of nervous vomit she had to swallow back. Her boss was clinically delusional. Mental illness was certainly an explanation for his low level of executive function, but she never would have guessed that he was so out of touch with reality. "Okay, so. You believe you're Merlin."

"You promised you would believe it, too," he reminded her. "And yes, I believe I'm Merlin. Because I am him."

She opened her mouth to respond, then closed it. There was no proper response.

"When I came here, I created a doorway. And that doorway is inside this book." He swallowed, but his voice was hoarse when he spoke. "It's been activated again. I can feel it. There was only one other person in this shop with us and now she's not here. Do you understand what I'm saying."

"No. I don't understand it at all. But I do follow it." It was absurd in the extreme, but she understood what he was trying to tell her. "You think that my best friend went to another world via your magic book."

"Exactly. And you believe me, remember?" He studied her face carefully. "Because if you don't, or if you don't have the capacity to at least try, what I show you next will come as a terrible surprise."

"I've already had a terrible surprise. My boss thinks—" She stopped herself. "My boss is Merlin."

He opened the book to a full-page illustration. For something clearly published before the advent of mass-market paperbacks, the picture was shockingly clear. Like a photograph. It displayed a mist-shrouded countryside with vibrant green hills and the shape of gray towers, indistinct through the fog.

She reached out a hand to touch it. Arthur—Merlin—shouted, "Wait!"

Tabitha tumbled forward, spilling onto the ground on her hands and knees. Her palms slid on the damp grass. A body collided with hers and rolled to her side with a loud "oof."

She sat back. Beside her, clad in a flowered shirt open over a ribbed white undershirt, hemp bracelets dangling from his wrist, was a dark-haired man of about forty, with rugged features and stubble on his sharp, square jaw.

Tabitha scrambled backward like a crab and shouted, "Who the *fuck* are you?"

Chapter Thirty-Five

The gargoyles brought Vanessa and Droguk to a small house a few streets from the main square. Whoever had left it hadn't taken their furniture, so at least there was a bed, but not a bit of food was left in the house. The Baron had been "kind" enough to return their packs to them, and the meager rations left inside would have to do for the evening. There was a well, though, and the gargoyles brought a bucket of water before barring the windows and doors to prevent their prisoners from escaping.

Alone in the darkness of the shuttered house, Droguk was the first to break the silence. "You can't accept his offer."

"I can't not accept it. I'm not going to let you die." She'd gotten him into this mess from day one. If this was the only way to fix it, then she would have to accept the consequences.

"We came all this way to cure you, not turn you into a monster," he said. "Do you understand that? You'll be a monster."

"And you'll be dead." It was noble of him to try to sacrifice himself, but Vanessa wouldn't have it. "Think about Drova and the kids. Are you really going to let her sit around, waiting for you to return, never giving up hope but hurting every single day, wondering if you're coming back? You have a family—"

"You are my family!" he roared. "You are my mate! I swore I would protect you."

"You swore to protect me 'until decay and rot robs my flesh of the oath mark I will bear for you.' I'm not going to be rotting in the ground. You heard what the Baron said. It's a living death. Which, by the way, is a much better option than actual death, which I'm very much facing." Grimly, she thought of all the times she'd hoped they would find a cure for her in her lifetime. Well, she'd gotten what she'd wanted. In the shittiest way possible.

"Yes, and you'll be living this living death away from me. What's the point of surviving if..."

The pressure in the air between them changed. He didn't have to finish his sentence for her to know exactly what he'd been about to say.

He didn't want to live without her.

She looked up at the exposed rafters and the straw roof above to get her bearings and blink away tears. It was the most romantic thing anyone had ever said to her. Also, the stupidest. "What's the point of me surviving, if you don't?"

For a long time, they simply stood there, looking at each other in the dim light seeping in through the cracks around the shutters, hopelessness binding them together but separating them at the same time.

"Vanessa," Droguk began, tears forming in his yellow eyes. "I can't let you go."

Her arms physically ached to hold him. She wanted to throw herself against him and cling to him, the way she'd intended to cling to the Baron when begging for mercy. But she had to stay calm. It might be the last time they were ever together, and there were things they needed to say.

"We came here to find a cure for my seizures. This isn't the magic spell I was hoping to find, but it's the one I got. The only other way to save my life would be to return to my world, but you heard the Baron. Only one other person has managed to do that, and he was the greatest wizard of all time." Did that make her a great wizard? It would be super helpful, if that were the case, but she doubted it. "And if I go back to my world, you lose me, anyway. At least if I stay here, there's a chance."

"If you become a vampire, you can never return to your world," he pointed out. "Unless you have vampires there?"

"I personally believe we do, but you're missing the point of what I'm saying." She took one of his huge hands in both of hers. "I don't want to leave Fablemere. Not now that I'm with you. And yeah, I'll be a vampire, but will that make me suddenly not your mate anymore?"

"Not in the eyes of the gods," he said sadly. "We won't be bound."

"Fuck the gods. In your eyes, will I still be your mate?" Her pleading gaze roamed over his face.

"You will always be my mate," he said firmly. "Even if you went back to your world, you would be my mate. And yes, even if you become a vampire, I will still belong to you."

"Until decay and rot robs your flesh of the oath mark you bear for me?"

"And an eternity after."

She sniffed back her suddenly runny nose, but the tears finally spilled over. He enfolded her in his strong arms and held her, bending his head to kiss the top of hers. She could give into her urge to cling to him, then, hold onto him and convince herself that nothing could separate them.

He lifted her in his arms, cradling her close, and kissed her. It was a shame they were going to be split up when he'd just gotten the hang of it. She put a hand on his cheek, the other against his neck, and swore to herself that she would memorize the feel of him. She wouldn't forget, no matter what happened when she left with the Baron. Not even if a hundred years passed without ever seeing Droguk again, she wouldn't forget his mouth on hers, their tongues slipping over each other, the crush of his arms around her or the low rumble of desire in his chest.

They only had one night together. For now, she reminded herself. For now.

It was too soon to give up hope while they were still together.

He lifted his head. "If this is our last night—"

"Yes," she whispered, brushing her thumb over his cheek.

She didn't need to say anything else.

The bed the previous occupants had left behind wasn't ogre-sized, but he carried her to it anyway and sat her on the edge. He dropped to his knees before her and took her foot in his hands to slip off her boot.

She bit her bottom lip, almost more nervous than she'd been when they'd sealed the binding ritual.

"This seems more important..." She swallowed as his hand caressed her bare foot. "Than the first time. Do you know what I mean?"

"Because it's the last time?" he asked sadly, removing the other boot.

She shook her head. "No. Don't say that. Please. It's not the last time. But it's the most real time so far."

He looked up at her, searching her face. "It's also just the second time."

"Hey, I was counting the fairy bath," she said, and shivered as his thumb massaged the curve of her calf over her breeches. "Did you forget about that?"

"How could I forget about that?" he slid his hands up to her thighs. "How could I forget how you tasted or what you felt like in my arms? The way you moaned? And knowing that it was me that gave you that pleasure..."

Her entire body trembled, and he hadn't even taken her pants off.

"Do you remember what I told you when we were there?" He reached for the laces of her breeches and swiftly untied them.

"That all you thought about, all the time, was fucking me?" The words made her lightheaded. "No one has ever said something like that about me before."

"No one has ever had the sense to?" He jerked at the waist of her trousers and she lifted her hips to help him pull them down her thighs.

"Nobody has ever felt that way, I think."

"Good," he huffed, tossing her pants aside. "Because the thought of anyone else feeling that way about you makes me want to find them and cave their skulls in."

"That's a little possessive," she said with a laugh, shrugging off her coat. "Which is not considered an attractive quality where I'm from. Outside of fiction."

"It's a good thing you think you're in fiction, then." He rose up on his knees and sank a hand into her hair, tipping her head back roughly. "Because you're mine. You'll always be mine."

"And no one else's."

His mouth descended on hers again, and she resolved to give up her sorrow. To forget the horror the morning would bring.

Tonight, and every night thereafter, she would be his, and his alone.

Chapter Thirty-Six

The daylight crept around the edges of the shutters once more, and a shaft of it fell across Vanessa's eyes. She flinched away.

"We should have slept," Droguk murmured, stroking her hair back. "We'll be exhausted for our travels."

Travels, plural. He would go one way, back to The Mire. She would go to the Sorrowlands with her captor, and they might never see each other again.

"Good," she all but snarled. "I hope I'm a huge inconvenience to him."

"Maybe vampires don't get tired," he mused. "Maybe the next time I see you, you'll have so much energy that you'll accidentally fuck me to death."

She tweaked his nipple in retaliation and he swatted her hand away.

"I never said it would be a bad way to die." He brushed his lips across her temple.

"You did say 'the next time I see you.' Will you still love me enough to get naked with me when I'm a vampire?" Her spine instantly straightened. He hadn't used that word. Neither of them had. And now it was out there.

"Of course I will." He frowned. "Why are you suddenly so stiff?"

"It was just..." She could let him misinterpret her reaction as fear of rejection, but that would be the same as casting doubt on feelings he'd already expressed to her. "I said love. I was being presumptuous."

"I don't think you were." His frown deepened.

"No, it's just..." She sighed in frustration. "Where I'm from, saying that word can have disastrous consequences. You can scare people away."

"I'm not people," he reminded her. "And after everything we said last night, love seems like an understatement."

She snuggled her head against his shoulder and shut her eyes tight. "I can't believe I have to go."

"But you do." The sad resolve in his voice had lost all of the anger that had tinged it the night before, when there had still been time to pretend things would turn out differently. "Go, do what the Baron asks, and we'll be together again. I don't know how, but we will."

She pushed up on one elbow to look down at him. "Don't try to rescue me. It sounds really dangerous."

"It is really dangerous, so I'm not going to try to rescue you," he said with a shrug. "You're going to have to rescue yourself. I know you can, so I'm not worried about it."

Vanessa flung her arms around his neck and squeezed him tight, trying and failing to subdue her tears.

There was a loud banging that almost burst the door off its hinges. "Time to go. By order of the Baron."

No. I'm not ready. Vanessa held tighter to Droguk, kissed him until he peeled her off him.

"We knew this was coming. Be brave," he whispered.

More pounding. Vanessa swore and shouted, "Hang on! I need to get dressed!"

They climbed from the still damp bed and sorted through the clothes they'd discarded. She scrambled to dress herself, her fingers shaking as she did up the laces of her breeches and tried to pull on her boots.

"Take a deep breath," Droguk said softly. "We can do this."

"Wait. Before we go." She looked around the little house desperately for something to write with and came up short. The fireplace. She rubbed her finger in the greasy ashes in the hearth and returned to him. "Give me your arm."

He did so without hesitation, but asked, "Why?"

"Our oath marks. I don't want to forget yours, and I don't want you to forget mine. It would be better if I had a pen or something, but for now..."

At least their marks weren't like Vikthor and Brentan's. She wouldn't have been able to replicate the intricate whorls and designs. She used her pinkie to sketch his mark around hers in the ash.

Her heart skittered.

"What's the matter?" Droguk asked.

"It's a book." She lifted her arm to show him. "Our marks. It's a book."

To demonstrate, she rubbed her mark into his skin. His eyes widened.

"It's how I came here," she said.

"I remember." He studied the mark a little longer,

then pulled his sleeve down over it. "As soon as I can, I'll make that permanent."

"Ooh, you're going to get a tattoo for me?" she teased him.

The door buckled under another onslaught of knocking. This time, it was forceful enough to dislodge dust and dirt from the ceiling.

"Oh my god, settle down!" Vanessa shouted. She gave Droguk one last glance. "I guess we have to go."

"We do." His jaw set firmly, he strode to the door and slammed it open so hard it cracked in two.

They stepped into the daylight, made cold by the gray-white of the city rising up around them. Vanessa thought about how the Baron had said the sunlight made him weak. *Maybe I can kill him. Maybe—*

The gargoyles would just kill *them*.

This was happening, and there was no way to get out of it.

"Droguk—" she began, and a sob closed her throat.

"Don't start crying now," he said in a low, firm voice. "You're brave."

"Okay. You don't have to talk to me like a dog at the vet." She closed her eyes, took a deep breath, and started walking. The gargoyles formed a moving fence around them, leading them through the empty streets, the deserted square, through the gates of Lua and down the stairs.

Waiting at the bottom, an ornate black palanquin enclosed in brocade curtains waited on the gleaming white stone. The Baron stood in its shade, hands folded in front of him. He wore black robes trimmed in white fur, and held another in front of him. "You may need this. It tends to get windy and damp near the coast."

"The coast?" Droguk's hands closed at his sides. "You're taking her across The Smuggler's Sea?"

"Do you think there'll be anything more terrifying than me on those seas?" the Baron asked. "Besides, it doesn't matter. The human is my property."

"The human has a name," Droguk shot back. "They're called Vanessa."

"Vanessa." The name sounded like an oily, black snake from his lips. "Let's not waste more time. Come along, Vanessa."

She turned to Droguk and cast her gaze up at his face desperately. No one was coming to save her.

She laughed.

At Droguk's confused expression, she said, "Even in a fairytale world, I'm not getting a fairytale ending."

"We will. It's just delayed." He lifted his hand to cup her cheek. "When you walk away, don't look back at me. I won't be able to let you go if you look back at me."

She nodded and covered his hand with hers, leaning into his touch. "I love you."

"I love you." He leaned down, but he didn't kiss her. He pressed his forehead against hers, took a ragged breath, and said, "Go."

She stepped back, lowering her eyes so she didn't have to see his face. Her hand lingered on his, though, their fingers linked as she turned away.

They held onto each other until the distance made it impossible. And when their connection broke, Vanessa's heart extinguished.

"Come along," The Baron said, pulling back one of the curtains. He offered his other hand and warned, "Mind your step," as she entered the palanquin.

The only thing that kept her from looking back was

her promise to Droguk. But she wanted to, with every aching breath. Adrenaline coursed through her, making her tremble. Her entire body screamed with the injustice of being taken from his side. Wild visions filled her head. Leaping from the palanquin and racing into his arms. Refusing to go, not caring if they both died, just as long as they did so together.

Those thoughts were tempting and dangerous. She pushed them aside.

The inside of the palanquin was dark, but she made out shapes of pillows scattered around the black velvet cushion beneath her. The Baron climbed in after her and reclined with a sigh. The palanquin lurched, and a gargoyle called out an order. They were mobile, carried by the stone monsters.

"You'll forget him, soon enough," Scylas said coolly. "Once I've brought you across, you'll be shocked at how differently you view things. What becomes important and what remains so. Your ogre won't be among those."

Her sorrow turned to hatred so intense, she thought it might burn her up from the inside.

"And they are simple creatures, ogres. He'll forget about you."

The agonized roar that tore through the skies told her otherwise.

* * * *

The sun set, and still he could not move. The stars came out, and he remained where he'd fallen to his knees on the stone. And when the sun rose the next day, he was still there.

Droguk knew he should get their packs and leave.

There was so little food left, since they'd planned to buy more in Lua. He would have to ration it until he found his way back to Shinewater, and simply hope he wouldn't starve to death along the way.

But he couldn't move.

If he went back to the house they'd stayed in, he would smell her there. He would climb into his bed-roll and breathe her in, and then he wouldn't be able to leave. If he left, it would be over. If he stayed, he would be over.

"You're going to have to rescue yourself. I know you can..."

Hadn't he said those words to her?

Wouldn't she have told him the same thing? He would be a poor mate indeed if he held her to a higher standard than he held himself.

Vanessa would uphold her end of the bargain. She would find a way out of the Sorrowlands. But it would be all for nothing if he didn't stay alive.

Wincing at the stiffness in his knees, he rose and cast a long look over the waving grass, which had already swallowed up the tracks the gargoyles had cut through it. Droguk had watched until he couldn't see the palanquin anymore.

He went back to the little house and did not climb back into the bedroll to give up. He did hold it to his face a moment, memorizing the scent of her. *The next time I see her, she won't be human. This might be gone.* If he was going to keep moving, keep breathing, he had to put those thoughts aside.

He consolidated their packs but wouldn't leave hers behind. Not out of sentimentality, he told himself. What if his pack got a hole in it? Or he stumbled onto an orchard and needed a way to carry food necessary for his survival? He could think of dozens of reasons to keep every piece of her equipment, from her bedroll to the sling he'd constructed to carry her on his back.

The Baron won't know how to take care of her. He shoved it into the pack, anyway. What if he needed to fashion a slingshot? Or bandage a wound?

He was grateful for all of these very good reasons, because he wouldn't be able to leave any piece of her behind.

In the tavern where they'd been taken prisoner, Droguk found the sword and axe he and Vanessa had looted from the corpses outside.

So many good memories.

He shook them off and found his way out of the city gates, down the steps, past the site of the worst moment of his life, over the bridge, and down the road that cut through the vast grass field.

A dark shadow stepped into the road, followed closely by another, both of them in black cloaks. The men the Baron had claimed he'd never sent. The hooded figures who'd been trailing them since Shinewater.

"You just missed him," Droguk said, never slowing his steps. They'd either move or get squashed.

Or, they could pull a sword from its sheath and nearly slice his throat to block his passage.

"Tabitha," warned a gruff voice from beneath the other figure's hood.

The sword-wielder pulled down its cloak to reveal an elfish, but unmistakably human, face capped with short, pale gray hair.

The furious human narrowed their eyes at him and snarled, "Where the fuck is Vanessa?"

331

The story of Fablemere continues in

THE VAMPIRE'S WILLING CAPTIVE

currently available on
Patreon, Ream, and Kindle Vella

in paperback and ebook July 2024

The world of Fablemere expands with the Fablemere
Fae in

**THE PRINCES OF
PLEASURE AND TORMENT**

exclusively on the Radish fiction app

Abigail Barnette is a pen name of blogger and USA Today Bestselling Author Jenny Trout. As Abigail, Jenny writes award-winning erotic romance, including the internationally bestselling *The Boss* series, as well as new adult novels.

As a blogger, Jenny's work has appeared on *The Huffington Post*, and has been featured on television and radio, including *HuffPost Live, Good Morning America, The Steve Harvey Show,* and National Public Radio's *Here & Now*.

She is a proud Michigander, passionate advocate of accessible and diverse community theater, mother of two, and wife to the only person alive capable of spending extended periods of time with her without wanting to kill her.

Milton Keynes UK
Ingram Content Group UK Ltd.
UKHW041000040324
438885UK00006B/375